DC BOOKDIVA PRESENTS

TRINA
HYDRO KILLER

DARRELL DEBREW

www.dcbookdiva.com
www.myspace.com/dcbookdivapublications

Published by DC Bookdiva Publications
Copyright © 2011 by Darrell DeBrew

ISBN-10: 0984611029
ISBN-13: 978-0984611027
Library of Congress Control Number: 2010932065

First Edition, February 2011
Printed in the United States of America

### Publisher's Note

*This is a work of fiction. Any names historical events, real people, living and dead, or the locales are intended only to give the fiction a setting in historic reality. Other names, characters, places, businesses and incidents are either the product of the author's imagination or are used fictiously, and their resemblance, if any, to real life counterparts is entirely coincidental.*

Edited by: Janelle Talley
Graphic Design: Oddball Dsgn

**DC Bookdiva Publications**
#245 4401-A Connecticut Ave
NW, Washington, DC 20008
www.dcbookdiva.com
www.facebook.com/dcbfanpage

# ACKNOWLEDGEMENTS

"Ms. Tiah Short" is first. Without your tenacity this wouldn't be possible. You definitely want this bad.

My daughter "Danielle Edmondson" and "Taylor"... What does the future hold?

"Ms. Freaky Old Lady (Harriet)"... Thanks for being there. You know what it means to call Tyrone.

"Iris"... You're scared of fire.

"Gabby" ... There are men who need to have as much heart as you.

"Lavon, Lady Boss"... Wherever you are, you are still in my heart and my thoughts. You are still my little sister. Now, say something slick.

"Nicole, Queen C"...Okay, you right—I've never met a female like you. Still, you haven't met a man like me.

"Ron Tae Ja Johnson"... Blue asked to have your name put in my next book. Most ask about their name. Wishing you the best. Your father is a good guy.

"Mr. Leo Sullivan"... Triple Crown will fall, giving you your rights back; a good writer like yourself shall survive.

"Twan"... What's good?

"Gary McKenzie The General"...You're better than Drake.

"Mr. Samuel Cornish" and "Mr. Kevin Roundtree"... I know y'all purchase books. Many cats in prison act cool while wishing death. Jealousy and envy come out in interesting ways. And true friendship doesn't require that I put a name in my book; if a person thinks otherwise, what does it require of him?

"Mr. Ernest Pitt"... Thanks for publishing my editorials in your newspaper.

"Linda Williams"... Maybe I'm important now.

"Terrance 'Gangsta' Williams"... Holla At Me Wordy.

"Kennedy Fountain"... You are special. Don't forget it.

# DEDICATION

Ladies … yes, you ladies who are constantly buying urban books, this book and others are dedicated to you!

I need your assistance for future titles, especially for Sally "The Pinstriped Bitch." If you don't know Sally, read " Keisha." "The Pinstriped Bitch" is about an older African-American homicide detective who loves young dick and a good murder mystery to say the least.

After writing more than fifteen books, I need to know about your freak, what you like, what you fantasize about and what turns you on. Just allow your imagination to run wild. It doesn't just have to be freaky. I'm interested in your romantic side and the passionate side too.

The pen is hotter than lava… just holla!
Darrell Debrew #14102-056
PO Box 1000
Butner, NC 27509

# CHAPTER 1

It would be a matter of minutes before Trina secured the last half of her $100,000 fee as a ghetto hit girl/homicidal maniac.

Goliath, a Colombian drug smuggler, had proven to be her most difficult prey. What should have taken a week had turned into three weeks. Though she was losing money because of the time, she always got her man. Trina wasn't about to let that change. And she always made sure that death was certain.

Usually, if her target was a male, she used her feminine charm to get next to him. Then a little poison in his drink would usually do the trick. Something like xyzzy, this worked instantly and left no chance of recovery. She also liked three shots to the head and a long gash across the jugular and the windpipe with a jagged-edged knife. A vein wound bleeds more—and quicker—if it's been ripped as opposed to just being cut with a sharp knife.

Unlike what she had been told about Goliath, he was on the go on a daily basis. She had been told that he loved to gamble and see prostitutes. She caught up with him in Miami. For three days, she watched his mansion to determine when would be the best time to go in. On the morning she decided to go in, when she arrived, he was leaving in his green Bentley, a car that wasn't included in the report she had. This seemed unusual, so she decided to just follow him.

After he hit I-95, he didn't stop until he got to South Carolina. Shooting him through the window while on I-95 wasn't good enough and was too risky. Drive-bys weren't her thing.

Getting him at the hotel seemed like the perfect thing to do. Her partner, Patrick, a computer genius and a retired FBI agent/assassin told her to get some rest. He didn't want her fatigue to cause her to slip. Plus, there was a chance that some cops had followed Goliath out of Miami.

Trina used her fake FBI badge to convince the clerk to call her when Goliath checked out of the hotel. The badge and a few hundred dollars were enough. Trina had slept for five hours in her car ,went shopping, and fueled up before he had awakened. The next stop was Memphis and then Chicago. In Chicago, she put a tracking device under his car so that she wouldn't lose him. It was Patrick's idea. She lost sight of him on the way to Arizona. She couldn't figure out what he was doing. He would stop at a hotel and stay for a day. Sometimes he would pick up a prostitute for a night, then leave out the next morning, usually just before dawn.

In Arizona, she found out all that she needed to know. It seemed that Goliath had a secret family on the other side of nowhere. She figured he wanted to make sure he hadn't been followed. She would have lost him for good in the desert without the tracking device.

It would be hard for her to sneak up on him where they were in Arizona. She would have to move at night because she was one of the few African Americans in the area. Killing the entire family—kids and all—was the least of her worries. All the drama would bring police from all around. All the highways were long stretches that would surely get her caught. Patrick told her to wait.

After a week, she came up with a plan. She would shoot him through the window at night. Using a silencer on her Uzi would give her a decent head start on the police, and nobody would be able to describe her in the dark. The plan was a bit risky, but she had to take that chance because of the time factor. If he could survive a barrage of bullets, so be it. She'd just have to come back to get him in the hospital if he survived. On the night she planned to do that, he headed out again.

His next stop was California. He stayed overnight in two different hotels. When he finally hit Las Vegas, she knew that she'd get him. Just like she thought, he was dropping big dollars at the tables. It would be a simple matter of waiting.

For three days, she watched him gamble, trick and drink like he was on a vacation. His behavior indicated that he wouldn't be leaving the hotel anytime soon. The night had come to do him in. She paid off a maid for a master key to his room. The maid had to be knocked off because she was a potential witness. The body wouldn't be found until the next day, when it was too late. Trina hadn't been taught to pick locks that were opened with plastic credit cards. What had to be done, had to be done.

She went in his room at eight forty-five p.m. and waited. The sun had just fully set.

She crouched by the window, just in front of the bathroom door. She hid behind a drape that covered the floor-to-ceiling windows. As she usually did when she was waiting, she rested the silencer on her lips, ready to jump up and out and shoot at a moment's notice.

Trina opened her eyes when she heard the plastic key enter the lock. She looked at her watch; it was twelve-thirty. Adrenaline went through her body. Though her legs were slightly numb from crouching, she was ready for action. That familiar taste entered her mouth. She loved that taste. The taste and feeling were things she could only experience just before she killed. She lived for the rush. It made her feel powerful.

She inhaled deep breaths, pushing her lungs to full capacity, and exhaled slowly. Since being sent to prison at sixteen, she had become a thrill seeker. Killing gave her the greatest thrill.

A smile came across her face when she heard the door open and saw light from the hallway shine on the carpet. All the waiting had made her feel anxious and impatient. Her emotions were pushing her to blast him immediately just for making her wait so long. But that wouldn't be professional because it could attract too much attention from the hallway, and she hadn't even made sure it was him yet. She knew better. She was too self-disciplined to act on emotion. Even before Patrick began giving her pointers, she had taught herself to do things perfectly.

By concentrating on her breathing—slow, deep breaths—she was able to get past the moment. She repositioned herself to let some blood run to her calves and feet. She hadn't stood up and had only straightened her legs a few times in the four hours she'd been lying in wait.

Her readiness went to another level when she heard the door close. Her smile widened when she heard a couple chatting. After all the waiting, she felt she deserved the thrill of a double homicide. Blasting three or four at a time didn't matter to her. She had killed women, kids and animals.

"So what's your name, big boy?" said the high priced prostitute.

"They call me Goliath, and I'm hung like horse I hope you can handle it." They were standing in front of the bed.

She threw her pocketbook on the floor with her left hand and lightly rubbed his crotch with her right. "If you can give it, I can take it," she said, adding, "in any position you like." Before she finished her sentence, she was pulling her dress down in a seductive manner. There was just enough light from the moon for them to see each other's faces.

Trina heard all that she wanted to hear. Surges of heat had started running through her body, just as they always did before she had a kill.

Goliath was thinking about how hard he was going to beat up the pussy. He already had an erection because of the way she was talking.

Trina could see them through the drapes as they climbed on the bed. She stood up to get herself ready and to finish letting blood run to her legs. Just a couple more minutes.

Goliath entered her from the back.

"Give it to me, Goliath!" She was thinking that he was quite large—one of the biggest she had dealt with.

"You shouldn't have said that." He started banging her as hard as he could. On a few occasions, he had put a few prostitutes in the hospital.

"Damn, Goliath, you are hung!" She usually faked her screams, moans and groans. "Oh, my God," she shouted. He had hit the top of her with all the force that he could muster. Each time he banged her, he pushed her closer to the head of the bed.

The sounds were turning Trina on.

The prostitute had her hands on the wall to keep from being forced through it. As painful as it was, she was enjoying the good fucking. Goliath continued pounding her, and she continued to scream. In the middle of her orgasm and screaming, two bullets pierced her skull, causing her to fall forward into the headboard. As Goliath turned after hearing the muffled sound of the shots, a bullet pierced his forehead, landing directly between his eyes. The second shot hit him in his left temple as he fell forward. Blood was everywhere.

Watching his body drop on top of hers made Trina hot. She stood there, almost motionless, panties soaked. Murdering made her cum all over herself every time. The smile on her face resembled that of a two-year-old who had just received a brand-new toy.

The feeling was extra good to her because she had gotten to knock off two for one. Just like in the movies, she fired off four pinpoint shots with nothing but the moonlight illuminating the room.

As a precautionary measure, she stood there to check for any movement. To be doubly sure, she walked over and nudged the bodies to make certain neither was alive. She took a few steps back once she was satisfied.

She pushed the.25 down the front of her pants until the silencer tickled her pubic hairs. The length of the gun made her think about something hard, long and strong going in and out of her. She thought about what it would have been like to take on that big dick of Goliath's. She didn't even get to look at it. Being asthough sexual pleasure was no comparison to homicide, it was just a flicker of a thought.

To finish enjoying her mission, after she cut their throats, she lit up a joint of hydro. It felt so good to be so bad.

# CHAPTER 2

It had almost been a decade since Trina committed her first murder. She and her identical twin brother, Troy, had done what they felt was the right thing to do.

For almost four years, their mother's boyfriend, Brutus, had been beating on them and their mother, Vanessa. It was one of those situations in which a female needed a male to help out with the bills. Because of this, Brutus felt like his money entitled him to do what he felt like doing. Their mother felt like she had to tolerate it and that Brutus was the best she could do.

It was hard for Trina and Troy to keep hearing and seeing Vanessa be verbally and physically abused. No matter how much they pleaded with her to leave him, she kept telling them she needed him and that he'd treat her better in the future. But he didn't. Two weeks couldn't go by without Vanessa getting a black eye or split lip. It was no secret on 165th Street in the Bronx on the Grand Concourse that she was constantly brutalized.

Things got worse as Trina, an attractive red bone, got older. Her body started to blossom. And her mother's boyfriend started taking serious notice and making verbal sexual advances.

By 14, Trina looked like a full-grown woman and was constantly turning heads. At Taft High School, she was getting more than her share of attention. Even her mother was getting jealous and she had become verbally abusive to Trina for no apparent reason.

The remarks from Brutus had started to scare Trina. She wanted to tell her mother, but was too afraid. She wished that Brutus would disappear.

"Troy, we have to do something," Tr
like it was more than a national emergen
"What are we supposed to do? Ma
to pay these bills" Though he didn't k
not to say that she loved him.

"He's going to get me, so we have to get hu.
screamed. "I'm not going to let him put his hands on m
time she saw him, it made her feel sick. It was bad enough u.
she had to wear clothes that he'd paid for—something he always
reminded her of.

Troy was usually aggressive when it came to his sister's
honor. But in this case, fear of what his mother might do kept
him calm. "What are you planning to do? " Troy exclaimed.

"I have a plan." She wanted to slap him in the face for not
stepping up. "We have to kill that bastard before he kills us or
our mother."

"How are we supposed to kill him?"

"With this." She pulled a paper bag out of her jacket. She
opened it to let him see a nickel-plated .25.

He sat up in the train seat. "Where did you get that from?"

"That don't matter. We got to do what we got to do."

"What about Ma? She's going to kill us." He didn't think that
he had it in him to kill, especially if it would make his mother
mad.

"Let me worry about that. Here's the plan." By the time that
they arrived back from Coney Island, they had gone over the
plan three times.

A week later they had worked up enough nerve to take care
of business. Troy was the main problem, though he only had a
small part to play.

As usual, the boyfriend came to their apartment on a weekend night about 7 o'clock to get something to eat. Troy told him
that Trina wanted to see him. This brought a smile to his face.

mother was in her bedroom asleep, tired from working as a library maid.

"What's up, Trina?" he said as he opened the door without knocking. She had her blanket over her, acting as if she was just waking up from a nap. "You're finally ready to let Daddy hit that?"

"Yeah muthafucka!" she said nastily as she threw the blanket aside with her left hand and fired two shots at him.

The first shot hit his right eye. The second hit his shoulder. He fell back and hit the floor. Half his body was in her room, the other half was in the hallway. Seeing him fall had her whole body tingling. There was a taste under her tongue she couldn't describe, but she knew she loved it. Instinctively, she got off the bed. She wanted to make sure that he was dead. She walked over to him slowly with her finger still on the trigger ready to fire if she saw one flinch.

She moved in closer, he grabbed for her leg. She fired five more shots. Three hit him in the head. One hit him in the throat. One hit him right in the heart. The chamber was empty.

As if on cue, Vanessa came out of her bedroom and into the hall.

"He tried to rape me. I could see it in his eyes." This was a preplanned act.

Vanessa screamed and was hysterical. It was hard for her to believe that he was lying there dead. Death was something she had never wished on him. Her feelings about what his financial support meant and her feelings for her daughter had her caught up. All the blood wouldn't let her reach out to him. She screamed and ranted. "What the fuck did you do to him?" she yelled. She hadn't even looked up at Trina to get an answer. She just walked back in her bedroom and slammed the door.

"I had to do it!" Trina hollered, though she knew her mother didn't hear her.

After his mother was gone, Troy came into the hall a few minutes later. "Damn, girl, you really did it," he said while looking down at the body.

"Yeah, that bastard is dead. I didn't miss a shot. I should have done it a long time ago."

"What did Ma say? I didn't want to come in because of all the hollering that she was doing." He glanced at his sister quickly to see her expression.

Trina was a darker shade of red, as if she had been in the sun.

"Just remember to say what you are supposed to say."

"I got that."

"We're finally rid of that bastard." Her energy level went down after she walked into the living room.

Fifteen minutes later an ambulance arrived with the police in tow. Just as the police got to the door, Trina's mother opened it.

"Arrest that bitch. She shot my man and killed him. I saw it myself." She was pointing directly at Trina, who was sitting on the couch with Troy. "Get that bitch out of my house."

Trina's mouth parted slowly. Instantly, she went into shock. Two officers picked her up off the couch and pushed her to the floor as they put her hands behind her back. She just kept staring at her mother.

Vanessa directed the officers and medics to the body.

Troy sat there as they took his sister out the door. It wasn't supposed to have gone down like that. He thought that his mother was going to be happy that she wasn't going to be getting beat up anymore. He hoped that things would be alright in the end.

Three days later, it came time for Trina to go to her bond hearing. This was the longest time that Trina and Troy had been separated from each other, and they missed each other dearly. Their mother had been acting so tense after the murder that she and Troy didn't speak for two days.

Things definitely were not working out as planned or expected. All that Troy could do was wait until his mother was not upset anymore. If she was mad at him, he couldn't tell. And he wasn't going to ask.

He knew for sure that his mother was mad with Trina because she wouldn't accept her calls. Their mother found out about the bond hearing when the court-appointed attorney called her.

When their mother and Troy arrived at the courthouse, the attorney told them that the court would let Trina go with them on the mother's word. It was a black-on-black crime, and Trina had told them that he was trying to rape her.

Troy wanted to go over and hug his sister. She was looking like she had been having a terrible time. Judging from the dark circles under her eyes, it was obvious Trina hadn't been sleeping well. Trina ignored the look and the fake smile that her mother gave. Trina was shaking and nervous.

About fifteen minutes later, Trina was at the defense table with her attorney. The attorney waved the mother over to the defense table to arrange Trina's release.

"Your honor," she hollered so that her disgust could be heard throughout the courtroom. "I don't want that tramp in my house. She killed my man. I saw the gun in her hand." Trina and Troy looked in amazement. A barrage of whispers broke out in the courtroom as the attendees questioned Vanessa's response. She looked at Trina with a look that needed little explanation. The lawyer's eyes were squinted to see if it was really Trina's mother. "So how the hell do I pay my bills? You little tramp. Worthless red bitch!" She walked out the courtroom, forgetting about her son, as if what she had just done was the thing to do with her head held high.

Trina ended up getting juvenile life. Her mother moved herself and Troy to South Carolina to get away from the city and make sure that they never saw Trina again.

# CHAPTER 3

J ason Scott joined the Federal Bureau of Investigation for one reason: to catch serial killers. Plain homicides weren't good enough, though that was where he had to start. Now it was time to move up to the big leagues and make his name as a great homicide detective.

While at Quantico, the FBI headquarters in Virginia, he cross-referenced all murders in the United States to find similar patterns. That's how he came up with the Hydro Killer. He had seven murders that happened in New York, Los Angeles, Houston, Miami, Atlanta, Memphis and Las Vegas. Ashes from a high quality marijuana bud had been found at each murder scene.

"Per your request, Mr. Scott, everything is just like it was two days ago, except that the bodies have been removed." Detective McGuire was a local cop who hated for the federal authorities to interfere with their cases. Most of the time they were just too pushy.

Scott walked in the room behind him. "Please show me where the ashes were found, if you don't mind." He had pictures, but he wanted to be sure.

Definitely a strange request in his opinion. "There's a circle in chalk on the carpet there."

Scott stood directly behind the spot and faced the bed. "He or she had to have been in the room before the victims came in, based on what you told me yesterday." He was referring to the victims being found in a sexual position.

"I can agree with that," McGuire said. "And I can assure you that it was a female." He pulled pictures out of his pocket. "We got them late yesterday."

"The time matches up with the time of death. Why didn't I know about this yesterday?" There was a bit of agitation in Scott's voice.

"It took a day to get the film from the hotel. It is owned by mobsters. They say they took their time getting it processed."

"That is definitely the shape of a female. We have a hit woman serial killer." This was the biggest break Scott had gotten so far.

"Would you mind filling me in on how you came to your conclusion?" McGuire found it strange that this kid didn't have a partner or a team of forensic specialists traveling with him.

"This is the seventh murder of a suspected criminal whose throat was cut after being shot, and again, ashes from a hydro joint were found to the right of the body. And always at a certain angle." With the picture, he was sure that he'd be able to get a team to lead an investigation. Twenty-three-year-old FBI agents are seldom taken seriously.

"I'll go for that. What do you think is the common factor among the victims?"

"That's what I'll have to investigate so that I can find her. I do know for sure that she loves doing what she's doing and is probably seeking credit for her work. That's how most serial killers are." He wasn't with the person who needed to hear the essential details.

"So what is your next plan of action?" He almost called Scott college boy.

"For now, I'm going to need this entire carpet."

"Excuse me?"

"The FBI needs this entire carpet. And I need it before the end of the day." His voice had risen. His attention went to imagining how she had pulled it off.

Trina had driven nonstop for two days to get back to Norfolk, Virginia. All the hydro that she had smoked had her wide awake. After most of her hits, she went on a binge. Usually for two days and that was it.

She was glad that Patrick had left the house for the afternoon, as he usually did. When she got in, she disposed of the silencer and the gun by placing them in a vat of sulfuric acid.

With that taken care of, it was time to get ready to get her groove on. To smooth herself out, she sniffed a line of coke. This would get her nerves back to where she needed them. She was already feeling sexy. A nice, long shower and listening to Erykah Badu would have her ready. She stayed in the shower for forty-five minutes, mostly masturbating and checking herself out in the mirror. If nobody else adored her, she definitely adored herself.

"Hey, Patrick," she hollered when she stepped out of the bathroom into her bedroom. She jumped on top of him and kissed his neck, ears, cheeks and all of his face. "I was scared that I was going to let you down."

"You could never let me down." He had been in the bed naked for more than fifteen minutes. He thought something might have happened to her since he had called her several times while she was gone and she hadn't answered.

Looking into his eyes with sexual hunger, Trina grabbed his manhood and slowly licked around the tip of it sending chills through his whole body making him moan. She smiled and whispered, "You like that don't you?" His eyes rolled back in his head as his moans let her know that he was loving what she was doing. Rubbing his balls softly she licked from the bottom of his manhood to the tip and said," I love Patrick, I love you so much. I'll do anything for you,baby. Anything you say." She went back to work and gave him the deep-throat treatment liked a pro.

"Oh shit baby, suck this dick, girl." He put one hand behind her head and eased her down on his dick. Up and down he guided her until it was just the way he wanted it. "Damn, baby, you gon' make me cum before I get in that pussy. Ahhhhh shit." He was fighting the urge to cum all in her mouth. The more he moaned and thrusted into her mouth made her pussy drip with anticipation of him sliding in and out of her.

"We have to get married, Trina." Sweat was starting to bead on his forehead.

She turned her head. "Am I good to you, Patrick?" She stopped sucking long enough to say that. She started up again. She started humming and sucking more intensely.

"You are the best, Trina." His dick was so hard that it felt like he was about to bust out of his skin. He was moving his left foot much faster. It felt like she was sucking on all the nerves of his body. The more he moved, the flatter he got on the bed.

"I love you, Patrick. Do you love me?" She stopped.

"Yes. I love you, girl." What else would he say with the bomb head she was laying down?

"I can't stand to be hurt, Patrick. I belong to you and only you." She caressed his balls with her right hand.

"I love you too, Trina. I know you know this."

She kissed from the shaft to his balls. She made sure that she didn't miss a spot.

"Please do that again." He wiped some of the sweat from his forehead. "Damn, Trina, that's it."

Quickly, she attacked the head again. First, she licked it to make sure that he was moistened up really well. She began sucking the underside of his dick, just above the balls.

"Oh, shit!" he hollered. "This is going to be a good one!"

She put her mouth back over the head and started sucking it until he was about to climax.

"Oh, oh, oh, oh," he moaned during the first spasm.

She felt his cum hit the back of her throat. This made her suck harder.

"Oh, Trina! Trina! Trina!" he hollered as he rose his mid-section up off the bed. He had to make her let loose.

She still made sure she got each and every drop.

# CHAPTER 4

When Patrick first met Trina, he and his wife were looking for a girl who was willing to be a love slave. Many perverted couples head to the nearest orphanage to find someone young and corrigible. But Patrick and his wife wanted someone a little older, someone with a great face and figure. The grapevine led him to Trina.

Trina had always been eager to get the approval of those in positions of authority. She learned that dealing with authority figures also helped her to get  money she needed to get material things with ease. But material possessions weren't her top priority, she was interested in easing her mental state by staying as high as possible to forget about her separation from her twin brother.

There was an incessant need for her to keep her mind at ease. She did all that she could to alleviate the pain from her mother abandoning her. It was a nightmare that she couldn't shake. And she wouldn't tell a soul what she was going through.

Trina wasn't fond of the idea of having sex with another female. But she was curious. She asked several lesbian inmates what it was like to be with another female because she saw so many female lovers in the prison. None of them had a steady supply of drugs, so she never experimented. Patrick and his wife, however, had plenty money and plenty material things. Maybe it wouldn't be so bad after all. Plus, she had a good idea.

The relationship started out like a marriage made in heaven. She kept them sexed just the way they wanted, from role-playing to kinky games. She just didn't go for being whipped and things of that nature unless they wanted the pain. She made sure that the both of them were exhausted after every round. They kept money in her pocket and gave her a brand-new Mercedes to drive. She even started going to college and kept a few boyfriends.

After about a year, Trina wasn't being stimulated by all the sex anymore.

There was only one thing that she could think of doing to fill the void. Her attempts to find her mother and twin brother had been fruitless. Committing another murder was the only thing that she knew to do. Just the thought of it brought a smile to her face.

She had been trying to suppress her urges, but the beast within just wouldn't have it any longer. "There are so many things that we can do without her. Don't I make you happy, Patrick?" Trina said to him in a sexy voice. She had just finished letting him hit it doggy-style. She had turned around and gotten in a kneeling position to make herself look submissive.

"We definitely have enough sex, so what is the problem?" Patrick sat in her recliner and lit a cigar. He was tired from fucking, but he was still hoping to gain another erection.

"So what good is she to you? She doesn't turn you on. And she's thinking about finding herself a young stud."

"Do you think that she'd do that to me?" He and his wife had talked about it on several occasions. He just wasn't having it. Why risk the embarrassment?

"She told me that you aren't giving her any dick. She's getting tired of me slapping on the dildo. She wants the real thing."

"That's what she needs to be satisfied with," he argued. The saggy titties didn't turn him on.

Trina giggled a bit. "So what are you going to do if she gets bold?"

Patrick blew out some smoke. He loved to smoke super-slim cigars. "I'd have to hurt her feelings for hurting me."

"If you let me hurt her, we could let the entire world know how much we love each other."

There was no doubt about her abilities. He had taught her much since she started living with them. He couldn't resist her eagerness to learn. "Do you feel that strongly about our relationship?"

"You don't need her. We don't need her. I'm the one holding you down." The cake was baking. All she'd need to do is put the icing on later.

"I've wondered at times what I need her for. She's just old and useless." He took a deep puff on his cigar. "What do you think that we should do to her?"

"We need to enjoy the million-dollar insurance policy that you have on her."

"It's better that I get it than her. What do you want to do to her?" He started grinning.

"A little poison. Who's going to question a retired high-ranking FBI agent?"

"Nah. We can't take chances like that. I need you to kill her with her own gun while she's on her way home. That'll be something that nobody will be able to figure out."

"You just rest. I got this. I'm going to make it look really good." She got off the bed and kissed him.

Three weeks later, Trina arranged for Patrick's wife to meet up with a 21- year- old male in a private place.

Trina waited three hours before she left on her mission to kill Cynthia. She wanted Cynthia to get all the dick that she could. She sensed that Cynthia was in there running her mouth too much, she did that alot. Besides, how much sex could a sixty-three-year-old woman stand?

Trina was riding a motorcycle through the woods and pushing it like her life depended on it. She hated that she had to ride a full mile through the woods before she could get to the road. She had just missed Cynthia by five- minutes.

She flew down the road without her headlight on. She didn't want anyone to be able to say that he or she saw one headlight at that time of night. Trying her best to focus her eyes in the dark Trina noticed that Cynthia's car stopped on the side of the road.

Cynthia realized that she had a flat tire. Dark and alone she immediately started to look for her gun, when she heard the sounds of a motorcycle getting closer.

The first shot knocked her brains all over the dashboard. Trina was supposed to make it look like suicide. So she placed Cynthia's missing gun in her lap.

"You just found your gun, and I was tired of eating that old-ass pussy. If Patrick hadn't okay'd my killing you, I'd have killed him along with you." She took all of Cynthia's money, her credit cards and jewelry. It wasn't a suicide but it damn sure was a robbery.

Fifteen minutes later, she killed the 21- year- old and took all of his money. She used a gun Patrick had given her. She emptied the entire clip of the .25 and cut his throat with a jagged-edged knife. Patrick had taught her to take precautions.

Two weeks later Trina walked into Patrick's room with two drinks in her hands and a joint in her mouth. "We have to talk, baby." She handed him a drink.

He slid over so that she could get on the bed. "I thought that you weren't going to be getting high anymore?"

Trina had stopped getting high for a second after the last murders.

"Things change," she said as she lit the joint.

"I knew that it was just a matter of time." He turned off the television and took a sip of his drink. Ten seconds later, he took two tokes of the joint when she handed it to him.

Seductively, she slid on the bed and started rubbing his chest. "Let's just say that I'm sick with it. I mean, I need a bigger thrill than getting high."

"What are you talking about?" He passed the joint back to her.

"I love being a killer." She took a long toke.

"Your killing had me at the police station having to answer lots of questions. You need to stop." All he could tell them was that he didn't know why his wife was on the road at that time of night and that he didn't know the boy in the cabin. He was telling the absolute truth. Still, he hated being a suspect.

"You didn't seem to have a problem depositing that $1 million dollar check" She gave him the last of the joint.

"No, I didn't, and I'm glad she's gone, but what's up with you?" He puffed the last of the 'dro .

"I found my passion and my purpose in life: killing people. You really taught me well. That's the only thing that makes me feel normal."

It was one of the most profound things that Patrick had ever heard. The way she killed his wife and that guy left no doubt in his mind that she was serious. He knew that she'd sooner or later find a reason to kill again. Having her locked up wasn't the answer. She could tell the authorities that they had conspired.

A few days later, after a meeting or two and a few phone calls, he put together a master plan to take advantage of her talents and desires. The Hydro Killer was born.

# CHAPTER 5

I t was late Wednesday afternoon when Jason Scott caught up with James Witherspoon, the FBI's assistant director. Scott had been walking by Witherspoon's office all day, just as he had done on Monday and Tuesday.

"We need to talk, Mr. Witherspoon. It's an emergency, and I do mean it's an 'emergency.'" He walked straight to Witherspoon's desk.

"You forgot to knock, and I don't have an open-door policy, so get the fuck out." Witherspoon had a nasty attitude when it came to his subordinates; it did keep many of them on their toes. He leaned back in his chair to enjoy the fear he expected to see in Scott's face.

"Sir, I need three minutes of your time. I have exactly what you need to make the FBI look good."

"I understand why a lot of people around here think that you are crazy. What the fuck do you have?" Witherspoon didn't care much for Scott because he was always skipping around protocol. Still, Witherspoon respected the kid because he had single-handedly solved a few murders.

"We have a female serial killer who is randomly killing people across the country. We need to go get her."

"Would you please sit down?" He waited for him to sit. "Didn't we talk about this a few weeks ago?"

"Yes. She struck again since then. She murdered a Colombian drug smuggler in Las Vegas."

"If I remember correctly, the last time that we talked, you didn't know that it was a female. What changed?" His tone and entire demeanor had changed. He was inquisitive.

Scott was surprised that Witherspoon was taking a genuine interest. "A camera caught her coming out of the hotel room of the drug smuggler. From behind, you can tell that it's a female."

"Do you have these pictures with you?"

"I have the entire tape in my office, sir. It's definitely a female."

"I assume you have done some other research into this matter, such as the time of death and things of that nature." Witherspoon turned a few degrees in his chair.

"The time of death is about the exact time that she's caught on the tape. She, whoever she may be, definitely did it." Scott leaned back in the chair. This was the most that Witherspoon had ever talked to him about anything. Most of the time, it was a quick pat on the back or a simple request.

"So refresh my memory—why do you think that she's the serial killer?"

"In all these murders, there are always ashes from hydro marijuana found in the carpet or on the floor."

Witherspoon started thumping his finger against his armrest. "Ashes from marijuana aren't a reason to connect a string of murders. You have to do better than that." His tone was a bit harsher.

"No problem. The ashes are always found on the right side of the victim. Just the same, the victims are also shot on the right side." He figured that was enough for the moment.

"I never heard of such a thing. What does this mean?" he asked, taking a deep breath. Witherspoon already knew the response.

"This is the third factor: All of the victims' throats were cut with some kind of jagged-edge knife. The knife rips as it cuts to make sure there's limited closing of the wound. For the past year, this serial killer has struck at least fourteen times." The case was turning into exactly the kind that he had dreamed about taking on. He had talked endlessly about it to anyone in the FBI who would listen.

"So why did you bring back that carpet from Las Vegas?" Witherspoon had been keeping up with all of his moves.

"As I suspected, somebody had been in the room waiting for the Colombian. She left indents in the carpet. Forensics say that she had to have been in the same spot for at least two hours." It only took a small amount of indentation to tell this.

"Is there anything else?"   "We're sure that she wears size eight in Avirex sneakers. This matches up with the tape." An idea came to him that would give him a good lead, but he didn't want to mention it.

"As you know, because of Homeland Security, we have to be careful with our budget and the cases that are taken."

"Are you telling me that you are just going to ignore these murders? She may be a homicidal maniac, which means there's no telling what she may do next," he said, raising his voice.

"Calm down. I take this very seriously. It's going to take at least one hundred agents. You only know that she's a female and wears a size eight Avirex." He came from behind his desk.

"I see." He stood up.

"Give me a few weeks. We are going to get this girl," he said, placing his hand on Scott's shoulder. They were eye to eye. "In fact, make me out a full report. Just forget about all the other cases that you've been working on." He walked him to the door.

"Okay, thanks. And thanks for listening."

Witherspoon waited for Scott to get out of earshot before he got on his cell. "We have to talk … like, immediately."

# CHAPTER 6

They called him the Car Master for a good reason. All a client had to tell him was what kind of car he desired and the color. If the money was right, he'd also get all the desired extras—rims, systems, etc.. In the streets, they called him T.R.

He learned the game in Greenville, South Carolina. When his money got right, he took the game to Atlanta. He had Car Master car lots and detail shops in Georgia, Florida, Alabama, Mississippi and Texas.

Just on the front tip, he was making millions. The real money was in stealing exotic rides and selling them for cash to hustlers. When he sold a hot ride, he made sure that all the paperwork was proper.

His water spot was Club 112. "Listen, y'all. We have to find two Lambos. There's a cat in Peru who says that he wants them, like, yesterday. He already gave me half the cash."

"T, we can't jack the cats we supplied with Lambos. You told us that was against the game. So we have to travel to fill this order." Mike was his number one man.

"We might as well start traveling," Calvin stated. "We're always able to get what we want in California." Mike and Calvin were two of the best car thieves T.R. had met. They were killers, and they were loyal. They stole the cars. He brokered the deals and fixed up the cars.

"Also, look on the Internet to see if there's anything in the Midwest. The closer the better." T.R. had been selling at least four cars a week. This order would slow things down because it could take three weeks to get a car back from California. Unless they stole at least ten cars, the trip wouldn't be cost-effective. That also meant sending a truck. Risk on top of risk. But he counted on the sale bringing more sales.

"Listen, T, we'll call you in about forty-eight hours," Mike said. They all dapped.

Calvin and Mike were also from South Carolina. They had all learned the trade under an Asian gang. It was T.R.'s idea to leave. He had been saving money, and, more importantly, he had made connections with the chop shops in Florida and New York. On several occasions, he had stolen cars on his own and laced his pockets. The chop shops didn't care where the cars came from as long as the paperwork was thorough.

To expand his empire, T.R. found cats who had done time for car theft. He caught up with most of them just before they got out of prison. He'd have a private investigator determine if the potential employee was a snitch or not. With ten good car thieves all only working on two-man teams, the money and the requests for cars wouldn't stop coming.

As many would say: He had the game on lock and he was the only shop in town.

"Hey, Patrick," Trina said as she came in the doors. "That dude in Maryland was too easy I didn't get a rush when I cut his throat though." It was a cat who had been rumored to be a confidential informant. He was getting ready to start working with the FBI.

"Damn. Maybe you were born for this kind of work." It was 4 p.m. She had left at 6 a.m.

"I told you that a long time ago. Where are you getting ready to go? You know that I'm wet.." She put her arms around his neck.

"I have to meet with somebody about your next gig." He kissed her. "You know how you get when you can't be on the hunt."

"We need to head to Vegas tonight and get married. I can't wait another two days." Since he had promised to marry her, she had only smoked one joint and went without any coke .

He turned them around so that he could head out the door. "I like the idea." He said that to make her happy. The way that she was doing things was scaring him. He wondered what kind of marriage he could have with a homicidal maniac.

"I love you, Patrick." She gave him a deep, long kiss. "I'll have dinner ready when you get back." She let him go.

He wondered two things as he left: if he should marry her and what his business partner wanted. Decisions had to be made.

To Patrick, Trina seemed absolutely normal, except for the murders and the lust to murder. He had yet to discuss with her why she killed her mother's boyfriend. In the beginning, it really didn't matter because she was just a sex slave. But she had become one of the biggest factors in his life. She had changed everything. He had no idea where her mental state was headed, but he had to keep her happy because she could bring him down and was helping him make lots of money.

Trina ran herself a hot bath and added bubbles and her favorite scented oil. It was time for her to think about her future. She thought that once Patrick married her she'd feel truly loved, which is what she wanted all her life. It made her feel good that they had secrets that created an inseparable bond. This also made her feel understood. It was time to start living a normal life.

But she wanted to do one last job before getting pregnant by Patrick. She wanted to kill four or five more people or somebody really important before she retired. She wanted to go out with a bang. That would get it out of her system. Then she could get married, have a baby and not look back.

She and Patrick had made plans to move to another state and have four or five children. She dreamed about this constantly, so much that she had been tempted to get pregnant against his wishes. But she couldn't do that to him. Patrick had never disrespected, mistreated or deceived her. She couldn't risk losing his love—the only love that she had.

# CHAPTER 7

Witherspoon had been at the meeting spot for fifteen minutes. He had arrived twenty minutes early. The situation was that serious. To make sure that their conversations were not recorded, they always met at an open field or a place that had lots of space. He always wore a device that alerted him to any electrical gadgets that were within one hundred feet.

Witherspoon was waiting for Patrick, who arrived exactly at sunset.

"My old friend, we have a rather serious problem. I need you to kill your future wife before we both end up in jail." Witherspoon remembered when Patrick had first stepped into the bureau.

"Damn, old man. You really need to retire. My wife has turned out to be one of the best killers that we've ever met." Patrick was one of the few whom Witherspoon could trust with his life.

"I'm only ten years older than you, so we must both be old."

"If you had a young girl like the one I have, you'd surely look a lot younger and be a lot happier." He was talking about the difference between paying young prostitutes as opposed to having a profitable relationship with one.

"Let me get to the point. The party has to come to an end. A serious hound dog is on the trail." He paused. "When I say 'serious,' I do mean serious." He turned to look at Patrick.

"I would think that is impossible. Please explain."

"She's being called the Hydro Killer, and there's a video of her leaving the hotel room in Las Vegas." He looked the other way.

Patrick had to think. He knew that Witherspoon wouldn't be lying or playing games. They had been making too much money off the murders—$100,000 apiece, minimum. Sometimes as much as a half-million apiece. He didn't know what to say.

They said nothing for five minutes.

"You're in love with her, aren't you? You are about to let her destroy us." His lips were puckered, the edges of his mouth pointed down. His eyes were as piercing as a cat's.

"No! Never! Why not have her kill the bloodhound? I can control her. I believe it's you who can't control the bloodhound." Witherspoon had started looking toward the moon.

Witherspoon pondered the idea for a few seconds. "I say we have them both murdered just to make sure there are no loose ends." He figured that it was more important to get at the bloodhound because he could find out many other things if he kept digging.

"There's another thing that we need to think about along with all of that."

Witherspoon looked at him with a look that couldn't be read. He was thinking about killing all three of them. "Did I miss something?"

"The Asians should have the $2.5 million wired in the next three days, unless they change their minds."

Witherspoon was silent.

Witherspoon picked the cases; Patrick made the propositions. They were both making twice as much as Trina. It was always an offer to get rid of the competition or get rid of an informant. Sometimes they were paid in cash. Most of the time the money was wired to an account.

The last sixteen months had been beautiful. They had made millions. Topping that off with another $2 million would be a lovely exit.

Witherspoon had to weigh the options. "Is there a way to stop the money from getting there?" There was little emotion in his voice.

"It took me three weeks to get a meeting with the head guy. I seriously doubt it." He exaggerated by a week. Patrick definitely wanted the money.

Witherspoon turned his entire body. "So we don't have much of a choice unless we want a war with an Asian Mafia?" These were just words because he knew the Asians didn't know anything about him. He also felt that Patrick would remain loyal. "No. They can get really crazy if that's what they want to do." He was debating what he'd do if pushed to murder Trina.

"We have to make a decision," Witherspoon stated dryly. "We'll have no choice but to have her do the hit. Otherwise, we'll have to do the hit." That involved way too much risk. He knew that Witherspoon would agree.

"We might as well get her to kill the bloodhound also. That should hopefully kill the investigation." He was thinking that he also had to kill Trina himself.

"That sounds really good to me. I'll meet with you tomorrow to get all of the information."

Witherspoon was thinking about all the things that could go wrong. There were things that he couldn't say at that moment, but he had to sign off on this.

"Yes, the bloodhound must be taken out of the picture. It must happen." Witherspoon took two steps then turned around. "I'll send you the information first thing in the morning. We don't have room for mistakes. Make sure you control her."

Patrick nodded his head, and they departed.

Scott had been working all day to put together his report. There were fifty murders and thirty-two murder scenes. Because he felt that Witherspoon was on his side, he started to look for some kind of pattern. It would be nice to know what she'd do next. Only insane serial killers killed at random.

Based on the evidence, she was always organized and always knew her target. She was definitely a professional, maybe an assassin. But the number of murders seemed too high for a hired killer. She was averaging two a month. But there wasn't a two-week period between the murders.

To establish a routine through locations, Scott ran lines on his computer as the murders happened. There was no discernable pattern.

Now that he had a chance to concentrate on just that, he skipped eating lunch. He had to have something else to connect all the murders.

He threw his feet up on his desk, closed his eyes and tried to come up with a new angle. "Hydro Killer, I'm going to get you," he kept saying to himself. To get more focused, he pinned the picture of her to his chalkboard.

Who are you, he asked himself. Where are you? Why are you killing all these people? Why are you getting high after each murder? What is driving you? There was one big question that kept popping up in his head: What did all these people have in common?

Scott put up all the pictures of the victims along with a little background information on his board. It took about three hours to compile the data from all the criminal files.

More than twenty of the names were connected with some kind of criminal activity. There seemed to be too many nationalities for all of them to be in the same group. A lot of them were rival drug gang members, but they had all been under some kind of criminal investigation.

He used a national criminal database to determine what agencies had been investigating the victims. The FBI came up more than any other agency.

As an FBI man, he had to sit back and think about this to make sure that he wasn't tripping. He ran the names again. There was no difference.

This left a few possibilities to look at.

The next thing that he noticed was that no agents had been named to many of the victims' cases and that the victims' names were mentioned in their rivals' files. This made the picture a little clearer.

Competition was being eliminated. He couldn't rule out that it could be a female FBI agent that was doing the hits.

He wondered if it was possible for him, an FBI agent, to commit all the murders. That was just too much traveling to do. Whomever he worked for would definitely notice that something was wrong.

He figured that an agent had to have gone in all the files, which meant that he had to use his access code. It would take some time to figure out, but he knew how to get information out of Quantico's computer system. It had been done in the past.

It was 10:30 p.m., and he was tired from all the thinking that he had done since that morning. He programmed the computer system to give him the name of who had had entered each one of the file the next day.

# CHAPTER 8

Trina was watching television in the living room when Patrick drove up. It was midnight. It was late for Patrick to be arriving.

He came through the door with a beer in his hand. He was out of his habit of just drinking at home and at social events. He took a long time coming in because he wanted to avoid her. There was a thought in his mind that he just couldn't shake.

"Please tell me what's wrong with you." She was sitting on the couch with her arms wrapped around her legs. Her face was resting on her knees.

He sat in his easy chair. He noticed that she wasn't dressed in some sexy lingerie as she usually was. "I had a lot of thinking to do. I just wanted to do it alone."

"I thought something like that. I stayed up to make sure you were safe. If you hadn't come in fifteen more minutes, I was going to start calling your cell. I just want you to know that you hurt my feelings when you didn't come back for dinner," she said as she began to walk out the room. She spoke in a concerned tone.

"Hold up, we have to talk," Patrick said, almost growling just as she disappeared from the living room. He had to get all necessary business out of the way.

She stopped in her tracks. She was about three feet into the hallway. The palm of her right hand was on her forehead. She didn't want to show him that she was angry.

He got up and followed to see why she hadn't come back. "Turn around. I need to talk to you." When he saw that she wouldn't turn around, he got closer. He turned her around. She didn't resist, nor did she hold up her head. "I'm sorry. We have to talk."

She pushed him back and held her head up. "So is this how it's going to be when we get married? I'm not going for it."

"Just please sit down. We have to talk. I'm dead wrong for missing dinner. I should have at least called. I'm sincerely sorry." The look on her face had him a little scared.

"This had better be good. I mean that." She walked past him.

He took a seat next to her on the couch. "It's time that the entire party comes to a halt and we leave the United States."

She got back into the same position. "Does that mean that we aren't going to get married?" She had a suspicious look on her face.

"We are going to do that, but first things first. Before we get married, something has to be done." He almost stopped talking because of the look in her eyes. "We have an emergency that has to be taken care of."

She stopped scowling and turned away from him.

"So you are trying to ignore me?" Patrick said.

"No," she said as she turned her head back around. "I feel that you are about to play me after all the loyalty that I've shown you. How long will it be before we get married? You know how I feel about that."

He looked down then looked back up at her. "There are two missions that have to be completed, then we can get married and leave the country." He was panicking on the inside. There were so many complications and potential complications that he couldn't think straight.

"These missions must be very important if you want to delay our marriage. Why not get married first?" She looked calm now.

"We have an emergency because you have been dubbed the Hydro Killer by the FBI. I got this information tonight. That's why it took me so long to get back." He got up and started pacing.

"They're calling me the what?" She leaned back in the sofa.

He stopped on the other side of the living room by the front door. "The *Hydro Killer*. What have you been doing at the crime scenes?"

She wished that he'd turn around. "I don't know what you're talking about." Deep down, she didn't care, and she almost said it.

He turned around. "No matter what, something has to happen." He aggressively walked back to the couch. "There's an FBI agent who's trying to put the pieces of the puzzle together. He has to be eliminated immediately. That's the way that it was put to me."

She liked the idea of killing an FBI agent. "It sounds like you are getting personal and jumping the gun. How can one agent be that damn dangerous? You've been smoking crack and didn't give me any?" She put her feet down and crossed her legs.

"It can happen. From what I was just told, this agent is desperate to get himself a serial killer. They say that's all that he talks about." He has visited a few agents to get info on the suspect.

"I understand why that may be important. So what is this other mission, and why is it so important? Is this another 'secret agent'?"

"No. The other is a hit that's worth $1 million to you. Then it's all over. Completely over."

Trina unpuckered her lips. "Why can't you take one of those hits?" The money didn't mean a thing to her.

Patrick was thinking that he'd have to kill her and do both the hits. "I think that you've forgotten who's in charge here. My wife isn't going to be disobeying me." He stood up.

"When this is done, I have needs." She stood up. "I'm ready to retire, and I'll love going out with a bang." "I also want to have some children by you."

"Okay." They hugged on it.

Scott went to his computer as soon as he woke up. He didn't want to wait to get to his office before he got the results. While his computer was logging into his terminal at Quantico, he went to get his morning coffee. It took less than five minutes.

Scott usually only slept five hours a night. He slept eight hours straight last night, however, because he had exhausted himself during the day. At eight a.m., it was late for him to be starting his day. His mother and father had gone to their real estate office in Richmond for the day.

On the computer, he had the names of all the individuals who had logged into certain files and when they logged on. He didn't want to believe what he was seeing. Witherspoon had logged into each of the files at least once.

He sat down. He had to give this serious thought. Just going out and accusing the assistant FBI director, let alone arresting and investigating him, was something that had to be done with care. Because of Witherspoon's position in the agency, there would be resistance from many. It would almost be necessary to catch him in the act. Thinking about what to do was a means to convince himself that it couldn't be true. The assistant director had an unblemished record.

He needed to know if the assistant director had been in other files. This required a little more poking around. There were several files that he went in. Half of these were eligible for investigation. All the victims had been murdered with the same kind of poison. Damn, serious work had been done to lots of people, Scott thought.

He printed out all of the information that he had. He decided to take a shower. It would help him figure out his next move.

He definitely couldn't just go up to Witherspoon and show him what he had found. Going to Witherspoon's boss wasn't an option either, but he had to go to somebody and he had to be smart about it. The hot shower helped him out a lot, it soothed him and helped him collect his thoughts. He had to make a trip to Washington to see the head of the CIA. He would love to investigate a high-ranking official in the FBI. As he got dressed, it made more and more sense to him.

He called his brother in the CIA and told him a few details.

He was extremely excited. Not only had he found the case, he had, in all practical terms, solved the case. It was a serial killer case that was like no other. The case was more than enough to satisfy his desires and make him famous.

He was expecting the investigation to last about six months. Once he found the female who was doing the killing, he'd be done. She had to be convicted with Witherspoon. He was psyching himself up as he put on his motorcycle helmet. A surge of energy went through Trina when she saw the garage door open. Whether it was a car, truck or bike, she would use her high-powered rifle to stop it and its driver. She knew that it could only be her target that came out of the house.

From almost two hundred yards away, she hit him in the head and knocked him off his bike. She had waited for him to get fifty yards away from his house.

The second shot missed, which didn't matter because the first spun him around.

If his helmet weren't bulletproof, he would have been killed instantly. Because of the speed that he had been going, he had been thrown about fifty feet. He hit the ground hard. That, along with the impact of the bullet, almost knocked him unconscious. He was willing himself to come out of his daze. The roar of a motorcycle put fear in his heart.

Just as he unzipped his leather jacket to pull out his weapon the motorcycle rolled by and he was kicked in the head. She let her bike fall to the ground so that she didn't have to take her eyes off him. It took her less than two seconds to unzip her jacket and get her 9mm out. In the next second, she fired two shots into his body. She approached him.

"Hello, Scott. I'm the FBI agent you're looking for." She had her left foot on his neck. With her left hand, she pulled out her FBI badge. He was looking at her with fear in his eyes. "I hope you like my identification." She flashed her badge in his face. With the barrel of her 9mm, she lifted the face guard of his helmet.

Her pussy was wet and throbbing from the thrill of killing a cop. She put the barrel of the gun up to his forehead and said, "I always make sure that my victims are dead." He was breathing heavily and shaking and sweating. His reaction was making her feel that much more powerful.

She was hoping he'd go for his weapon, but he didn't. "You ain't that much fun, but I'm still enjoying this. Good night." She let off two shots into his skull.

She looked around to see if anyone was on any of the country roads. After she wiped the barrel of her gun off and put it in its holster, she pulled a joint of 'dro out of her pocket. She didn't think about checking the contents of his jacket.

"I'm going to smoke this down the road, Mr. Scott. Maybe I'll see you in hell when I get there." She revved up her bike, did a wheelie in the dirt and headed for the woods.

Doing a cop was just what she needed. Him being the cop who was trying to bust her and Patrick meant everything in the world. If she never murdered another person, she felt that she had released all of her anger and frustrations. It also made all the difference in the world that her murdering spree was with the man at the center of her life. Now she could raise a family with him.

She laughed all the way as she rode through the woods. Her satisfaction was so immense that she didn't smoke the hydro. Patrick not wanting her to get high anymore had a lot to do with that too.

He didn't want her to continue to leave a trail. He told her she needed to get her body together to have a healthy baby. She went for it.

Before the night was over, she planned to be in Atlanta. She would wait there for Patrick to tell her what to do. She told him that she was doing this last mission to show him how much she loved him.

# CHAPTER 9

When Scott's parents got in from work at 5 p.m., they saw their son's body. After calling the FBI and the local police, they called his older brother, Gerald. Gerald had left Washington immediately.

An hour later, the entire area was swarming with police and FBI agents. They were canvassing the area, asking people if they had seen anything. There were absolutely no leads.

"Hello, Gerald," Martin Jackson said as he opened Gerald's car door. "We were waiting for you before we put the body in the ambulance." Martin Jackson was the agent in charge at the scene for the FBI. Because it was an FBI agent who was murdered, the Virginia police knew the feds would want jurisdiction. "Thanks, man." Gerald replied.

He had his eye on the body. "Walk with me.

He called yesterday and last night about the Hydro Killer. He said that he had a package for me to look at." They were about two feet from the body.

"He was always talking about catching a serial killer. That was his biggest goal. He was a good kid."

Gerald had stopped listening. Seeing his brother spread out like that was causing him pain in his chest. His heartbeat had sped up fifteen beats per minute. It was hard to believe that somebody had gotten to his brother. Scott had been overly cautious about everything. Instinct told him that the killer must have had something to do with what his brother was working on.

"Whoever got at him had to have been a professional." Gerald was shining a flashlight on the helmet. "This is a bulletproof helmet. I remember when he got it. He must have been working on a serious case."

"I can't disagree. Let us take care of the body. We'll have a joint task force formed in the morning—the FBI and CIA." Now that Gerald had seen the crime scene, it was time to close the thing up.

"Let me see if there's something on him that he wanted to give me." He kneeled down.

Martin leaned with him. "Use these gloves. There's no need to make my superiors mad with me."

Gerald took them without looking up. After he put them on, he unzipped Scott's jacket. There was a white envelope that had a CD in it.

"I bet that whatever he wanted to show me is on this CD. Do you want to go inside and see what's on this? My brother has a great computer system."

"Sure, Gerald. Let's go see what's on this. It can't hurt." He was taking the chance that he'd get chewed out by his boss for letting evidence get out of his hands.

"Let's go." Like many cops, he was trying not to show much emotion. His mother and father were standing on the porch. He hugged them and introduced them to Martin. He also told them that he had to use his brother's computer for a minute. They knew that Gerald would hunt the killer down on his own if he had to.

Getting to the contents of the CD was easy. "He was working on a serial-killer investigation," Martin said.

"He also came to a lot of conclusions."

"This is the first that I've heard of the Hydro Killer. There are a lot of dead people because of this person." In Martin's experience, serial killers didn't get away with all those murders; they eventually got caught.

"My brother did a lot of work on this thing. I'm going to the end of the file." They started reading all the conclusions together.

Martin wasn't sure what to say. He started reading it again.

"This has to be investigated very thoroughly," Gerald said. His first thoughts were that Witherspoon had his brother murdered. He looked up at Martin.

Martin sat in the chair that was next to Scott's bed. "All I can say at this time is that it's a serious matter. It's an FBI thing, and we need to deal with our own. You can trust me like that."

"First, I'll need to have a copy of this. I'll need to be kept up to date on everything."

Martin stood up. "I promise you that." They shook hands. "This has to be checked for fingerprints and everything else. This is a big case."

Gerald had already started sending the contents of the CD to his computer in Washington.

"Thank you for meeting with me on such short notice." Witherspoon had waited a mile down the road from Patrick's house. Witherspoon had the hood of his '57 Chevy raised like there was something wrong with it.

"It isn't a problem. We have many things to attend to." Patrick hoped that nobody was watching them.

"As we speak, they're probably putting the bloodhound's body into an ambulance and getting ready to pronounce him dead on arrival."

"I know that. That can't be the reason for this meeting." This was the first meeting that they had that wasn't out in the open.

"No. I need to know a few things."

"The money arrived at three forty-five, and the mission should be taken care of by the weekend."

"That isn't the only thing that's on my mind." He put the hood of the Chevy down. They were both standing up straight and staring at each other across the front of the Chevy. "You understand that you have to kill her, don't you?"

Patrick sighed, his expression was one of discomfort. He said, "What makes you feel that is necessary?"

This thing doesn't need any loose ends. What makes you think that she'll be able to stop killing?" He almost called her a homicidal maniac.

"She says that she's tired. She and I are about to leave the country." He had been struggling with this decision since the last meeting.

"I see. And I disagree. Please tell me how a serial killer can stop killing. Did you think about that?" He had seen many agents make mistakes because of their feelings for a female.

"If I'm not mistaken, we have several killers who are loose cannons, and we haven't killed them. Isn't that correct?"

"None of them has killed more than six times on six different missions. She has killed more than fifty people. I'm sure she's addicted. She could easily take you down." He was speaking through gritted teeth.

Patrick didn't want to show his anger. "I have control of her. She just wants to get married and have a few children." He wanted the same thing. She had breathed new life into him.

Witherspoon walked around to the driver's side where Patrick was standing. "I hope that all of this doesn't come back to haunt us." He got in his Chevy.

Patrick stood back to give the Chevy enough room to move. He watched the Chevy ride down the road.

Patrick knew that he was supposed to kill her without giving it a second thought. He had rationalized in his mind that he had control of her by giving her what she wanted. He could also see and feel her loyalty. If it weren't for all the love that she was giving him that he couldn't get anywhere else, he probably would have killed her. The loving was that good to him. Giving it up was a hard thing to do. He was straight-up whipped.

He had to take that chance.

Lil Wayne's "Everything" was pumping through the club's sound system and moving the crowd.

Trina found herself a table and ordered a bottle of Moët. She wasn't about to drink anything heavier than that. This was her first time being in Atlanta, and she wished that she weren't there on business.

Several men tried to join her. She refused all of them by saying she was waiting on her man. She hadn't yet seen any of the people she was looking for.

A dark-skinned model chick came over. "May I join you until your party arrives?"

Trina looked up at her. She figured that the girl had to be a lesbian or something. "Yeah, you can chill with me a bit."

"Your man must be crazy to stand you up at this club so late. My name is Chancey." She stuck her hand out. Trina gave her a feminine handshake . "Girl, where did you get that dress?"

"My man bought it for my birthday." She wanted it known that she had a man.

"So where is he at?"

"Well, I'm not waiting on him. I'm looking for a guy called the Car Master. Can you point me in his direction?" That was her purpose for the conversation.

"So you're one of his girls or something?" She took a sip of her drink and hoped to hear a "no."

"No. I'm in the market to get myself a '64 Corvette. I heard that he's the man who can make it happen." She was still keeping up with the people who went into the VIP section.   "I   like classic cars too. I'll tell you what—I'll get you into VIP with me. He's been up there all night." She winked her eye.

Trina winked back. "So what are we waiting for?" She put her drink down.

"Let's go."

All the rejected fellas egos were salved a little bit. Chancey went both ways, newcomers to her club was a regular thing. They looked like two models heading for VIP.

Trina made it a point to look at as many men's faces as she could. She knew to make eye contact and to smile a lot. Club 112 was packed to the max, and there were lots of faces.

Trina was definitely thinking she had to come back to Atlanta to party. She always heard about Hotlanta.

"That's him with the red leather jacket on and the yellow baseball cap. Those are his top boys that are with him." Chancey was waiting for the perfect moment to present her offer of bump-ing pussies.

It was all three of them. She could tell by their haircuts and complexions. They were all sitting at the same table they were at when the pictures were taken. If it weren't for Chancey, she might have missed them.

"So how do we get to talk with them?"

"As good as you look, that's going to be very easy. Just stay right here."

"Okay." Trina struck a sexy pose.

Chancey sashayed her way over to them like a runway mod-el. "There's a lady here that needs to see y'all about getting a classic car." She turned and pointed to Trina.

"Oh, yeah?" one said, curiously. They eyed Trina and liked what they saw.

"Get here, over here," another said loudly. Chancey waved at Trina to come over.

Trina thought that it had almost been too easy to meet them. Because of the table she was headed for, most of the people in VIP had their eyes on her. She walked over, moving a little slower as she got closer to their table. She wondered if she'd be able to poison all of them in the club and get it over with. Sexing all three of them wouldn't be cool, at least not on the same night because so many people would remember that she was with them.

"Hello, gentlemen" Trina said. She decided to keep it gangsta because they and others were staring so hard. "Y'all don't know how to invite two ladies to have a seat?"

T.R. began to stand, and the others followed suit. He spoke first. "Please have a seat, ladies. We were caught off guard." He motioned for the waitress to bring his favorite—two bottles of Cristal.

"Thank you, T.R.," Chancey said as she sat.

The name made her eyebrows raise. She sat down and looked directly at him. She couldn't tell what he really looked like be-cause his baseball cap was pulled over half of his forehead.

"Damn, girl, you look familiar," Calvin said.

"Yes, you sure do," Mike stated loudly. Something told him he should have spoken first.

"She's trying to get a car, not a date, fellas . Y'all aren't going to embarrass me." Chancey was getting a little jealous.

Trina hadn't taken her eyes off of T.R. Just as she was about to say something, the waitress came back with two bottles of Cristal and five clear glasses. Trina felt the need for another drink.

Trina and T.R. were locked in a trance. T.R. pulled his cap up to let his face be seen. He waited for the waitress to finish. She poured the ladies' drinks first.

T.R. turned his hat backward. "What's your name, and what do you want?" He leaned back to get a good look at her.

Mike and Calvin looked back and forth at Trina and T.R. They were looking at Trina now.

Trina looked at them, then at T.R., then back at them, then at Chancey. "I'm not sure." T.R. didn't act surprised. After a little thought she spoke up and said, "I know what kind of car it is that I want."

"So tell him. You aren't going to embarrass me," Chancey said loudly. She sounded disgusted.

Trina gave T.R. a funny look and raised her eyebrows like something was up. Chancey caught the look but didn't understand what was going on. T.R. caught the look as well and felt a little uneasy.

"Is something wrong?" Chancey asked Trina.

Trina shook her head and said, "Nah, I just had a crazy thought, T.R. looks just like my twin brother, Troy."

"That's why she looks so familiar!" Mike and Calvin hollered. They all looked at T.R. Trina took a sip of her drink.

When you feel like you're looking at yourself in a different version, it's a must that something be said, especially with the situation at hand. If it turned out that she was wrong about T.R. being her brother, she would play it off by flirting or just saying that T.R. looks like her twin brother who had disappeared years ago. But she was almost sure it was him. And killing her twin brother, even for a million dollars, just wasn't happening.

T.R. took a long look at Trina. She definitely looked like his sister. He didn't want to handle this in front of Calvin and Mike and definitely not in front of Chancey. "All of y'all leave. Let me talk with her alone," T.R. said. They stood up slowly and looked at each other. "I said goodbye," he said sternly.

He clasped his fingers in front of him and rested his face on them, letting his legs take all of his upper body weight. He waited until they were out of earshot.

T.R. and Trina were examining each other's faces. All kinds of thoughts and emotions were running through minds and hearts.

"You need to say something, T.R. People are going to start thinking that you're crazy or something ." She wanted to make up her mind. If that door didn't have to be opened, she didn't want it opened.

"Okay." He started taking off his jacket. She sipped all of the Cristal in her glass and started pouring some more. She only took her eyes off of him for a fraction of a second. "What I have to say will make this matter very simple."

"So say it—if you ain't scared." She liked the expression that came to his face.

He was rolling his shirt sleeves up to his elbow. "Okay, I'm ready. What state were you born in?"

"I was born in the Bronx, and we went to Taft together."

"When is your birthday?"

"We were born on December 15. I came out fifteen minutes before you did." "Tell me—"

"Nope. May I ask a question, Mr. Car Master?" She felt that she had a bigger interest in this than he did.

"Why not? It might make this quicker," he answered angrily. He was planning to beat her ass for pretending to be his twin sister.

"How did we become separated? And please give me details." She took another drink.

He reached over and took the drink. "I might not want to be hospitable to you." She looked at him, amazed. She was angry because of that and his anger. "I hope that you aren't playing with me."

"I'm not. So answer the question. Like, now!" She put her pocketbook down and was ready to kick her stilettos off. "My sister caught a murder charge, and I never heard from her again. Can you tell me any details about that?"

"Sure, I can. It happened halfway in and halfway out of my bedroom."

"That's public information. That was probably in the police reports that you read."

For years, T.R. had been trying to track down his sister. He had hired several private investigators. None of them could get any further than the prison that she had served time in. One of the prisons had burned down, thus ending the paper trail.

If she had the nerve to play like she was his long-lost twin sister, it meant that she had major game. T.R. wasn't taking any chances.

"We planned the murder when we rode to Coney Island," she said. "The alibi was supposed to be that he tried to rape me. Need I say more?" She placed her right arm on her right thigh and pointed to her birthmark.

He was trying to think of something else that only she and he might know. "Let me look at your elbow." He rubbed it hard to make sure that it wasn't just makeup.

"That hurts. Would you like to cut it off and take some DNA tests? We can do that."

He stopped. "You just might be my sister."

"It took you three days to get your—" She was about to mention his hesitation before the murder, but he cut her off.

"That's enough." He pulled up his shirt sleeve and showed his birthmark, which looked just like hers. "I believe you, but we'll do that DNA thing on Monday."

"I don't need any further proof. Can your twin sister get a hug?"

If she was running game, he felt like he had to go for it. The expression on her face said she was telling the truth. He thought about it for a few seconds and then stood up.

She had started crying by the time she wrapped her arms around his neck. He wrapped his arms around her and began crying. Once she started, it was hard for him not to.

"I missed you, Troy. That's who you are to me, you will always be Troy. I prayed every day that you'd write me. I never gave up."

"I tried my best to find you. I swear I did." People had started to stare at them. "It's all good, though."

"We're making a scene." She pulled away and backed up. "Let's go outside and talk. It's really important."

It was the happiest she had been in years. He was the person that she loved the most in the world. She was glad that she had talked to him before she saw him alone. She was wondering if she would have killed him. She knew that she could have never forgiven herself.

They got in his white Escalade. "I need you to drive to an open parking lot, like, on a dirt road or a really dark road," she said.

"What's up with all of that?"

"Please, just listen." She turned up the volume on his stereo.

The more she talked, the more he knew that she was Trina. He thought that her request was really strange, and that scared him a bit. He planned to grab his 9mm when he got out of the truck. He was paranoid.

It took about fifteen minutes for them to get to the airport. "Is this cool?" he asked her.

"This is really cool," she said as she started to get out of the truck. He hadn't heard her because of the noise from an airplane that was landing. She headed to the front of the truck.

He got his gun from under the seat as he stepped out. He was glad that she walked to the front of the truck. He wanted to keep his eyes on her.

She reached the front of the truck and placed her pocketbook on the hood. He was just about to turn to face her.

"Put your hands up, whoever you are."

She complied with a surprised look on her face. She was staring at the gun as if it could be fake. "What is wrong with you? I know you aren't going to kill your only sister that you haven't seen in ten years?" If her voice were any higher, she would have been screaming.

He just stared at her.

"Troy put the gun down. I have something to tell you."

"What could you have to tell me if you didn't know that you were going to see me? How could you have something to tell me?"

Is it wise to tell a person who has a gun on you that you are a hit woman and you were hired to kill him? She definitely had to figure out the right thing to say.

He was holding the gun at shoulder level. "You need to think of something to say." Two SUVs pulled up.

She noticed that the vehicles were driven by his boys.

"You have ten seconds to say something that's going to keep me from killing you."

"I'm your sister! What the hell is wrong with you?" she pleaded.

"Six, five ..."

"Stop, Troy!" She looked at his boys, hoping they would help.

"Three, two ..."

"The FBI started an investigation on you and your organization. When I heard your name, I volunteered to lead the case."

"Say what?" he hollered.

"Look in my pocketbook. You'll see my badge." That was a close call, she thought to herself.

"You had better be telling me the truth." He waved to his boys to come.

"What's up, boss? The area is empty. We need to rush."

"Open her bag. She says that she's with the FBI."

"Yeah, she has an FBI badge. It's her alright."

"Okay. Step back." He put the gun down. He definitely wasn't about to kill an agent. She had to have a partner or a crew in the area.

"Thank you, Troy. This is what I get for trying to protect my twin brother? You could at least say 'I'm sorry.'"

"I'm sorry." I didn't understand why you wanted to come out here so that we could talk. He wasn't going to shoot her. He felt that he had to protect himself from getting robbed or kidnapped. There was still the possibility that his sister could be being used to set him up. The game calls for a man to think like that. Troy put the gun in the small of his back.

"You scared the fuck out of me. You were about to kill your sister in cold blood." She had her hands on her hips.

"I was just protecting myself. I couldn't shoot you. You look just like Ma. So tell me what's happening with the FBI investigation on me." He waved his boys off because he now fully believed her.

"Hell to the naw. Get me the hell out of here." She was walking while she was talking. Now just wasn't the time.

He just stared at her sitting in his passenger seat. What else could he do but drive her up out of there. He respected that she was rattled.

It was the first time that somebody had pulled a gun on her. She didn't care for it at all. She made a decision that they should get DNA tests before they went any further. She wasn't taking any chances that he might do something else irrational. Since she felt that she needed to make a few more decisions, she didn't say much else to him. What to do was a big thing.

# CHAPTER 10

"It hurts my heart that one of ours has been murdered in cold blood." Witherspoon was concluding his eulogy. "There is no way that we'll be able to bring Scott back to life, but we sure can bring his killer to justice." Out of the five hundred agents in the crowd, one hundred of them were investigating the murder, thinking that the murderer might show up at the funeral. "We are the Federal Bureau of Investigation. That means that we are the best at conducting investigations. There shall be justice. I personally promise that."

More than a thousand people were attending the funeral. Most of them had never met Scott. Many of them didn't live in the state. Their attendance was about support. It was standard procedure for a cop's funeral.

Gerald and Martin met up at the back of the crowd. He wanted Martin to fill him in on what was going on with the investigation.

"Have a seat, and let's go for a drive." Gerald motioned to the passenger side of his Porsche. They got in and headed toward I-95. Nobody at the service missed them.

"We figure that Witherspoon has to know something about those murders," Martin said. He had reviewed the documents at least seven times. It was that important because it was his immediate supervisor he was investigating.

"I feel the same way," Gerald said. "What is your reasoning?" The CIA was on back-up status because it was an FBI in-house matter. Gerald's supervisors were ready to jump on the case. Special clearance would be needed to investigate another agency.

"It seems that he was in each of those files about thirty days before most of the murders occurred."

"That's a pretty deep calculation."

"There are a lot of missing links in this puzzle," Martin said.

"I wouldn't say that. We know that he knows something and that he's involved. So he has to lead us to the rest." He noticed that he was pressing the accelerator a little harder.

"We need the other links to make a case. We can't rush this, so be cool. We want him as badly as you do."

"So tell me what's happening. Have y'all started surveillance yet?" He had been spending a lot of time with his family.

"We've been watching him since the night the murder was committed. I put a few of my most loyal agents on the case."

"So what has happened so far?"

"Earlier that night Witherspoon met up with a former agent who stays in the area. His name is James Patrick. He was at the funeral."

"So do you think he has something to do with it?" He was ready to see James Patrick.

"It's hard to say. He's been hanging out near Patrick's house for the past few nights. They haven't met up with each other since the murder, though."

"So what's y'all's next move?"

"We're going to have to do some illegal taps and things of that nature." There wasn't a federal judge or magistrate in the area who didn't know Witherspoon on a personal level.

"What about surveillance on this Patrick cat?" Gerald asked.

"We are going to do that also. It's all going down before midnight tonight, but we'll probably get there if we just keep watching Witherspoon. He just isn't hanging out on that road for no reason."

"That makes a lot of sense. Would you mind telling me what road this Witherspoon is hanging out on?"

"I can't do that. Let us handle it. In a few days, I can tell you that this is going to be over with. Now, get me to my house."

"Do you think Witherspoon murdered my brother alone or do you think he had help? I'm just curious."

"I've been tangling with that myself. If he didn't, he definitely knows who's involved. Just like he said: The killer shall be brought to justice."

Gerald couldn't ask for any more for the time being. The FBI was on top of the prime suspect, though he was an FBI supervisor. Though he was satisfied with the FBI's efforts so far, he had to put some of his own effort into the investigation. He also wanted to make sure that his brother received credit for solving a major serial killer case

"It isn't like you to not call me. What the hell is going on?" Patrick hadn't heard from Trina since she had left Virginia.

"Why are you cursing at me? That's how you plan to treat your future wife?" She was expecting him to be mad.

"I hope that you're calling me to tell me that you did something and you're about to come home."

"No. I ran into some serious complications. You need to know about this."

"So tell me." Patrick was shaking his left fist in the air.

"I have to tell you face-to-face. I'll be back in a few days." What she had to tell him was too serious to be discussed over the phone.

"That isn't good enough. I need to know today. You are making me look really bad."

Trina was caught in a terrible position. She wasn't going to kill her brother, but she didn't want her future husband mad either. Unfair was the only way that she saw it.

Frustrated she stated, "You act like I'm not important to you."

"What does that have to do with you being important? We're talking about business here. Trina tell me what the problem is."

She put the phone by her hip. She was thinking about hanging up. She would have to do a lot of explaining about Troy, especially because she had never told Patrick that she had a brother.

"Trina. Trina. Talk to me," he said angrily.

"I'm here. I have to go. I'll see you in a few days."

"You had better do more than that."

Click. He looked at the phone as if to say that she couldn't have done that to him. To no avail, he called her cell.

Trina walked into the VIP at 112.

"Where have you been, girl? This party is for you," Troy hollered while walking toward her. "This little party is just for you." He put his arms around her. They had done the DNA test at his doctor's office.

"I had to make a phone call. I'm sorry."

"You look great. And I don't want you messing with any of these busters. They're all lame and broke as can be. You feel me?" It was a brotherly thing. He also felt that he had let her down when she caught her case.

"I have a man, Troy." They got on the stage.

"Ladies and gentlemen, I want y'all to know that this is my twin sister who I've been searching for for four years. She walked in here last night to see the Car Master. You fellas need to be careful. This is my baby sister. Y'all party up. Everything is on me." The crowd clapped out of respect.

Trina had to go through the ritual of shaking hands and kissing cheeks with all of his friends and associates. That took a half hour, and she was tired.

"Let's go, Trina. I have something to show you. It's outside." Troy pulled her by her arm.

He was not feeling the way that cats were looking at her, so to avoid problems, it was best to get her out of their presence.

It was sitting in front of the club waiting for them—a 1976 Corvette Stingray.

"I picked this up for you today. All I had to do was go to Texas. This is what you came to see me about. My gift to you."

Trina smiled like nothing bad had happened that night. "Let's go for a ride. I'm driving since it's my car."

"Well, let's go, little sister."

"I think I was born before you," she stated before she sat in the seat and laughed.

He got in the car quickly. "You don't have to tell the world," he said. "Just drive. You were always hardheaded."

She put the car in motion and put the pedal to the metal. The tires hollered *"Scrchhhh."*

"Did you have to do that, Trina?" Troy joked. "The FBI is after my ass."

"Big brother, we have some serious things to talk about."

"Somebody trying to put me in jail is a rather serious thing. But you got my back."

"Things are much worse than you think." She headed toward I-85.

"What do you mean? Are they getting ready to arrest me in a few days or something?"

"No." She looked over at him before she blended with the traffic.

"So do I have to wait all night for you to tell me?" He yawned because he'd been running all day.

"Somebody is trying to kill you," she stated dryly.

"Stop playing. If you had said rob, I'd have understood, but kill? I don't have any competition in this state." He started laughing.

She got off I-85. When she got to the bottom of the ramp she said, "I want you to listen to me real good. Let me pass this vehicle first."

"I know for sho' that yo' ass drive like a madwoman. I'm not riding in a vehicle with you anymore. It's a good way to get killed."

She looked at him and smirked.    "That wasn't a joke." He was glad that she was heading off I-85. He was looking at her thinking about how bodacious she used to be.

"I wasn't laughing. I couldn't stand to see you get murdered." She turned left at the light. They were at the same spot that they were the night before. "We need to have a heart-to-heart talk. Get out of the car."

"Okay."

She got to the front of the car first. There was a slight breeze, making it chilly. She looked him up and down, appreciating how much of a man that he had become. Tears welled up in her eyes.

"What is wrong with you? We did this the other night." He smiled because he felt the same way.

"Just be quiet and let me hug my brother." She pulled him tight and pulled herself up. He had grown to be about seven inches taller than she was. "I missed you so much."

"I missed you too. Why didn't you ever write or something?"

"I wrote you at least a hundred times." She sobbed a few times and laid her head on his shoulder.

"None of the letters got to me. I would've written you back."

"I understand." She let him go and stepped back. She wiped the tears from her cheeks. "So how is she?" Saying the word "mother" wasn't happening.

"She's doing okay." Troy hadn't called his mother and told her about Trina being alive and well.

"We'll get to that later." She coughed to get some bass in her voice. "I have to tell you something."

"You've already told me enough. Me and my crew are going on a long vacation, so stop trippin'. We have to go see Ma." He wanted to get it over with.

"What I have to tell you is much more pressing."

He took his Gazelles off. "Please tell me."

"There's an extremely large hit out on you. Somebody wants to kill you."

"So the FBI is supposed to be protecting me or something?" As far as he was concerned, he didn't have any competition or enemies.

"No, it isn't like that. Stop asking questions and let me explain."

He shrugged his shoulders.

"I was hired to murder you and all your boys." She held her finger up. She wanted to explain how she had become a hired killer. Most of the details were vague. She told him that the FBI badge had been given to her. To make him believe her, she showed him a few newspaper clippings for murders that she had committed. One was for a murder on the outskirts of Atlanta. It just so happened that he knew the cat. He had to put his head down and close his eyes to let it all sink in. Primarily, he was trying to figure out who would pay that kind of money to have him killed. If she was getting a million, there had to be more money and other people involved. It was frustrating trying to figure out who was behind this because he didn't know of many cats who could afford to spend that kind of cash.

All the thinking made his head cloudy. He hadn't ever thought about his life being saved because of his sister being sent after him as a hit girl. He couldn't get the thought out of his head that he could have been murdered.

"There's no way that you could've killed me and my peeps. We don't be slippin'—ever." This was an emotional and egotistical response.

"I just followed a man across the country before I put two in his head and cut his throat. After I killed her boyfriend, it became just a matter of procedure."

"I'm still not buying it." He was mad with himself. His sister's game was still tighter than his.

"Your boys wanted to fuck me. I would've fucked the both of them to get the other half-million. They would've been relaxed, and all I would've needed to know is where you rested your head."

"Oh, yeah?"

"If blowing up your house is what it would've taken to get at you, it would've been done, but I can't kill you." She hugged him again to make him feel better.

He hugged her back. The look in her eyes kept him from arguing any further. The intensity in her eyes, the stance and leaning of her hips, the sternness in her voice and her unwavering gaze were unlike anything he had seen in females he'd met. His brain was still on lock otherwise.

"Now listen good," Trina said as she pulled back from him.

"What's up?"

"We have to leave tonight. We're going to go see the person who can tell you who paid for the hit. We have to leave now. Just trust me." She didn't want to take the chance that Patrick or anyone else might come to kill her and her brother.

"We have to pick up some artillery first."

"No, we don't. My SUV has everything in it that you can think of. Even a fifty cal. I always get my man, little brother."

She hated that she had to show her bad side to her brother in order to save his life. She had been fully prepared for the killing to stop. She was thinking to herself what she'd do if Patrick tried to kill Troy. At that very moment, she didn't know what she would do. It would be nice if they could give the money back and help Troy establish himself elsewhere. It would be wonderful to marry Patrick, skip the country with him and her brother, have a few babies and never look back. But that was no plan. That was more like a dream.

Witherspoon pulled his head from up under the hood of his 1964 GMC truck just as Patrick stopped behind the truck.

They established eye contact. Patrick moved in front of Witherspoon. Their dance last for ten seconds.

"It took you way too long to get here," Witherspoon said. They were actually supposed to meet in an open field up the road a half hour earlier.

"I've been trying to iron out the problems. We do have a big problem." Patrick didn't look his best.

"What exactly is the problem? I need to know about these things."

"We'll be pulling up close to them soon. We can hear everything that they are saying, loud and clear," an FBI agent said to his superior.

"Okay, stay with the plan. Just keep going down the road and get as much as you can." Martin had all of Witherspoon's cars bugged. With five vehicles doing surveillance in rotating shifts, none of the conversations would be missed. "Just stay on the plan."

"You need to be careful about how you talk to me. This isn't an FBI operation." Patrick was hesitant to come to the meeting because he knew that it would not be pretty.

"Where is that crazy female of a killer of yours?" A black Durango truck with tinted windows drove by. It slowed down when it got closer.

"You still need to be careful. And she's coming back."

"There are millions on the line, and you are about to get the blame for this. She's your responsibility." His voice had risen considerably.

"Relax, she should be back in a day or two. I'm sure that there's a good reason." He noticed the truck making a U-turn.

"This is surveillance unit five. We have a suspicious black truck that's making a slow U-turn in the vicinity."

Martin squeezed his eyebrows closer together and looked up to the right. "Maybe it's just a coincidence. It is a public road."

"It started slowing when it got close to the targets, sir. It was going so slow that I had to pass it."

"We'll just watch it. That's all that we can do."

"Please call me the minute that you see her. Call me at home. We all have to talk," Witherspoon said with authority.

"Just remember this: We may have to give the money back." How Witherspoon answered would determine how he handled the rest of the situation.

"I don't have that in my plans. We must make sure that this thing is taken care of without any loose ends." Witherspoon and Patrick eyed the black truck as it passed.

Patrick made sure that he got a good look at the truck. The rest of what Witherspoon was saying didn't register. Patrick sensed that the truck wasn't a coincidence. He just walked away without saying a word.

"The parties dispersed. The truck took off at a high rate of speed. What should we do?"

"How fast is the truck going?" Martin didn't want to make any grave mistakes.

"It's moving pretty fast. Way over the speed limit. At least eighty."

"Just relax. Let's go over these tapes at headquarters. Lots of decisions to be made."

Patrick had been placed in a terrible position. He figured the black truck had to be part of the Asian gang that paid for the hit. He promised them that they'd be able to take over Car Master Inc. and not have a problem with the FBI. It had taken him months and a few trips to New York to close the deal.

It was definitely an emergency that called for damages to be issued. Whenever Trina had a problem, she always asked for his advice. He was thinking about killing her and the targets. The Asians told him that if the target didn't get hit, that he—and all the people he loved—would get hit.

# CHAPTER 11

Troy had just woken up from a nap. All the information that he'd been hit with put him out. He felt safe riding in Trina's SUV. It was bulletproof and much more. She gave him a loaded 9mm so he could put it in his waistband and feel manly.

"Hey, Troy, you need to wake up. It's your turn to drive."

"Are we in South Carolina yet?"

"Yeah, we crossed the state line about fifteen minutes ago. There are a lot of state troopers in these parts who hate blacks. They still use the rebel flag." She wasn't worried too much because she had her false badge. She was in a rush to get matters resolved some kind of way.

"We should have brought my main boys along. We may have to go to war with somebody." He felt this way because he was in an extremely peculiar situation.

"That's too much to be carrying. Believe me, I can handle anything that comes our way. Plus we'll be able to do what we want. Trust me." She winked her eye at him.

"What are you, a Navy Seal or something?" He figured that she could shoot at the most, just like his boys.

"I have all kinds of training. I'm not just some ho from the ghetto. How many bitches you know from the 'hood who have a traveling war machine and the know-how?"

"But we don't know who put out the hit on me and my crew," Troy said.

"Who'd benefit if you got murdered? It has to be somebody in the same business that you're in."

"I'm the largest thing in the area and five states."

"There has to be somebody big enough in one of those states to benefit. They put out a lot of cheddar to get you bro', so think."

"Okay. This is a stab in the dark, but the next biggest thing to me is the Asians from this state. But me and them are like family."

"When it comes to money, only blood relationships can stop a covered hit, so don't overlook them," Trina said.

"When I say that we are like family, I mean that," he said. "They taught me everything I know about the business."

"Well, you had to have left them and got out on your own to make it as big as you are. You have to be taking food out of their mouths." She looked at him to see his expression.

"I'm still not feeling that," he said. "Get off at this next exit. I have to get some clothes. This may take more time than we think."

"Okay, but what about the Asians? Are you bigger than them?"

"Yeah. I'm pulling in close to $750,000 a week just selling hot cars. Everybody comes to see me. I'm the Car Master." He had gotten slightly excited.

"So if you disappear, who else is going to be able to make the best come up?"

"I would think them—the Asians. They were making a pretty penny when I was with them, but they were just like blood family to me. It's hard for me to believe that."

"This is how we do things. Patrick is a slick-talking white man who gets his money for the hits and protection. He probably convinced the Asians that they could make millions with you out of the picture. Money makes people go against family."

"Turn left at this corner," Troy said.

"Is this going to take long? I'm in a rush."

"Turn right at the next corner and pull up behind the green Bentley."

"I don't like strange places. At the moment, I'm very tense and in a rush." She backed the truck into the driveway.

"Just relax. Nobody knows about this place, so, please, just be cool."

Though things had been moving fast, Troy hadn't totally forgotten about his duties. There was something that he had to do.

He knew he was heading into a dangerous situation and that he might not get another chance to take care of this. He wasn't sure if this was smart, but he had to do what was right.

He knocked on the door before he opened it with his key. When he walked into the kitchen, he saw whom he was looking for.

He grabbed her up and hugged her as hard as he could. She hugged him back. "Mama, I have somebody that you need to meet," he said as he put her on the floor.

"You want me to meet one of your girlfriends this early in the morning? Boy, what is wrong with you?"

"Nothing. I'll be right back."

She sat down to drink her coffee.

"Hey, man, thanks for returning my call, especially this early in the morning." It was about nine thirty a.m., and Gerald had left a message for Martin to call him ASAP.

"That was your brother. I'm sure you'd do the same for me."

"So tell me what's up with Witherspoon." Gerald had taken leave from the CIA to keep up with the FBI's investigation.

"We have him under constant, super-tight surveillance. If he utters a word in his house about the murders, we'll know about it."

"So what do you have so far? I know that you have something."

"Well, he met with Patrick yesterday evening. We have the entire conversation."

"Please tell me more."

"They are really mad with each other, and there seems to be something serious going on," Martin said. He was expecting him to ask for a copy of the tapes.

"So what's going to be your next move?"

"We are going to plant bugs in Patrick's house just as soon as we get the chance. Whatever it is that they are up to has to be illegal and has to deal with the murders." Martin wasn't going to tell Gerald about the female. That's who he really wanted to watch because he had evidence there was a female involved. He thought she was the one carrying out the hits.

"So do you think that they are the only people that are involved? This thing seems to be a little more complex for just the two of them." Gerald had gone over all of the evidence and felt that there were many missing links.

"I think that Witherspoon is going to crack sooner or later. I'm a patient man."

"I understand that. It sounds like you have enough to make an arrest. Witherspoon is going to tell all that he knows, and I'm pretty sure Patrick is going to do the same." His voice had taken a commanding tone.

"Hey, man, it may be a little early for that. What is the rush?"

"Let's say Witherspoon gets a whiff that you are investigating him. What do you think that he's going to do?" Gerald asked.

"That isn't going to happen. All of the agents that work with me are loyal." He had raised his voice a notch. "What is there that he can do?"

"In case you haven't heard," he said, standing up to make his point, "an FBI agent has been murdered because of this Hydro Killer. What makes you think that it can't happen again?" He was pointing his finger in the air as if they were in the same location. "He might even decide to leave the country."

Martin ran his hand across his face. "Maybe we should talk later. You seem to be really upset about this thing."

"Hell yeah, I'm upset. My brother has been murdered, and we both know that Witherspoon had something to do with it." He wanted to say that Patrick had to be his brother's murderer. Who the female was didn't matter to him.

"Call me back later." Click.

Gerald was in the black truck and had also made a recording of Witherspoon and Patrick's conversation. As far as he was concerned, Patrick was the one who killed his brother. Plus, Patrick had the experience as a killer to do it.

Patrick's coldness had Gerald thinking that they just might skip town or something. He wasn't about to let that happen. At a minimum, he decided to put his surveillance efforts on Patrick. He had no intention of allowing his brother's killer to get away.

"Mr. Patrick, it took a long time for you to return my phone call. Joey Lee really doesn't like that." Joey Lee was an up-and-coming member of the Asian mafia. Most of the members of the Asian mafia lived in New York, California and abroad. This is why so few knew that an Asian mafia existed. They only knew about the Asian gangs.

"Please accept my apologies. There are simply going to be a few delays." Patrick had promised that he'd make it all happen in less than forty-eight hours after the first payment. It had been much longer.

"Make sure that you call me in the morning." His voice was nasty and straight to the point.

"Before you hang up, I need to ask you a question." Patrick looked side to side.

"Please make it quick. My time is precious." Typical of a gangster who hasn't exactly made it in life to be arrogant when the chance is presented.

"If we aren't able to pull this off, will you accept the money back? Maybe even with a little extra."

Being trapped among the Asian mafia, Witherspoon and Trina wasn't a pleasant position. His instinct told him that something was wrong with Trina and that something may have changed her attitude about murdering people. It had happened to him. Giving the money back—even if it meant allowing Witherspoon to keep his million—was the only solution that would work.

"No, that isn't an option."

Joey Lee had promised his superiors that the five million would be a worthy investment and pay back three-fold in one year. With Troy and his top two car thieves and lieutenants out of the way, he and his soldiers would easily be able to take over the rest of the operation by strong-arming the other top people. They planned to use a black dude as the figurehead. Nobody would know that the bulk of the money would be going to the Asian mafia.

Joey didn't plan on failing, no matter what he had to do. His honor and dignity were on the line. Failing at this mission would mean a major loss of respect with the Asian mafia. To him and his kind, death was a better consequence.

Trina was mad suspicious when Troy finally came out the house. He walked to the driver's side of her SUV. She was clutching her .380 just in case somebody came after them. What she didn't know along with being anxious had her leery.

She looked him up and down to let him know that she was pissed. She waited for the window to come all the way down before she spoke, "Why are we still here Troy? We have something very important to do."

"But we have to do something first. It isn't going to take that long."

"Troy, I don't have time for these games. I need to get all this over with." She figured he was trying to get her to see their mother because it popped in her head he was from South Carolina.

"I'm sure that we have time. I'm in a rush also to get this hit off my head." He had a puppy-dog look on his face.

"You want me to go in there and talk to ..." She pulled her cap down further over her eyes.

"Our mother." They hadn't spoken about her. He had been waiting for her to bring up the subject.

Thoughts of her mother had been thoroughly blocked out a long time ago. She leaned her head on the headrest.

"Little sister," he said as he stepped closer to the vehicle, "if what you told me is correct, the Asian gangs aren't a joke. We may not come back."

She turned her head to look at him. "Don't ever say anything like that. I already told you that I always get my man. There are no other options," she snarled.

"She's still our mother."

*"No!* That's *your* mother. My mother abandoned me over *some trash!"* she yelled, as she sat up in her seat and pointed her finger at Troy.

He had already prepared himself to remain calm. "I understand how you feel and I don't want to change that, but I have to make things better."

"Well, maybe you should have written me a few times. My address was on the Internet." She was looking him dead in his eyes and praying that he didn't say the wrong thing.

"When you didn't write—"

"I wrote you a bunch of times. I told you that yesterday." The anguish could be heard in her voice.

"May I finish? I was so busy wildin' that I didn't think about finding your address on the Internet. I was too busy making moves, sexing chicks and getting high. When I thought about it, you had left the prison. Plus, I hadn't heard from you. I figured you didn't want to hear from me."

"Something must have happened to the letters because they didn't come back to me." She looked out her front windshield.

"I'm telling the truth. I decided to look for you a few years ago. Just come inside for a few minutes."

"I can't do that." The things that her mother had said and done after the murder and in the courtroom were flashing through her mind. She hadn't thought about her mother for more than five years.

"Yes, you can. You have to. The healing process has to start somewhere. We can all be a family if we work at it." He had thought about all of this a long time ago.

*"No!* Nothing can make me forgive her. Nothing. So let's get the fuck out of here before I leave you here." She rocked back

and forth in her seat. Her love for her brother was the only thing that kept her from rolling up the window.

He placed his arm on the roof of the vehicle to rest his head on his arm. "Damn, sis'. Just do this for me. I can see in her that she truly misses you. Just come in to let her know that you are alive. Just do that for me." He was using his most convincing voice.

"No. I'm not going to do it. Am I leaving with you or without you?" Just the thought of being in the vicinity of her mother made her ill.

"You are going to regret this. She still loves you."

"You have ten seconds." She cranked up the SUV and started rolling up the window. As the window went up, she revved the engine and looked at her watch.

Troy started walking toward the front of the SUV. He was confident that she wouldn't run him over nor leave him there. He took his time getting in.

Just as Vanessa was about to come out the door, the SUV pulled off. She decided to use her cell phone.

"Answer your cell, Troy. It isn't that bad, now is it?" Trina said in a sensitive, high-pitched feminine voice.

He cut his eyes at her. "So you want to start giving orders?" He flipped his phone open. "Hello." It was their mother, and she wanted to know who was making all that noise. "It was your daughter." She hung up.

The word "daughter" made Trina look at him. "You just had to say that it was me." She made a right turn.

"What does it matter?" He reclined the seat a bit so he could relax.

She remained silent until she pulled on the side of the road. Just as she put her SUV in neutral, she said, "So why do you want to make me look like a coward?" She had turned a little so that they were face-to-face.

He looked up at the ceiling as if to seek guidance from another source. He wished that he could avoid answering her. "How did the word 'coward' come into play? She needs to know that she's fucking up also."

"I'm not about to let you make me look bad." She put the vehicle in gear.

"So you want to see her? Is that the catch? You had to do it on your own terms, just like always." He was thinking to himself that it had to be a woman thing.

"No. I'm not going to look bad in front of her. I'll never let her think that I'm scared to face her." She was turning the block. "I bet she can never punk me."

"So I know what to say to get you to do something." He made his seat come back up. "Are you sure about this? That was the quickest turnaround that I've ever seen." They pulled up in front of the driveway.

She cut the engine off. "I want you to stay in the truck." She looked over at him.

"If you leave your gun in the truck, I'll do that. You look really angry."

"I always have a gun on me. I'm not going to shoot her, no matter what has happened. I still have love in my heart," she said as she looked at him.

He wasn't sure of what to say. Though he wanted to be there to mediate, he felt compelled to respect his sister's wishes. Hell, she was doing her best to save his life.

She opened the door and got out of the truck without making eye contact with him again. She puckered her lips as she walked up the driveway to the front door. Under any other circumstances, she wouldn't have been visiting her mother. There was too much pain. There were too many bad thoughts. Being abandoned had a grip around her heart.

As she knocked on the door, she thought about leaving. What good could come from this visit, she wondered. What was there to gain besides proving she was every bit as much of a woman as her mother? But maybe that was enough. That was important to her because it took years for her to reestablish her self-esteem and self-worth. She wanted her mother to know that Trina wasn't a little girl anymore.

She knocked again, this time a little harder. She took several deep breaths and composed herself. She was in complete control of her emotions.

Troy hit the speed dial key for the house on his cell. Just as it started ringing, his mother opened the door.

"Who are you, and what do you want?" Vanessa asked as she puffed on a cigarette.

Trina took the cap off of her head and let her hair hang. She and her mother looked each other up and down. She didn't say anything. She figured whatever she said would be the wrong thing. What does one say to the mother who abandoned her?

"Who are you, and what do you want?" She took another drag.

"It's me, Trina, your daughter." She could not believe that after all those nights of crying and the negative emotions that she was now facing her mother and saying that she was her daughter. She didn't understand that she was trying to show her mother that she was the one who had power over herself, not her mother.

"I knew that!" Without warning, she slammed the door. It made a loud, crashing sound.

The sound shook Trina and made her jump. Troy jumped out of the truck.    Trina grunted as she let out a deep breath. Impulsively, she kicked the door. Hard. It sprung open, slammed against the wall and slammed shut again.

"Let's go, Trina," Troy said as he grabbed her from behind. "Let's go, Trina." He turned her around.

"Let me go," she said as she lifted her arms in the air. They began walking toward the truck. "Drive. I'm ready to get the fuck out of here."

They hopped in the truck and put their seatbelts on. Troy cranked up the truck and began pulling out the driveway. Trina couldn't take her eyes off the door.

Trina wiped beads of sweat from her forehead. "I lost my hat back there."

"I'll buy another one." He glanced at her to check her expression and gauge her temperament.

"That's okay. We should not have done that. I feel like I just started my jail bid all over again." Unloading her 9mm into somebody was all that she could think about.

"I can change things. We all need to be able to have good relationships with each other." He was hoping for the best. When he got a chance, he'd call his mother and tell her that she was dead wrong.

"She still hates me. I could see it in her eyes. It was never a fun situation." She always told herself that she did what she had to do.

"There's just one thing that I need to know."

"What's that?" Trina asked.

"If she just apologizes to you, do you think that you'd give the relationship a fair chance?" He was prepared to ask this question again and again if he had to. He wanted his mother and his sister to repair their relationship. Family was important to him.

"I don't want to feel this way ever again. I don't think that's a good idea." She was looking out the window, thinking about some of the kills that she had enjoyed the most.

"Just think about it. And keep an open mind for your brother."

She reached into the glove compartment and pulled out a small manila envelope. "I'll think on it. For now, I have to smoke this hydro." She fired it up just as they hit the highway.

# CHAPTER 12

"Yo, Joey, Patrick just left out his house. What do you want us to do?" Anthony Chin was Joey's most trusted lieutenant. He had been watching Patrick's house from the woods all day. Two FBI agents were doing the same thing from the front and they had fallen asleep. It was eleven-thirty at night and they had gotten lazy.

"Just follow him. We have to find the other target and kill all of them." Click. Joey Lee was infamous for being blunt and straight to the point.

Patrick was heading toward Norfolk Beach's parking lot. To get there, he took an intricate route by going in the opposite direction on I-95 and getting off and riding around in a wooded area to make sure he hadn't been followed.

After making two turns and backing onto a path, Patrick lost the Asians.

Gerald parked in a path and laughed. With an opaque tracking device, he'd be able to find him. Gerald noticed that some foreigners had also been following Patrick. He wrote down their license plate numbers like any good cop would.

He sat for fifteen minutes before Patrick finally moved. Patrick went farther into the country and parked again. He parked on a long strip. In the daytime, it would have been extremely hard for Gerald to camouflage himself. On a bluff move, he parked directly across from Patrick and acted as if there was something wrong with his vehicle.

Gerald did a good job of making it look like there was something wrong with his vehicle. He made eye contact with Patrick several times. If Patrick came over, he planned to say that his oil was low. Gerald made sure his oil check took an extremely long time, and Patrick finally pulled off.

Gerald pretended to pour in a quart of oil. There was the possibility that Patrick could be watching him from down the road.

When he got in his vehicle, he saw that Patrick was heading toward I-95.

Gerald made sure to stay at least a mile behind him.

"Where is this man of yours at?" Troy asked. He was still driving. "It's 12 o'clock, and he was supposed to have been here an hour ago." Troy was in a rush to find out who had put out a hit on him and handle his business.        "He's really big on being safe when it comes to an operation." She took a sip of her coffee. After smoking three joints, she wasn't feeling as edgy about what happened with her mother.

"But he doesn't seem big about being on time. We'll have to talk to your man about that." Ne-Yo's "So Sick" was playing.

She giggled a little and turned the radio down a bit. "Troy. Tell me something." She looked over at him to make eye contact. "Did you really miss me? I mean, did you *really* miss me?"

"You are the only sister that I've ever had. How could I not miss you?" She wondered if she had to kill Patrick to save Troy.

"I used to dream about you, little brother. Do you remember the time I poured honey in all of your underwear?" She started laughing.

"That isn't funny. I never got you back for that." He had to go to school without any underwear on. Troy thought to himself that she always had a lot of heart.

"Since I just saved your life, I'm sure we're even." She rubbed her left hand on the side of his neck.

"I guess that means that God never wanted us to be separated. But I don't think that it's all over." A wave of paranoia went through him. "He needs to show up."

She looked out the front window while drawing her hand back. "I'm glad I didn't kill you. I had to think about it a lot after you pulled that gun on me. I knew then that I still had love for you. That really pissed me off." She glanced at him.

"Again," he said, pausing, "I'm sorry. Stop being so sensitive. A lot of things happen to people in the ATL. I'll make it up to you."

"I didn't want to be a killer. I was at the point that I was ready to stop. Now I really don't know. I just wanted to be loved and not abandoned again."

He squeezed her shoulder. "Look at me." He waited for her to face him. The pain in her expression touched him in a manner that he couldn't describe. "There is nothing that will be able to come between us. I love you, little sister."

She turned her head, then looked down at the floor. Her cell phone went off. The sound took her from the thought that she was having. Before she answered her cell, she said, "If you let me down, I'll have to kill you." She answered her phone like what she had just said was part of protocol. She didn't say anything during the call. She briefly held the phone to her ear and then hung up.

"Listen to me, Troy." She had to make sure that he didn't want to continue the conversation. She was putting one in the chamber of both of her nines. One was in her shoulder holster. The other was on her hip. She looked at him when she finished.

"I'm scared that he might try to kill you himself." She looked over at him. "This truck is bulletproof, so I want you to stay inside and be ready." She was praying that they wouldn't end up going after each other. She knew that Troy didn't have a chance. But never would she tell him that. "Okay."

"So what are you going to do?" He looked toward the figure that had just exited a vehicle about fifty yards away.

"Protect my brother." She slid over and kissed him on the cheek.

As she was getting out of the truck, she took a deep breath and scanned the parking lot and surrounding area. She was happy to see few cars and no movement other than Patrick getting out of his vehicle.

Patrick was thinking about pulling his gun on her. Betrayal was the first thought that went through his mind. Why was she in the SUV with another individual? Why was this individual in the driver's seat? There was too much of a chance that putting her at gunpoint could make the situation worse. And he could tell by the way she was walking that she was ready to pull out. He had taught her all that she knew, and he knew all of her habits.

The entire time that she was walking toward him, she was rubbing her palms together. After scanning the scene, and being satisfied, she kept her eyes on him and his hands. His drinking coffee and sitting on the hood of the car didn't present a threat.

She stopped about three feet in front of him. It was a tense moment for her. Usually when she looked at him, she was looking to please him. She was certain she would get a negative reaction on this occasion.

"I want you to know that you've placed my life in danger. I thought you loved me." Patrick went straight for her emotional center.

"It doesn't look that dangerous out here. And you are still living, and you know that my love is true. That was nasty of you." What he said made her mission easier.

"Please tell me why you didn't complete the  His voice was dry. The tension between them could be seen in how he folded his arms and sipped his coffee.

She took a deep breath and crossed her arms also. "The target is my twin brother."

He leaned forward a little bit and stood up. "Did you say that he's your twin brother?" She had never told him about having a brother or her mother. She had always avoided the topic.

"That's exactly what I said. We took DNA tests and everything. I know that you don't expect me to kill my one and only brother." She backed up from him a bit. She was beginning to feel uncomfortable.

He didn't want her to kill her brother. Later might be a better time, if it here would come a time that it could be said. "Is that who's in the truck?"

"Yes, that's who is in the truck. So you want him yourself?" She was wishing she had a pattern to follow to guide her. Where she usually got her advice from was where her problem was. She was praying that she wouldn't have to kill Patrick to save her brother. That is, if she'd even be able to do that.

"So what are you expecting me to do?" Her nervousness was causing him to be cautious. His plan was to do the hit himself and possibly kill her if he had to.

"You need to tell me who put out the hit so that we can squash this or something." She felt tense because he wasn't acting like himself. A couple hits of heroine would be nice.

Gerald had listened to most of the conversation. He was pretty much satisfied that Patrick had something to do with his brother's murder. The solution to his problem was easy. Still, he wanted to hear a bit more.

Patrick had started getting angry because she was standing up to him. "You placed both of our lives in jeopardy. So you want to sacrifice my life for your brother's, and we'll probably all get killed."

She rolled her eyes and let out a deep breath. Troy didn't know if he should stay or go. "That isn't fair. Would you kill your brother for any amount of money?"

He turned to his right and put his right foot on the bumper. "Didn't I let you kill the wife I had been with for forty years?"

She puckered her lips and looked up at the stars. "That isn't the same thing, and I think that—I know that you were tired of her anyway." His cynicism made her more determined to save her brother's life.

"So what do you suggest we do? The Asian mafia isn't going to accept the money back. It sounds like you want to get us all murdered."

As Troy was about to pull the latch on the SUV door, he saw a figure walk by the passenger's side. The figure was moving rather fast.

"We could just leave the country like we planned."

"We have company. Spread."

Trina went to her left while she placed her hand on the gun that was attached to her waist. Patrick pulled his weapon from his sock.

"Freeze! This is an arrest," Gerald hollered as he was still walking at a fast pace. Gerald had a bead on Patrick. "You killed my brother, you bastard. I heard the entire thing." In the middle of his sentence, he had started firing shots at Patrick. His Glock had the beach parking lot lit up.

Trina fired at Gerald as she ran. She heard her shots, his shots and other shots. Through her peripheral, she didn't see any fire coming from Patrick's direction. She was satisfied with what she saw. Gerald had fallen about ten feet away from Patrick's vehicle.

Making sure he was dead was the only thing on her mind— whoever he was. Troy was standing over the body when she got there.

"I think I hit him about three times. He was walking really fast and was acting like he knew y'all." Troy had slid over into the passenger seat to get a good shot and not to let the interior light in the truck warn him.

"So those were your shots." She had her hands on the side of Gerald's neck. There was a slight pulse and some movement of his arms. Troy kicked his weapon to the side. He must have hit Patrick.

"I'll go see while you figure out who the he fuck this is. He isn't Asian, that's for sure. I know that much." Troy was leaning over and looking him in the face.

"No. I'll check on Patrick. He's my man." She walked toward Patrick without saying another word. She felt like something was compressing her chest. Though she had been thinking about killing him, she didn't want him to die by someone else.

Troy started searching Gerald. It only took a few seconds to determine that he was a CIA agent. If Trina hadn't sounded so down, he would have hollered it out.

This called for serious thinking. Why would a CIA agent want to kill an FBI agent? And what did that have to do with him and the hit that was put out on him? He was positive that neither the CIA nor the FBI had a reason to want him dead. He recognized that this thing was getting deep, and he still didn't know who had put out a hit on him.

As Trina got closer to Patrick's body, more and more tears welled up in her eyes. He was not moving or making any sounds. As she knelt down, she put her weapon back in her holster.

Her heart had started beating so fast and hard that she could feel her pulse in the palm of her hand.

"How did this happen?" She knew he was dead because of the blood that was seeping out the back of his head. She looked over at Gerald's body with an expression that wished that he wasn't dead. She smiled when she saw Troy fire two shots into his head at point-blank range.

Troy started walking over.

Trina looked back down at Patrick's body. She didn't want to believe that he was dead. It had all happened so quickly. It was hard to believe that Patrick had been caught slippin'.

She looked up just as Troy walked past Patrick's car. The sight of him gave her the strength to wipe her tears away before she started crying heavily.

"So is he dead?" Troy asked.

"He got hit right in the back of the head."

He felt that he shouldn't have said that after seeing the expression on her face.

She put her hand against the side of Troy's face. With her other hand, she held the other side of his face. "Yes. I need to hug you."

He stepped closer to her and stood up as she stood up. They embraced. By the way that she hugged him, he knew that she felt a great loss.

She cried for a while. "Troy," she said while still holding onto him.

"What's up, little sis? I got you."

"You are all that I have. All my love has to go to you. I can't stand the pain."

"I love you, little sister. Just like you love me. Nothing is going to come between us. Now we need to get out of here before somebody comes."

She let him go. She looked around and was glad that nobody was in the area. "Let's go." They started running toward the SUV. "Hey, who is the other guy? Or who *was* he?"

"He was with the CIA."

"He was with the CIA," was the last statement she made as she opened the driver's door.

As they were about to make it out of the parking lot, Troy handed her Gerald's identification. "Why did this cat want to kill Patrick? That's really weird to me."

She looked at the identification before she pulled onto the highway. "There are a lot of things happening. And Patrick told me that the Asian mafia put out the hit on you."

"Oh, yeah?"

"Yeah. We're headed to my house." She cut the music up so she could think to herself. "Survival" by Grandmaster Flash and the Furious Five was playing.

# CHAPTER 13

"Guess what," Anthony Chin said into his cell phone. It had been an hour since he had lost Patrick. It would be nice to relay some good news.

"Why should I guess when you can tell me?" Joey Lee was thinking about cursing him out again.

"Troy just walked into Patrick's house. He's with a female."

"Are you sure about that? Do you know what it is that you just said?" Joey Lee saw himself firing him or maybe even killing him.

"I'm in the woods, and I'm not more than fifty yards from the house. I saw his face as plain as possible in the lights from the house." If he could have, he would have taken pictures with his cell phone.

Sarcastically, Joey asked, "So what do you think that you are supposed to do?" How Troy wound up at the hit man's house was a question he'd love to have an answer to. Having Troy dead would be much better than having the hit man dead.

"In a few hours, I'll be able to bring you a beautiful present, so relax." That was Anthony's way of making things up to his boss.

"Call me back in an hour." Joey Lee was making plans to go to Plan B. He hung up the phone before Anthony could respond.


Trina felt like it had been months since she had been home. With Patrick dead, she felt a terrible void. The kind that meant life and death. It didn't help that she didn't understand why the CIA was involved. It didn't help that she had had to deal with her mother in a negative way.

"Trina, we need to be getting out of here. What are you doing?" Troy had just walked up on her.

"I'm transferring money out of accounts and putting them all into one. Patrick had about $10 million that he didn't think that I knew about. I just put all of my money and his in a brand-new account in Brazil. Where are we headed?" The computer was whirring and clicking.

"How did y'all get all of this?"

"They call it murder." She looked up at him to make eye contact.

The sound of fire truck sirens started going off.

Troy looked around. "What the hell is that?"

Trina looked at the ceiling and starting smiling. "It means that I'm about to have some fun." She made the alarm stop with a few commands of the computer.

"What are you talking about?"

"Look. We have four people who broke the perimeter. Isn't that so very interesting?"

"It looks like two for you and two for me." Troy was taking his 9mm out.

"No. I want you to stay in this room and watch the computer and the front door. We only have one of these." She held up an i-Pod that worked as a personal computer.

"So what does that mean? It's a man's world, you know."

She started screwing a silencer onto her gun. "I'm a professional killer and a homicidal maniac. They'll never get to fire a shot." She started toward the back door.

Troy wanted to argue. But the way that she was acting and the fact that it was her house made him listen. He didn't feel like taking a backseat to his sister. At Taft, they used to always tease him about his sister having more heart than he because she caught a murder beef. This had an effect on all the things that he did in South Carolina. It was the main thing that had made him a gangster.

Trina could see every move that all four of them were making. Two of them were almost to the back door. She was just in time to unlock it without them hearing it. The screen door was always unlocked, so that wasn't a problem.

She smiled when she saw the first one step onto the patio floor. She could have easily opened the door and shot him, but that would make it harder to get the second one. Two seconds later, the second one stepped onto the patio. The other one had his hand on the back doorknob.

She checked for movement to see where the other two were. They were walking on both sides of the house and heading for the back. They seemed to be checking for open windows.

From where she was standing in the kitchen, she couldn't be seen in the dark from the back door, but she could see two people clearly.

She took a deep breath. The first one was in white. He was looking around. There was no more time to look at her monitor. She had to make accurate shots. Using her peripheral vision was the key. With her weapon raised, she waited for the second one to poke his head through the door.

Just as he looked to the left, she fired and hit him just below his left temple. No sooner than she could pull the trigger and aim, she fired two shots at the other one's head. One shot hit him in the neck; the other hit him in the side of the head.

Trina's monitor let her know that she had hit the both of them. Still, she moved in carefully, just like she had been taught. Any movement called for two quick shots. They were completely out.

To make things proper, she pumped two shots into the base of each of their skulls. She smiled as she looked at her monitor. No time to celebrate.

She had to make a quick decision. They were about to turn at the same time. She knew that letting them walk through the door wouldn't work too well because of the time that they'd be walking through. One would turn around and cause her to chase him. That was a bit too much for the situation.

Her idea told her to lock the back door. The one who was on the right side of the house had just stepped onto the patio. The other one was twenty feet behind him. She was looking through the window as the first one approached the door. She backed up and knelt on the floor.

Her plan was to catch both of them before they turned around and stepped off the patio.

One of them rattled the door to the point of practically pulling it off the hinges. Anthony Chin was the last man. He decided to shoot the lock off. The other one kicked the door open.

They both received bullets to their foreheads before the door was able to make any noise. Both bodies fell back onto the patio. Trina had scoped their positions with her mini-computer. She finished them off like she finished off the first two.

On her way back to the front of the house, she went in her room and grabbed an attaché case and all her credit cards. She paused for a few seconds to think about all the love that she and Patrick had exchanged there. She felt bad that she couldn't have saved his life. Most of all, she felt bad because of the void that had been created. But she knew that she had to keep it moving.

She had to make one last stop in his bedroom. She hollered to Troy to let him know that it would be time to leave in a minute.

Trina cleared out most of Patrick's safe. The only items that she left were diamonds and other jewelry that weren't valuable to her. There was $250,000 in cash that would come in handy on the road.

"Damn, sis. You are good as a motherfucker with a gun." He was grinning like he had just seen an exhibition.

"I'm glad you said that. We need to make our guns disappear. They both have been used, and we don't take chances." She extended her left hand to him. "Let me have your 9mm." She was already holding hers in the other hand with the barrel pointed to the floor.

"What are you talking about? You gave me this gun."

"That gun links you back to the murder to a CIA agent. It has to be destroyed. In the morning, the police are going to be all over this house like the president got shot here."

He took a deep breath and 'umphed' as he let it out. "It's hard for me to argue with that." He handed it to her slowly.

"Follow me." They headed for the kitchen. There was a vat of sulfuric acid under the sink. She opened the cooler. "In an hour, these guns will not be evidence." She placed everything—two guns and a silencer—in the acid. "Out the back door."

"Where the hell are we headed to?" He was thinking about all the loose ends that he had.

"We are headed for Brazil and Peru to live up in the mountains. All hell is about to break loose." They arrived at the SUV. She got in the passenger's side.

"What the hell are you talking about? I can't leave the country just like that." He cranked up the SUV.

"The Asian mafia and the FBI are going to be at our asses. Patrick and I did a lot of dirt, and that's the FBI that's sitting across the street from the driveway." A thought popped in her head.

"How the hell can they link you to Patrick? I can't see that happening. Patrick is dead, and I know that you are thorough." He wasn't thinking at the time. "We need to handle the Asian gang. That's what's on my mind."

"When we came in here, a car was parked across the driveway. Do you remember that?"

"Yeah, I remember." He put the vehicle in motion. "I figured those were the Asians."

"My instinct says that it's the FBI. I figure they have been watching Patrick. That's the reason that Patrick was probably so late. He had to lose the tail."

"But he didn't lose all the tails." They were almost to the entrance. The gates had started opening.

"I haven't figured that one out yet. They're still there. I have to get in the back." She had formed a plan to get them off her tail without any repercussions, such as them calling other authorities and putting out an all-points bulletin.

He looked at her. "What are you getting ready to do?" The gate had fully opened. He pulled up to the street.

"Go left."

"Okay." When he looked straight ahead, he saw the faces of two white men. He noted that they looked at him pretty intensely. He took off.

"Did they look at you?" She was lifting up the very backseat. "Yeah, they did." He had the SUV up to forty-five and climbing.

"Well, we have a tail." She saw their headlights come on.

Troy was thinking to himself that he was involved with more drama than he had ever expected. He looked in his side-view mirror to see how close they were.

"When you get to the next road, I want you to turn right. We are going to play a trick on them." She was sitting in the far backseat with an M-16 in her lap. The M-16 had a rocket launcher attached to it.

"Trina."

"What, little brother?"

"Do you like doing this?"

"No. I love it." Her pussy was on fire. "Just as soon as we dust these dummies off, I'll need me a joint and some of that boy to bring me down." She also wanted to say something about getting laid, but she felt that she hadn't known her brother long enough to talk like that around him.

"I can tell. What the hell are we going to do?" He was starting to respect that his sister was that vicious.

"Patrick taught me that when FBI agents do surveillance by themselves, they don't have backup. We'll lead them a few miles down these dark country roads and surprise them. They probably think Patrick is in this SUV, so they have to follow it."

"Just tell me what to do. Hey, they are getting ready to pass us. What is up with that?"

"Relax. They're doing that to make us think that they aren't following us. Turn the radio down. They just might attach a bug to the truck." She was rubbing her M-16 and watching them through the tinted window.

She watched the hands of the one in the driver's seat. She was thinking that she could blast both of them without any problem, but there was a chance that the driver could also drive them off the road. With four kills today, she was already on overload. Plus, Patrick had taught her to never place herself in any kind of unnecessary danger. She could hear his words in her head. She had started missing him.

"Did you hear that, Troy?"

"Nah. What da fuck was I supposed to hear or have been listening for?"

"It was a small thud. That was a magnet. They figure that it wouldn't be heard. Or they may not care. It's hard to do one-car surveillance on a country road." The car had already sped up way ahead of them.

"So what do we do now? They are going to turn around, don't you think?"

She stayed quiet.

Through his rearview mirror, he could see that she was in deep thought. He was thinking that the FBI agents would turn around and circle back sooner or later.

"Say something, Trina. We have to make a move."

"Stop the truck in that path. I'm about to really put it on them." Because it was 2 o'clock in the morning, she was certain that they didn't have any backup.

He backed into the path because he wanted to be able to see them if they came back.

"I'm going to get the bug off the truck." She got out and went to the back of the truck.

It took her less than a minute to find it. She was thinking about how badly she wanted to sit in a hot tub and get a few orgasms. She figured that masturbating would have to do for tonight.

She attached the device to her M-16. She tapped on the driver's window for him to roll it down.

"Did you find it?"

"Yeah, it's a temporary device. That means that they are going to turn around."

"So what is the plan?"

"It's simple. Go down the road exactly two miles and cut your lights off. Plus, park in a path."

"That's it?"

"No lights and no music, and keep your eyes open. We don't fully know what's happening. And give your sister a kiss on the cheek." He kissed her.

"What the hell are you going to do?"

"What I know how to do best. *Kill 'em!*"

Trina looked back and forth as Troy made it down the road. She didn't want to get caught off guard if they drifted back up the road with their lights out.

A soda can on the side of the road gave her a great idea. She put the can in the middle of the highway, in the middle of the yellow lines.

The perfect resting spot would be the length of three cars from where they should stop.

Just down a small embankment, she rested behind a tree. She kissed the weapon, like she always did.

She closed her eyes and started to meditate. She prayed that this would be the last time that she'd have to take a human life. With her brother back in her life, she just wanted to show him love and receive the same from him. Finding a strong black man would also be a nice thing.

With Patrick dead, she figured there was no connecting her to anything and that she just needed to leave the country with her brother to keep him alive. She figured that if somebody was willing to put out a $5,000,000 hit and go after Patrick, he had to be determined enough to kill Troy.

She planned to spend so much money on her brother in overseas countries he wouldn't want to come back.

Several cars passed by in the next half hour, but none of them stopped. Fifteen minutes later, a car came from the direction that she hadn't expected. It was moving slowly, and a flashlight was scanning the woods opposite her. She could tell that it was them by the headlights.

It didn't matter to her that they had come the long way around. Catching them from the front or the back didn't make a difference.

The closer they got to the car, the slower they moved.

It was time to move. She moved from behind the tree and fired two rockets at them. A second after the driver flashed a light in Trina's face, the first rocket hit the roof and exploded. The night was lit up like the Fourth of July.

A split second later, the other rocket landed on the trunk of the car and caused a louder explosion. *"Vroom."*

The entire vehicle was on fire with the agents cooking inside. She could feel the heat from where she was standing. She was tempted to masturbate right there on the spot, but it was time to get the hell out of the country.

"Okay, little brother, we have to leave the country as fast as possible." She had just run two miles in twelve minutes flat.

"I thought that you were joking about that. I need to make sure that things are secure before I leave." He put the SUV in motion.

She grunted at him. "Listen. The CIA, the FBI and an Asian gang are involved in this, and we don't know what the hell is going on."

"So that means that we are just supposed to leave the country and do what? There are people on the other end that need me."

"I need you also, big brother." She cut her eyes at him and smiled.

He wanted to say that he wanted to make sure that their mother was straight. "I got you. So when are we going to come back? I'm from da 'hood and need to keep it gangsta." He went to the club at least four times a week.

"We'll have to make sure that it's safe first. We won't need a thing. We'll do whatever you want on the other side of the world."

"Okay. The spot is hot. Can I make a few phone calls?"

"Yeah, do that. We have to take the back route to North Carolina, and then steal a car."

"We might as well rob a few banks while we're at it."

She laughed, though she also took him seriously. Robbing a bank presented a new challenge. By morning, they were almost in Georgia. They were in a stolen vehicle. Instead of killing the owner, she simply knocked her out and left her a few thousand dollars.

# CHAPTER 14

I t was a little after 9 a.m. when Martin arrived at the scene of Patrick's murder. Another unit had been sent for the two agents in the car—it hadn't been discerned that they were agents until the vehicle was searched.

The beach had been taped off and had twice as many police on the scene as the usual murder scenes. More than half of them were from the CIA and FBI. Martin had been called because of Patrick.

When he heard that Gerald Scott had been murdered at the scene, he knew that it was all related to the *Hydro Killer* case.

He just walked up behind Gerald Scott's body. He saw Gerald's gun a few feet away from his hand. Then he saw Patrick's car and body.

"What's up, boss? I'm sorry that I didn't know that you had arrived." Franklin was Martin's most trusted man and the officer in charge of this investigation.

"Did Gerald have a vehicle, or did he just pop up?"

"His vehicle is less than three hundred yards away, at the end of the beach. He was in a black truck with tinted windows."

"Did you say a black truck with tinted windows?"

"That is correct, sir." Franklin didn't know the significance of the black truck.

"What is the big question here that you see?" He started walking over to Patrick's body.

"Well, sir, by the way that Agent Gerald Scott fell to the ground, he had to have been shot from behind. In fact, he was shot in the back. Who else was here last night is the question." He looked at Martin to see if he had missed anything, but he knew that he was definitely on point with his observation.

"That sounds like a good assessment. It looks like he shot Patrick before he got shot. We'll know when we get the ballistics."

"Do you think that this has something to do with the *Hydro Killer* case? Agent Scott must have suspected Patrick of something. It all definitely happened at night. What were they doing here?"

"I believe you are on the right track. We need to check out his house to see what we can find. Those other dead officers were supposed to be watching Patrick's house and him." Martin felt the need to voice this.

"That hadn't come to my mind. How did Patrick get past them and they all ended up dead? Somebody has put in a lot of work in the past twenty-four hours."

They stopped at Patrick's body. "He didn't even get a chance to pull his weapon out."

"Me and my crew are going to Patrick's house. We'll let ballistics and forensics tell us the rest," Franklin stated.

"I know who I have to go see. I'm taking two of your officers."

He slammed the cell phone to the floor and stomped on it. "Damn, they must be dead or arrested." Joey Lee had been calling Anthony's number for three hours.

"So what are we supposed to do, boss? Do we get them or go to South Carolina and Atlanta as planned?" Tommy Lin was Lee's best man all the way around.

"Let's ride. Troy has to die. Or my ass is going to be out. That just isn't happening. And we have to get that money." He grabbed another cell phone out of his desk.

"I'm ready. I need some action. Seek and destroy is my favorite thing." He held the door open for Lee. Tommy Lin was trained in guerrilla warfare and as an assassin when he was in Vietnam.

"Do we have more than what we'll need to handle this?"

"Yeah. We have enough weapons and ammunition to take on a small army if need be. You know I love my job, so relax." He straightened out his boss's collar and brushed off his shoulder.

"Let's ride. Anthony Chin would have probably messed things up anyway." They started heading for the door.

"I loaded the car up with whatever we might need to make it all happen. We only have to knock off three cats."

They hit the Triborough Bridge in Queens and headed south. They were riding in a brand-new, white-on-white, GT Mustang.

They waited for Witherspoon to get two blocks from his house. Martin was the lead man and pulled his car in front of Witherspoon's.

Surprise caused Witherspoon to frown and stare blankly as he pulled his car to the curb. As Martin was getting out of his vehicle, Witherspoon yelled, "You are making a grave mistake!" He had just put his car in park.

Martin and the other officers had their weapons pulled. Martin didn't bother to holler that it was the FBI. One of the other officers opened the driver's door.

"Please get out of the vehicle," Martin said in a calm voice. He was doing this with as few officers as possible because of possible loyalty problems.

Witherspoon put his hands up to eliminate any possibility of him getting shot because of an itchy trigger finger. "What is this all about? You are about to get fired." He had placed his feet on the ground.

"I'll tell you in a minute." He kept an eye on the rookies to see if they'd get shaky. He threw a pair of cuffs at Witherspoon. "Put those on with your hands in front of you."

Witherspoon was looking up and down as he cuffed himself. His feet were moving about erratically. It was a situation that he hadn't fathomed happening. He had devoted most of his energy to figuring out how to destroy Martin.

"Are you happy, Martin?" he snorted. His instinct told him that Martin had lost his mind and was preparing to kill him. "You know that you are in a lot of trouble," he stated confidently, trying to rattle Martin.

"Now stand up." Witherspoon stood and shook himself to get his pants to fall in place. "Walk to my passenger door. Real slow like. I'm not in a bit of trouble."

"So what the hell is this about?" He felt uncomfortable with three 9mms pointed at him. He stopped at the edge of the door.

"Let him sit in the front seat," Martin ordered to the closest rookie while he walked around to the driver's side. "That's it, Witherspoon. Nice and easy." He put his head back up. "Hey, fellas, follow me in his car." Martin re-holstered his weapon and got in his car.

With the other officers in tow, Martin took off. His first goal of causing Witherspoon as little embarrassment as possible had been accomplished. This coincided with preventing Witherspoon from being alerted by the wrong officers.

Martin waited for them to ride two blocks before he spoke just to see if Witherspoon would speak first. "So tell me why you did it. We have a solid case against you."

Witherspoon didn't feel the need to turn his head. "What are you talking about?"

"I'm talking about the *Hydro Killer* case." Martin would have preferred to wait at least another two weeks to make a more solid case. An important element was missing—direct evidence.

Witherspoon gave him a nasty look. "What is there that I can have to do with that? I'm at the top of the FBI."

They took a right turn. "That's exactly why y'all were able to do this thing."

Witherspoon looked out of the window on the driver's side to see where they were. "That sounds like the imagination of a lunatic." It was meant to be an insult.

"It's just the work of lunatics. There are almost seventy murders in this case. That includes the four Asians who were found in Patrick's house. I think that you need to make things easier for yourself." They had hit a country road.

"Agent Martin," he stated with a touch of authority.

"Yes, sir."

"This job of yours is about to make me extremely mad. Get me out of these cuffs, and I'll forget all about this." He looked mad enough to spit.

"That kid Scott had all the needed evidence to indict you, which I intend to do."

"What the fuck are you talking about?"

Martin looked at him with an unemotional stare. "You need to calm down, sir. You might as well get used to this."

"*Martin*, you are about to lose your job and be prosecuted for this treasonous act that you are committing."

Martin straightened himself up. There was a bit of guilt in arresting the assistant FBI director. But he had reviewed the evidence no less than twenty times since Scott's murder.

"With all due respect, sir, if you calm down, I'll tell you a few good things."

Witherspoon kept the same look while still facing the window on the passenger's side.

"Your name is connected to every file that a murder occurred. Scott programmed the computer at Quantico to give him the information. In all the files that you went in, a murder happened less than sixty days later."

Witherspoon still had his head turned toward the window. He had to accept it all as a bluff, though he couldn't discount it.

"If I were to believe that, how would that put me in the case? I think that you are about to make a grave mistake. I'll be looking to sue you when this is over," Witherspoon commented.

"We know that you didn't pull the trigger."

"What the hell does all of that really mean? I'm not in the case." He felt that there couldn't be any more information.

"We also feel that Patrick didn't pull the trigger either. So who the hell is the trigger person?"

"It sounds to me like you brought that kid's crazy-ass theory because you don't have any other leads." Witherspoon's satisfaction with the measly evidence caused his arrogance to come out.

"Just to let you know how serious this thing is, Gerald Scott killed Patrick, and somebody killed Agent Gerald Scott."

"So you have some more irrelevant information to put out there? Take these cuffs off of me and save yourself lots of trouble."

"Oh, yeah. Four Asian gentlemen were murdered execution style in Patrick's house. That's really strange, but I think I have it all figured out." He took a left and headed toward headquarters.

"You can't be serious. All of that was just as flimsy as can be. You seem to have lost your memory."

Martin looked at him and thought about saying he had more evidence. Instead, he picked up his radio. "I'm getting ready to bring in an accomplice of the *Hydro Killer*. Please make it known to all that it's the assistant FBI director."

Martin stared at him while they were at a stop sign. Witherspoon just looked forward.

Martin had been working under Witherspoon for more than fifteen years. Nobody could have made him believe that one day he'd be arresting one of the men whom he respected the most.

Part of him wanted to find a way to drop the investigation and act like it never happened. This is exactly what he told his investigative team. What Scott had found was just too strong to ignore. Plus, if they hadn't jumped on it, the CIA surely would have. That would have been a major embarrassment for the entire FBI. Martin was being pushed from many directions.

His hand had been pushed to the limit when four agents got murdered in the same night, and it all seemed connected to the *Hydro Killer* investigation. His mission couldn't be that hard. He was looking for a female. A female who was a cold-blooded killer.

He sensed correctly that it was about to be a long day. His trump card was making Witherspoon talk. It would be tough.

When he booked Witherspoon, he felt bad enough to call himself a traitor. He had given the agency a warning so that no questions would be asked when Witherspoon was brought in.

All eyes were on Witherspoon. By the look in everyone's eyes, he could tell that anything that he had to say would be useless. Most of them looked at him as if he had already been found guilty. He was grateful that no media had been invited to the event.

Just to make sure that Witherspoon didn't receive any assistance from loyalists, Martin stayed in place until the U.S. marshals came to transport him to FCI Petersburg. Witherspoon was placed in isolation and basically treated like a terrorist.

Witherspoon waited to see his lawyer.

It was 2 o'clock in the afternoon when Martin arrived at Patrick's house. He had Franklin meet him there. A report on Witherspoon had to be completed first.

"I think we have the person who pulled off the murders." Franklin was a little excited about the situation.

"Let me hear what you have to say." Like a professional, he was looking at all the surroundings. Getting to know the victim or suspect was always the first place to start.

"Patrick had to be the hit man. He was a trained assassin and he and Witherspoon were the best of friends. They wanted to make a bit of money and they did."

Martin was expecting him to say that. "What size shoe did he wear?"

"I don't know. We can go in his bedroom, but what does that have to do with anything?" In his haste to close the case, he hadn't thought about the rest of the evidence.

"It might mean something." He headed for the back of the house. "Where are the wife and the young girl who lived with him?"

"We were thinking that the young lady was sent away because the wife is deceased." They had just entered Patrick's bedroom. Franklin had too many conclusions in his head.

Martin reached under the bed and to look at shoes. "He has pretty big feet—and he should be six-feet-one."

"You still haven't told me what that means. You must think that he isn't the *Hydro Killer*." He watched Martin walk to the other side of the bed.

"There are no female shoes in this room. Let's find her bedroom."

"I know you don't think that young girl is the killer."

"No. I can't say that yet, but we'll know a whole lot more when we have all the times of death. Did you go to the crime scene for the two FBI agents in the case?" Martin was heading out of the bedroom to find the young lady's bedroom.

"Being cautious is a good thing, but we don't have a lot of people to pick from who could be a professional killer. Those officers got blown up in their car. All the Asians were murdered execution style." He was selling himself his own point of view with what he thought was perfect deductive reasoning.

They had just walked into her bedroom. "I don't see any textbooks that tell me that she was a college student. We need to meet this young lady."

"Her name is Trina Lattimore. It seems that she was just living here. He was probably screwing her. She does look good." Franklin was looking at a picture of her on the wall.

"She wore a size eight shoe." Martin put the shoe back down.

"You act like that may mean something."

"The imprints on the carpet that came from Las Vegas were from a female who wore a size eight. Scott had measured the indentation in the carpet." He was imagining what Scott could have done with the case.

Franklin started doing some rethinking.

"What are you going to do with ten million dollars in cash? Don't you think that these people might rob us?" Troy was feeling pretty good about not being in America up until now. They had already spent a million dollars shopping.

"We are just going to go across the street and redeposit it. That way, there isn't going to be a paper trail," Trina said. The bank clerk inspected the account documentation.

"That will merely be a matter of fifteen minutes, if you are able to wait," the bank teller politely stated. "Please have a seat."

Trina headed for the sitting area. "Stop tripping, Troy."

"I'm not used to this kind behavior from a female. All that we are doing is a little strange to me." He sat down next to her.

"Well, I hope that you are getting used to having a gangster-ass twin sister. I'm not changing."

So far, his sister had put an expensive watch on his arm and purchased the most expensive clothes that they could find. He had to admit that he was amazed and pleased. "When we get back to Georgia, you can't be acting like a gangster. It'll be your brother's time to shine." He almost said South Carolina, where he knew he had to head.

"I'll just use my time going to school and being by my twin brother's side." She kissed him on the cheek.

"So how long are we going to stay in Belize? This place doesn't look like it's as much fun as Morocco."

"As African Americans, we need to go to Africa at least once in our lives." She couldn't think of a time that she had been happier. Just hanging out with her twin brother meant so much to her.

"That sounds good to me, but you know that I have a very lucrative business to get back to and to run."

"We'll just wait to see if some foreigners come looking for you. They're the ones who put out the hit. Us being here gives you the upper hand."

The clerk walked over to them with a silver attaché case. "Here's exactly what you asked for." She placed the attaché case on the table. "You'll have to sign for it."

"Well, that will be all." Trina opened the attaché case. It was slightly larger than most.

"Thank you much, madam. Please come again if you need us." The clerk walked away with the same sexy strut that she walked over with.

"Damn."

"Does she look that good?"

"No. I'm talking about all that money. Back in the United States, the banks just can't go to the vault and let you have ten million in cash." He was beginning to believe that his twin sister was really a hit girl.

"You have to call in ahead here also. I e-mailed them before we left the United States. Let's go."

"Whatever you say." They had a rented Rolls Royce. A driver was outside waiting.

"Three million of this is yours. So you can carry this."

"I love you too, big sister." He took the attaché case and headed into the sunset with his sister.

A lot of people were looking at them because they looked like they belonged together. A few had complimented them on being a handsome couple. Trina would always just thank them. Troy didn't take that route because there were too many attractive females in the vicinity.

Trina could not have thought of a better way to spend her time. On occasion, she thought about Patrick and the plans that they had made. She wished that the situation could have been resolved without Patrick being murdered. How it had happened was bothering her.

Right now, having her brother by her side was making her feel better than any man could make her feel. Because he was the man in his area of expertise, she had decided to give him her loyalty. So far, he had shown that he was able to deal with her and her abilities and strengths. She had also decided that she wasn't going to let him see her act like a ho.

Hanging out with her brother was the damage control that she needed. Thoughts of sex, killing and getting high were absent from her mind. She was living in the moment and enjoying it.

Troy was enjoying himself. All the work that he had seen his sister put in had him in a daze. She was the baddest thing he had ever seen with a weapon. Her saving his life was really trippin' him out.

He had respect for her game to the fullest. Being out of the country was the best thing because they really didn't know what was happening. He had told his main people to lay low and to watch the Asian gang.

Because Trina was enjoying herself, he didn't want to press her too much about heading back to the United States. He also made sure that he didn't say anything about their mother. He had been trying to talk his mother into sitting down with her and talking about the problem. She just wasn't having it. His mother didn't even want to talk about it.

He planned to keep trying because he had nothing to lose.

# CHAPTER 15

Witherspoon's preliminary hearing had been set for the last day possible—three days after the arrest. So far, nobody in the FBI had confirmed for the media that Witherspoon had been arrested. It was an embarrassing moment for the FBI, as it was for Witherspoon. Nobody in the media would dare print something about an arrest unless he or she had concrete evidence.

"Good morning, Mr. Witherspoon," Martin said when Witherspoon and Mr. O'Malley, Witherspoon's lawyer, entered.

Witherspoon shot him a nasty look as he took a seat.

In a stinging and assertive tone, O'Malley asked, "What can we do for you, Martin? We have a bond hearing to attend. He's definitely pleading not guilty."

"We want to offer Mr. Witherspoon the opportunity to skip the bond hearing and keep his arrest from the press. Isn't that correct, Mr. Lovett?" Mr. Lovett was the head federal prosecutor for the district, and he planned to personally prosecute this case.

Mr. Lovett affirmed by shaking his head.

"I don't understand," O'Malley stated. "This case is very weak. I mean, very weak."

"On the tape, we have evidence that Mr. Witherspoon knows who the killer is. In fact, we think that we know who the *Hydro Killer* is. If he goes in that courtroom, we are going to play this tape and let the media have a field day." Martin felt he had to keep the upperhand.

"Okay, Mr. Martin." O'Malley crossed his arms. Witherspoon had leaned back in his chair. "Are you going to allow us to listen to the tape, or are you just trying to bluff?" He was only entertaining Martin because he was ethically required to unless Witherspoon told him something to the contrary.

"First, I want to tell you what we want before you listen to the tape." He looked over at Lovett.

"Would you mind hurrying up?"

"We are certain that Mr. Witherspoon knows the identity of the *Hydro Killer*. All we want is his testimony and cooperation in this investigation, and we'll make sure that he only does a small amount of time for a white-collar crime." Martin had diagnosed the case with Lovett at every angle. They decided that their main goal was the girl.

"That's a rather generous offer, but how can you bargain with something that has not been revealed? All of this sounds like a bluff to me. My client declines." He was about to reveal how badly he wanted to hear what was on the tape. "Let's go, Mr. Witherspoon."

"This is a tape of a meeting with the now deceased Agent Patrick. On this tape, Agent Patrick is telling Witherspoon that a hit didn't take place. Witherspoon keeps telling him that he needs to kill the girl." He hit the play button and let them hear a few sentences.

Martin leaned in on Witherspoon to get a reaction. A weak reaction would be good enough.

Witherspoon sat up straight in his chair. When he looked up, he noticed O'Malley looking at him. So far, he was keeping a poker face.

"I'm making bond, and there's no evidence in this case." Witherspoon stood up. How Martin had played him and investigated him had put fear in his system, but letting that show was the last thing that he'd do.

"Mr. Witherspoon, you are making a mistake." Martin knew that he had him. "All you have to do is tell us who the girl is, and you'll be out of prison in less than ten years."

*"No!"* Witherspoon hollered. He was turning red, and his eyes seemed about to bulge out of his head. What Martin said about giving him a deal bypassed him.

Lovett stepped close to the table and used a calm voice. "Once the court hears about the particulars of this case, he isn't going to allow bond. This is a death-penalty case."

"I'm innocent, and y'all can't prove differently." He turned toward O'Malley. "I'm ready to go, counselor."

O'Malley smiled. "Thank you for the discovery preview." He stood up. "I look forward to the battle." He had a sadistic grin.

"Mr. Witherspoon, there is something that you need to also remember." Martin stepped forward and hollered, "We have all your bank records, and we're sure that we have you! Your plea bargain is going to be a few life sentences if you don't accept now!"

Witherspoon turned back and started looking at him after the first sentence. "You're a good cop but not good enough to frame me." He turned and went out the door. A guard had to let him and his lawyer out the next door.

Martin was frustrated with the situation. His only lead on a female was Trina, but so far, he didn't have any leads to find her. The only things that he knew about her were that she had been in jail for murder and had been living with Patrick for a few years. None of that made her fit the role of a serial killer/professional hit girl.

He also had the feeling that Patrick had been the *Hydro Killer*. The murder in Vegas could have just been a coincidence or something of that nature. There was the possibility that Patrick was trying to frame Trina for the murders by standing on female shoes while he was in the room. He had been entertaining that thought since being in Patrick's house.

Though the times of death said Patrick died before the Asians did, he had to try to make his theory work. How could Patrick be dead and commit six murders? All the evidence said that there had to be another person. So far, it was a super-big mystery that had him pulling at straws to convict Witherspoon.

His only options seemed to be finding Trina and questioning her or getting Witherspoon to talk. Not the greatest options when time is a factor.

He felt like the entire reputation of the FBI was on his back. If Witherspoon didn't get convicted, it would make him look bad and cause a call for his resignation. Everyone would feel that he let an agent's killer get away.

The store clerk almost jumped when she saw the end of an Uzi pointing at her. Intense fear made her drop money on the floor and stick her hands in the air.

Tommy Lin had a devious smile on his face. "Thank you for not making me say 'put yo' hands up.'" He wanted to rape her because of her sexy figure.

She had been working in the South Carolina Car Master since it opened. As the manager, she opened and closed it six days a week. She was too scared to talk.

"I don't want any money." He fired a few shots to the left of her, shattering the glass case that held thirty-inch rims.

"What do you want? What do you want?" she hollered, slightly jumping up and down.

Joey Lee walked into the store and locked the door. "We want to know where Troy, the *Car Master,* is at." They had grown tired of hanging in Atlanta. A few people told them that Troy stayed in South Carolina.

In a high-pitched voice, she said, "I don't know where he is at." She couldn't stop shaking her hands and arms.

Joey Lee had his gun pointed to the floor. He walked up to her slowly and pulled her to her knees by her weave.

"I told you that I don't know where he's at. He hasn't been around here." She was praying to herself that they didn't kill her. She screamed when she felt a gun barrel at the back of her head.

"She's lying. Go ahead and waste her." Tommy Lin loved scaring people.

"No, no. Don't do that. If I knew, I'd tell y'all." Her eyes were squeezed tightly.

"Boom!" Joey Lee fired a shot through the floor, right next to her left hand.

"I swear, I don't know," she screamed.

Tommy Lin laughed.

Joey Lee kicked her right side. She ended up against the counter. "Listen to me really good. I mean, really good. I know who you are and where you live at."

She sat up against the counter. She was shaking all over, lips and all.

"If you don't get this message to him, my friend and I are going to come to kill you and your entire family." Joey Lee was getting frustrated with the situation.

Tommy Lin fired his Uzi at the ceiling.

Each shot made her jump and pushed her to the point that she started hysterically screaming.

"Thih yow," Joey Lee's hand sounded against her face. "Shut the fuck up." He grabbed her by her jaws so that she couldn't make any noise. "Let him know that some people are looking for him. If you call the police, you are going to have some dead relatives." He let her mouth go.

Tears were running profusely, and she couldn't stop saying "Okay."

Joey Lee was satisfied. It didn't matter to him that his face was seen. He planned to put so much fear in her that she'd be too scared to tell the police. He felt that his mission had been accomplished.

Before the day was out, they planned to hit two more of Troy's stores. The objective was to either draw him out or punk him out.

As soon as Witherspoon walked in the courtroom, the cameras made it seem as if he were a movie star who hadn't been seen in years and it was a major event. Stepping in the courtroom meant that he was definitely charged with a crime, and the reporters were there to get the particulars firsthand.

Witherspoon kept his stone face. Inside, his heart had dropped to his knees. On so many occasions, he had watched defendants escorted in and out of the courtrooms. With the tables turned, there was no satisfaction.

He had no choice but to think about the tape that he heard fifteen minutes ago. He wondered what else they knew. He wondered where the girl was, if she had been caught and what she told them.

To say that he was tense didn't begin to describe how he felt. After almost fifty years of service, it wasn't supposed to happen this way. It was hard for him to dismiss that he had shaken hands with all members of this court.

"This case is United States v. Mr. Calvin Witherspoon," the prosecutor stated with a bit of pride in his voice. "It's his preliminary hearing and bond hearing." Martin was sitting directly behind him.

Judge Goldsmith turned to the defense table. "Is the defendant ready to proceed?"

Judge Goldsmith was sixty years old and considered the most efficient adjudicator in the Fourth Circuit. He was also extremely pro-government. Goldsmith had been picked for the case because one of his nephews worked at the FBI.

"Yes, sir, we are ready to proceed." O'Malley had already started thinking of how to get Goldsmith off the case. Witherspoon took a seat and a deep breath. Having a staring contest with Goldsmith wasn't in his best interest, but he just couldn't help it.

"Your honor, Mr. Witherspoon is charged with fifty counts of murder for hire and fifty counts of obstruction of justice." There wasn't a person in the courtroom who hadn't turned to look at Lovett. He had done that intentionally. "Count three is the murder of a federal agent in the line of duty."

A silence-the-people bomb had been dropped. Everyone's attention had been heightened. They knew that the details had to be juicy with all of those murders. The charges would have had the same effect even if it weren't a high-ranking FBI official who was being charged.

Goldsmith was shaking his head. "Would you please tell me what the probable cause is for me to hold this case over?"

"We have two pieces of evidence for you to consider that reveal that there was a conspiracy."

"Would you please?" Goldsmith had been briefed thoroughly about the tape and its contents.

"This document states how all fifty murders have similarities and that Mr. Witherspoon had involvement in each case. We also have the transcript of a tape that the defense has heard." The document was about fifty pages.

"It seems that I won't be making a decision until the end of the day." He turned to look at the defense table. "Does the defense have anything to say?"

"Yes. We need this court to remember that there isn't any kind of direct evidence to link Mr. Witherspoon to any murders, and I can safely say that the word 'murder' isn't on the tape. I think that after you thoroughly review the evidence, you'll be inclined to throw this case out." O'Malley had done a good job of making an argument that sounded good. "The defense also moves for bail."

Goldsmith shook his head and turned his seat to face the prosecution. "What does the prosecution have to say about this?"

"The biggest factor that needs to be kept in mind is that four FBI agents and a CIA agent have been murdered. One of those FBI agents was working on this case." Many eyes went to Witherspoon. He and his lawyer were surprised that Lovett put that in the case. Witherspoon now knew how it felt to be found guilty before the trial.

"Does the defense have anything they'd like to say?" Goldsmith was doing a good job of acting neutral.

"Yes, your honor. We do have a few things to add." He was talking noticeably louder. "The prosecutor hasn't presented any evidence that proves all of these murders are connected to this case or to Mr. Witherspoon. I pray that this court keeps in mind that Mr. Witherspoon has been a prominent citizen for a very long time and has served his country for almost fifty years. We argue that bond is the least that is called for."

Goldsmith shook his head while he looked around the courtroom. With his best posture and hands clasped, he stated, "This is an unusual situation all the way around. I can't say that I'm delighted with having responsibility over this case. Though I haven't decided to hold this case over, I still have to make a decision about bond. This is a death-penalty case, and bond isn't appropriate." He hit his gavel.

Witherspoon's shades of red were very noticeable and dramatic. With a look of shock on his face, he looked at O'Malley. O'Malley looked down at him. O'Malley didn't feel like it was a good time to give an explanation. If it weren't for the marshal walking over, Witherspoon would have sat there all day.

Martin and Lovett loved what they were seeing. It was all about pressure. Considering Witherspoon's stature, position and age, they felt like it wouldn't take much for him to give in. They were counting on Witherspoon not wanting to be in isolation for two years.

Martin loved that Witherspoon walked out of the courtroom without making eye contact.

At the end of the business day, Goldsmith had ruled that the case had sufficient probable cause. He had written a thirty-page decision that would be published.

# CHAPTER 16

On the other side of the world, Trina and Troy were having a great time at the casinos. It didn't matter to them that they had lost more than $200,000.

"They're trying to catch me riding dirty. Trying to catch me ridin' dirty," sounded on Troy's cell phone.

"I bet that's one of my boys on the line," Troy stated.

Trina responded by saying, "Answer it while I throw these dice." When the dice hit four, she hollered, "Let me get some of my money back!"

Troy had stepped away from the table. "Yeah, what's up?" He told them to call him every few days.

"So you don't know how to call your mother anymore?" She put her cigarette back in her mouth.

"A day hasn't gone by that I haven't talked to you. So why are you tripping?" He had stopped walking after he found out his mother just wanted to spaz.

"So when were you going to call me today?" There was a ten-hour time difference, and it was 10 o'clock in the morning in America. Things were poppin' in Egypt.

"I was going to call you. Be easy, Ma. Don't I take great care of you?"

"That slut you are hanging out with seems to have you twisted. When is your ass coming home?" Troy had spoiled her in every possible way and was always there whenever she needed him.

"She happens to be my twin sister and your firstborn, and she hasn't said one bad thing about you." He and Trina made eye contact.

"So you are about to sell your mother out for a murderer? I knew it. I knew it. Ain't this a—"

"Be easy, Ma." Trina was still rolling the dice and losing. "Nothing is going to change between you and your son. What has you all riled up today? Somebody must have done something to you."

"Well, if you weren't with her, you'd be here handling your business. Some people are trying to shut down all of your stores."

"I know, Ma." Trina put her arm around his waist. He covered the transmitting end of the phone.

"So why are you disrespecting your sister? Do I have to lose my money and my brother at the same time?"

Troy kissed Trina on the cheek. "No. This is important. Can I have about five minutes?" He smiled to make her feel good.

"Okay." She stepped a few feet away to wait on him.

"I'm back, Ma."

"I bet you were talking to that no-good slut who killed my man ten years ago." Being ignored was very high on her list of things she wouldn't tolerate.

"Stop trippin', Ma. There's a thing called forgiveness that you need to use."

"That's your opinion. I haven't found a good man since Brutus got murdered by your sister."

"What's done has been done. What about having a sit-down with your daughter?"

She sucked her teeth. "When are you coming back home? She might try to kill you also just to hurt me."

"Bye, Ma." He hung up.

He went over to Trina and hugged her from behind. "We need to find some weed so that we can catch a buzz. Are you down for that?" Troy asked.

"Not really, but if that's what my brother wants to do, I'm with it."

"I need to relax and think. You know that we may have to go home soon?" Getting pulled in three different directions was stressful.

"What is the rush? We are having a really good time." She was wearing an elegant black dress that revealed her entire back.

"Things are happening, and they've been on my mind all day." They started walking toward the entrance.

"Is that the reason you have been acting funny all day? Remember that I'm your sister and part of your team." She was looking up at him with a sincere expression of concern.

He held open her door as they got in a cab. "Get in, and I'll give you the details." They told the cab driver to take them where things were really happening.

"It's like this, sis." He put his left arm across the seat. "Three of my stores got shot up today. It was two Asian dudes who did it."

She squinted her eyes. "So why are you just now telling me?"

"Because you are having such a great time, and I didn't want to spoil it. What does it matter?"

She sat back in the seat so that her right shoulder was on the seat. "You seem to forget that we are in this thing together. So how is this about to be handled?" It didn't need to be said that the incident had something to do with the contract.

"My boys said that they'd handle it in the next few days, so I felt that it would be best to relax until then. I planned to tell you one way or the other." He had been trying to avoid the look that was now on her face.

"Next time I would like to be informed a little earlier. If they can't handle it, we can." Trina was ready for whatever for her brother.

"But what about the *Hydro Killer* case? The police might be looking for you or something."

"That's true. What I was worried about was the Asian mafia coming after you and catching us off guard. Plus, we haven't seen anything on CNN or in the American papers about them wanting me."

He thought about what she had said for a few minutes. "All of that seems to make sense. I'm going to call a few other people to find out some more details. These Asians don't sound like the Asian cats I know."

"What do you mean?" Trina asked.

"What these cats did to my people and my stores was on a terroristic level." His heart beat faster as he thought about the situation.

"All men can die. So that includes them."

For the rest of the night, they got high back at the hotel room. She enjoyed it because she was doing it with her brother. She was also certain that whoever was causing havoc was trying to do the hit on her brother or another hit person. Because it was a problem that wouldn't go away, it had to be handled.

As far as them nailing her for being the *Hydro Killer*, she felt that, at best, they'd want to talk to her because she was living with Patrick. She was fully prepared for this and knew how to handle being interrogated. But it might take a few weeks, months or even years for them to find her.

Regardless of when it happened, her main goal was to enjoy life with her twin brother. That meant she had to keep him alive.

"Oh, yes," Joey Lee stated when he saw the passengers of a burgundy Suburban enter the Car Master shop. They had waited five hours for at least one of the three of them to show up.

"Are those the targets?" Tommy Lin was playing with a butterfly knife.

"That's the number two and number three man. We still have to find Troy." He was trying to do some quick thinking. He had to think about the police looking for them. The police had left the store only a half hour ago. Surely, they had some descriptions.

"We'll take those two out and get Troy later. If we have to come back or flush him out, it doesn't matter."

"I like that idea, and I have a great idea of how to flush him out. It's guaranteed to work." Joey Lee put one in the chamber of his 9mm.

"So what's the idea?" Tommy Lin smiled.

"For now, we need to think of the best way for us to knock them off. What do you think their next move is going to be?"

"Umm ... " He turned his attention back to the store. "If I was them, I'd be looking for a place that has a lot of people who look like us."

"Oh, yes." Lee started rubbing his hands together. "I have to make you a permanent part of my crew. Take it a little further."

"We might as well make it look like the Asians did it. That would be perfect, so when they leave, we'll just follow them."

"Yes, indeed. That's one of the reasons that we have not been in contact with them," Lee said.

"Okay, what's the idea that you have? We need to make all of this happen before the police start a hard investigation." Lin knew that being in a suburban area made it easier for them to stand out.

"Let's follow them. If they go to the Asian gang's spot, we kill them. If they don't, we kill them." Lee cranked up the Caprice and put it in drive. It had been purchased in Georgia to use as camouflage.

Lin reached in the backseat and pulled his AK-47 off the floor. Lin hoped that it would be pitch dark when—and if—they arrived at the Asian gang's spot. It was about twenty miles away.

When Joey Lee saw them make a turn and head south on I-95, he decided to pull ahead of them.

"There go one of those Asian motherfuckers right there. I ought to blast his ass right now," Calvin said disgustedly.

"If we let them get to their spot, we'll also get them along with the rest of them." Mike was thinking about all of the cars on the highway also.

"Yeah. You definitely have a point there. We are about to run these Asian cats right out of town, like we should have a long time ago." Calvin slowed his SUV a little.

"We should have known that one day they'd be making some moves against us. People hate for a black man to be on top."

"Before Troy gets back, we are going to have this entire thing settled. If we knock off about twenty-five of them, the other seventy-five are going to leave."

"So we might as well take over their operation. That's probably what they wanted to do to us."

Calvin leaned down in the seat. "I've been hating them bitches since we left them and started rolling with Troy."

"Troy has treated us real good. He deserved to have a vacation with his sister. I know she's finer than a motherfucker." Mike couldn't stop thinking about her.

"You think he'd mind if I hit it?"

"I'd wait a while to see. He had been hoping to find her for the longest time. He might be real sensitive." Mike was thinking how to sex her first.

"Well, I'm about to meditate on what I'm going to do to those Asian cats. We are going in straight blazin'."

"We'll be there in ten minutes."

It was almost that long before they arrived. In half an hour, it would be dark—pitch black. Based on the activities that were happening outside the building, they seemed to be partying.

Each of them had two Uzis, six clips and two 9mms. They figured that there were about fifty of them at the most. To go through the entire place, they figured that it would take about ten minutes. They were both wearing bulletproof vests just in case there were any surprises. It was mandatory that they be fully strapped once they heard about the first attack.

It came down to being a simple process: drive up as close as possible, step out and start firing. No questions asked.

They only had to drive about fifty yards to get to the building's entrance. They looked at each other and pulled their masks over their faces. Their adrenaline was overflowing.

With its high beams on, the truck arrived at the first entrance of the spot. In a split second, both were out of the vehicle and firing at everyone that they saw.

Mike got shot in the chest when he walked through the door. The impact and velocity of the bullet pushed him back and made him fire a few shots in the air.

The Asian cat who shot at him was standing directly in front of the door. He missed the other three shots he fired.

Mike's shots missed by a few feet.

The shooter went down. Calvin shot him from behind Mike. He pushed his man to the left while he went to the right.

There were about twelve others, some of whom were females who had no place to hide.

Some tried to hide behind a few objects.

More shots went, bullets flew in all directions. It didn't help at all. Mike was back on his feet and firing.

They took a few steps forward and kept shooting until they had hit everyone they saw.

It was time for them to reload again and leave.

"Clak, clak, clak, clak," the AK-47 sounded. The bullets went right through Calvin and Mike. Lee and Lin had been standing directly behind them the entire time.

Their bodies fell backward. Their Uzis went up in the air. Their Uzis sounded for the last time. Neither had enough control to fire at what was behind him.

More fully automatic gunfire hit the air. Their bodies were cut in half.

Lee and Lin laughed because of how easy it had been to kill them.

"Damn, Joey Lee, you should have hired me in the first place." He had on a McDonald's smile.

"Let's get the hell out of here." They had walked through the woods.

"Might as well. What's the rest of the plan, boss?"

"When we get to the car, I'll fill you in." They headed toward the door. "We have to make this thing totally foolproof."

They trotted across the parking lot and through the woods.

A scandal is what Witherspoon would have preferred to be in. Instead, he was stuck in a bad situation all by himself. In FCI Petersburg's hole, he had far too much time to think.

At seventy years old, any kind of lengthy sentence would be like putting him in a coffin. He knew that at any given time his health could start declining and then start snowballing. He had witnessed it happen to many. As a high-ranking FBI official, he knew that he'd have to serve his sentence in isolation. It would be unlikely they'd send him to a low-security facility when he started his sentence. That might mean being in isolation for at least five years. He had already started to envision himself going crazy.

With his picture plastered on every magazine cover and newspaper's front page in the country, there was no way to be undercover in the federal system—that's if he went to a penitentiary. More than likely, he would probably end up with the death penalty and placed in Colorado's underground prison, never to see daylight or touch another human being again. He'd even have to read his mail on a screen.

When you go from calling major shots to having to wait for your meals, it's a rather frustrating situation. None of the guards who worked in the prison was qualified to be in the FBI. The tables hadn't just been turned, they had been turned upside down.

"So what does this case look like to you?" Witherspoon had been waiting for this visit since he had been denied bond.

"This is a tricky case. They have you linked to a lot of files. In all of the files, a murder happened in thirty days, on average, afterward," O'Malley stated.

"So what? I'm the FBI assistant director. I'm supposed to go into those files."

"I understand that, but we're going to need access to Quantico's computer system to show that you've been in several other files." O'Malley wanted to do some additional research before he stated that he had a defense against the files.

"That should be easy enough. I still have a few friends over there. What are you planning to do?"

"We are going to need an expert witness to go up against their expert witness. That'll be a crucial part of the case."

Witherspoon nodded. "Just get the best, and let's take these treasonous bastards to trial."

"The most dangerous part of the case is the conversation that you had with Patrick. That entire tape is going to be played for the jury. That's what they are going to use to establish a conspiracy."

Witherspoon stood up and started to pace the six-by-six room.

O'Malley remained quiet. His instinct told him that Witherspoon was definitely involved in something. It was the only thing that had him worried.

"Is there a chance of getting that suppressed?"

"There are no privacy rights when using open spaces. They also have pictures." O'Malley would have preferred for Witherspoon to have read over the discovery before their meeting.

"We still have to try, right?" Witherspoon stopped pacing to establish eye contact.

"No doubt the motion has already been put together." He was lying.

"Keep it absolutely honest with me, counselor." He turned around. "What are my chances with this thing? What are my chances?"

"This is also a big factor. The money that you have in foreign bank accounts. Why did you use your personal computer at your house?"

"You sound like you think that I'm guilty." He was still facing the wall. This conversation was making him doubt his attorney.

"We both know that the amount of money you have in those foreign accounts is going to look bad in front of a jury."

Witherspoon looked at the ceiling. "Perhaps, but I'm not connected to any murders." He didn't even waste time trying to make it seem like he was totally innocent.

"This is a conspiracy case. You don't have to be caught at the crime scene." O'Malley was praying that they didn't come up with any more evidence.

"Answer my question. What are my chances? What are my chances?" He was at the door looking out into infinity.

"It won't be that easy."

# CHAPTER 17

W hen a detective has only one lead, he has to make the most of it until something else comes up. Trina Lattimore was still, so far, the only lead that he had.

What he knew so far didn't add up to what he needed to crack the case. At best, he knew that she had committed murder at the age of 15. It all happening in the Bronx presented a lot of questions.

How did she come to live with Patrick? What was their relationship? Where was she at?

The biggest factor that made sense to him was her shoe size. The transfer of several million dollars was the only other thing that seemed suspicious. Plus, when the transfer was done on their computer, it was around the time of death of the Asians. If she wasn't the one in the house who killed them, who else could it have been?

In his gut, he knew that it was her. Logically, it just didn't add up.

He had gone through all of her belongings several times. She seemed like a normal female. He didn't get much out of her college buddies. They told him that she loved to party and party hard. None of that fit the profile of a serial killer/hit girl.

Asking the neighbors didn't help any. Neighbors who live miles away usually don't know too much about their neighbors.

This case was his top priority. And he had to come up with a foolproof way to get a conviction. The publicity for the case was snowballing, and everybody would be keeping score. It was time to talk to Witherspoon again. Might as well because he had gone through Patrick's house at least three times.

Troy and Trina decided to go on a deep-woods safari to get their minds off everything. It was Trina's idea. They hadn't seen anything that resembled civilization in days. They had a great time smoking weed, kicking it and laughing all that they wanted to.

"Hey Trina, you need to come in here and see the news." They were chilling in a luxury suite.

"Boy, I already told you that we don't have any more weed." She walked in the room brushing her wet hair.

"This cop said that the *Hydro Killer* is about to get convicted. Just listen." He had been watching television for an hour. He was really waiting to see some rap videos.

Trina was intrigued that they were about to convict some-body for the crimes that she had committed. She smiled at being a part of history, though she was certain that the FBI didn't know the truth. She grabbed her computer to get some answers. Troy went to get his cell phone while she did her computer search.

Troy was fully dressed when he came back in the room. "So what did you find?"

"They've charged the FBI's assistant director with conspiracy to commit murder for hire." She paused to close her laptop and turn around. "I have no idea who this cat is."

"So why do you have that look on your face?" He sat in the leather chair.

"Let's say that he decides to put my name out there. He must at least know Patrick." She wasn't going to take the situation for granted.

"Has he ever met you?"

"No."

"If you all have never met or talked, what could there be for you to be worried about?"

She stood up and walked the length of the couch that she was sitting on. "He may know me and lots of other things. That means that he will probably give my name up."

Troy started laughing.

Instead of saying that she felt disrespected, she stared at him.

"Why are you getting mad? They ain't got no evidence. And they ain't got no case. So just relax." He was still laughing a bit.

She sat back down. "Forget about it, Troy. What's happening with the situation with the Asians?" There was no need to discuss with him what he wasn't ready for.

"I was just thinking about that. Let me call my boys to see what's happening." He hit number three on his speed dial. "The work should have been a piece of cake." If he would have checked his messages, he would have known that his boys hadn't called him.

Somebody answered on the third ring. "Oh, yeah ... thanks ... I'll call them."

His heart rate had slowed considerably. "My boys are dead." He put the cell phone up to his forehead. "What in the hell is happening?"

She just sat there and waited for some of his pain and shock to wear off. She was also being affected by it.

"Let me see if I can find out what the hell really happened or what the word on the street is."

He called about ten people. They all kept telling him the same thing. He wasn't able to get in contact with his lawyer. It was time to call his mother.

She picked up on the first ring. "Finally, you decided to call your mother. What the hell is wrong with you, Troy? I haven't heard from you in days, and the task force is looking for you."

"Please ease up, Ma. I'm under a lot of stress."

"Don't you think that I'm also under stress? I haven't heard from you in days. The entire world has been looking for you. People 'round here are dying."

"Ease up, Ma. Tell me what happened. Why aren't Mike and Calvin answering their phones?" He was in deep denial.

"They're dead, baby. The funerals were held yesterday."

Troy sat straight up in his seat. "Did you say that they are dead? Did you go to the funerals?"

"That's exactly what I said. Chopped them motherfuckers in half. It's a good thing that you weren't with them." She took a pull on her Newport.

"Please explain."

"They got chopped in half at the Asian gang spot on Port Royal. Some Asians got murdered also."

"That doesn't make lots of sense, Ma. I'mma be home in a few days."

"Don't bring that heifer with you to my house. Leave her in the street where she belongs."

"Ma, that's your daughter, and I need you to get your ass out of town. Do you understand me?"

"Boy. I'm yo' mother, in case you have forgotten. I bet that bitch has been whispering in your ear." She was lighting up another Newport.

"We are having a war, and that may mean problems. They may come after you because they can't get to me. Don't you understand that?"

*"No.* Just don't bring that bitch to my house." Click.

"Why is this shit happening," he hollered.

Trina turned around and started looking at him.

Troy started walking around. In all his years of hustling, he hadn't encountered any major problems or setbacks. With that backdrop, the current events were just too much. Troy had lost his cool.

It was hard for him to believe that his boys got murdered at the Asian spot. They were smoother than that. Something else had to be up.

A rush of emotions kept him from thinking that he could have been with them. He was mainly thinking that his boys were gone and that he had to have revenge.

The situation also made him mad at Trina. If it weren't for her, he might have been able to save their lives, he thought. A hit still possibly being out on him wasn't registering.

He was walking back and forth with his hands on his head. With each step, he grunted and growled.

"Would you please tell me what happened?" She had been watching him for the past ten minutes.

"It ain't good." He was still pacing, taking large steps. "It ain't good at all. I have a major war on my hands."

"What are you talking about?" She could see that his problem was bigger than hers.

"Somehow, the Asian—" He stopped pacing to lean on the back of the sofa. "Somehow Mike and Calvin were murdered at the Asian gang's hideout."

"I didn't do it. So why are you acting like you are mad at me?" She stood up and put a unit on her face.

He turned around. Admitting to these feelings wasn't the thing to do.

"Say something, Troy. Don't play with me." She took all things seriously. They both had problems and they had to work together. Being insulted was the thing that had her ready to flame up. "This isn't the way to handle this, Troy."

He looked at the ceiling. "You don't understand. Those were my boys. We built an empire together. They were like my brothers." The last statement came out in a high pitch. A tear came out of his left eye.

"I lost my twin brother one time. I cried about that shit on many nights. You ain't told me nothin'. I mean nothin'." Whenever the time came, she could be as unemotional as needed. Whenever she thought about killing, that was always her state of mind.

He snorted hard and wiped his eyes and the tears off his left cheek with his right forearm. Though she was a professional killer, he still saw her as a female, and he couldn't allow a female to be tougher than he was when it came to his reactions. He had to be a man, even if he couldn't be a straight cold-blooded like her.

After he snorted a few times and spit in the trash can, he faced her.

"We have to get back and handle this. The *Car Master* isn't about to go out like that."

She smiled and went over to him from the opposite side of the couch. He hugged her fiercely. It was a pleasant moment and a meeting of the minds.

She pulled back from him. "Can a sister get a high five?"

"Sure." They high-fived about five times.

"All we have to do is find out who the killer is and handle it accordingly. So chill, bro." She was totally fired up.

"But what about the case? We can't let you get caught."

"Shit. I ain't charged. Somebody named Witherspoon is charged. I don't know him and he doesn't know me. We have to get back to America."

She wasn't about to disrespect the reality of the case. Because she had been living with Patrick, she knew they would be looking for her. She counted on them not looking for her in South Carolina or Georgia. Her plan would be to play the background for her brother until the serial killer case cooled down. She would go to the Midwest to live for a while.

"Why in the hell are you protecting her? Just tell us who she is and we'll give you a bond," Martin said after banging his fist on the table. They had been at it for an hour.

O'Malley leaned back in his chair. "If my client maintains that he's innocent, how is he going to know something about some girl? If Lovett doesn't show up in a few minutes, then we're ending this meeting."

Martin had told them that they would be discussing bond arrangements in exchange for an interview. Lovett had confirmed the negotiations over the phone.

"Listen here, Witherspoon." Martin looked away from O'Malley to Witherspoon. "You are not going to have a chance at trial. You know how this thing works."

Witherspoon touched O'Malley. "I got this," he whispered in O'Malley's ear. He turned back to Martin. "I taught you all the things that you know. What makes you think that you can put me in jail?" He stood up to act intimidating and powerful.

Martin stood back a little bit. He was reminded of the times that Witherspoon barked orders at him.

"If this case wasn't weak, you wouldn't be here now trying to trick me into giving you information. I was putting killers in jail before you were born."

"Nah, this case isn't weak at all. There are just a few necessary links that have to be found. I know that you were getting money off those murders."

"Can you tell me who gave me the money? Can you say exactly what the money was for? If you could answer these questions, you'd have more than one defendant, wouldn't you?" Witherspoon's confidence had grown since he had adjusted to the situation.

"It's going to be a while before you go to trial. We are going to find that girl. I promise you that. She just didn't disappear into thin air, but we don't need her for a conspiracy charge, now do we?" He was now more determined than ever to convict him. He could almost taste it.

Witherspoon laughed out loud. He took his seat. "While you are resigning, I'll be retiring. I don't have any information for you. We'll see you at the suppression hearing. That part of the evidence is about to be thrown out."

Martin felt that he had no choice but to just shake his head at the situation. Speechless, he walked out.

Martin was beginning to think that he was in a must-win situation. Little did he doubt that Witherspoon was in some kind of conspiracy. He was having doubts, however, about getting a conviction. The way that Witherspoon was acting made him think that Witherspoon had something up his sleeve. In a sense, the ante had been pushed up.

Losing wasn't an option. It would mean that his fifteen years with the bureau would mean nothing. No retirement, no pension, nothing but embarrassment. He had to think about the significance of the evidence being suppressed.

Whether or not the evidence was suppressed, Martin knew there was a more pertinent determining factor: finding that girl. He needed more information on the shooter. Finding her was the only thing that would make him feel comfortable.

Lovett told him that O'Malley would likely punch holes in the theory about Witherspoon looking in all those files. There were thousands of other files on murder victims. O'Malley would argue that it was plain coincidence and create the necessary reasonable doubt. If Witherspoon couldn't be connected to the serial killer, it would definitely be hard to convict him for Scott's murder.

Usually a cop is obsessed with just putting a man in jail. Martin was obsessed with keeping his honor.

# CHAPTER 18

Vanessa opened the door like she was pissed off. "Who the fuck are you? I didn't order any piz—" Her eyes bulged wide open.

"Tell me where your son is at." Joey Lee started backing her into the house. He had robbed a pizza delivery boy to make it easier to get to the front door. Lin was walking up the path and making sure that there wasn't any traffic on the dark street.

"What the hell do you want?" She stopped at the wall. She had regained most of her composure. It wasn't the first time that she had been held at gunpoint.

"I want to see your son," Lee said in an authoritative tone. Lin locked the front door. "Check the house to make sure nobody is here. They had been watching her house since she went to Mike's and Calvin's funerals."

"He's not here, and there's no money in this house. I swear that to you." She figured they were part of the Asian gang.

"In the next room please." He wasn't feeling that comfortable in the foyer.

"Would you mind holding that gun toward the floor?" She started walking. "If you hurt me just a little bit, my son is going to kill you."

He pushed her in the back with his free hand after he dropped the pizza box. "So you are a tough old lady, huh?"

"I'm from the Bronx, so be careful." She sat in the chair. "My son runs a lot of shit around here."

Joey Lee sat down also. He was amazed at her tenacity. "Your son must be a coward or he's out of town. We've been tearing his shit up and killing his main people, and he hasn't shown his face."

Lin came back in the room. "The house is clean." He stood behind Joey Lee.

"My son isn't a coward. What the fuck do y'all want?" She had a nasty tone.

Joey Lee glared at her. "Let her know that we aren't playing."

"I'll be glad to do that." He pulled a blackjack out of his pants pocket and started walking toward her.

"You had better not put your hands on me." She turned toward him and put her hands up.

The first blow hit her in the right forearm.

"Ah, shit," she hollered as she stomped her feet in a rhythm.

The second blow hit her on top of her head with his right arm also connecting with her right wrist.

"Stop hitting me, motherfucker."

The third blow landed on top of her head.

"You son of a bitch!"

He kicked her, making the chair and her fall backward. Joey Lee smiled at the exhibition.

Her head hit the floor with an audible bang that reverberated throughout the room. "Y'all are cowards beating on an old lady." Things were blurry, and she was losing consciousness. She had hollered at them from the bottom of her soul.

Joey Lee stood and walked over to her. "I hope that she doesn't die. You kicked her pretty hard." He could see that in a few seconds that she'd be out.

"She's pretty tough. She might die before she tells us where Troy is at." Lee was hitting his left palm with the blackjack.

"This is what I'm thinking: One has to call the other sooner or later. That's how we'll flush him out."

"That was the same thing that I was thinking, but how the hell are we going to do that? We can't stay here. There are too many neighbors around here for us to hold a hostage." It wasn't possible for them to stay held up hostage in the house for days without drawing suspicion to the house.

"We'll wait for tonight to take her out of here. In the meantime, we need to find her cell phone."

"I'll tie her up." He took a few long plastic straps out of his pocket and started binding her hands.

"Good. I'll look for her cell phone."

Joey Lee hadn't expected to have to put in so much work and spend so much time down South. So far he was satisfied with the results of his mission. As far as he could see, there was only one more step that needed to be completed: flushing Troy out. With his mother under their control, that shouldn't be that hard.

All that he had done went well with his overall plan. Troy's top men were dead and the rest were scared. Without Troy in the picture, Joey Lee could call in his people and soldiers and do as he wanted. But his superiors wouldn't be happy until the leader was definitely out of the way. They had financed the hits.

Making sure that Troy was taken out was his responsibility. He had another idea to go along with that.

"I must really love my sister. I do not want to be in New York at the moment." Troy had to give in to his sister because she had been so good to him on the trip.

"All I want to do is ride around the Bronx with my brother. This really means a lot to me." They were in a limousine and had just passed Yankee Stadium. "Do you remember the first time that we came to a Yankee's game?"

A smile came to his face. "Yeah, that was when Daddy was alive." Their father died when they were 5 years old.

"Little brother, I've been fortunate because nobody ever really came after me or somebody I have love for, except the night that you saved my life." The limousine turned left on the Grand Concourse.

"What the hell did all of that mean? You didn't even sound right when you said that. Break that shit down." His being ready to leave also added to his mood.

"I've just always known what I was dealing with. I always had a target. In this situation, we are the target." She made the statement like it should have been obvious.

They had just gone by their old building. "It's a bunch of squinty-eyed Asians we are dealing with. They aren't the smartest in the world."

She pointed. "There's the Kent Theatre." She started crying. She was thinking about all the good times she used to have with her girls and just hanging out.

What he heard in her voice alarmed him. "Yeah, we used to go there a lot." He looked at her face. They were past that intersection. "What's wrong with you?" He didn't believe that she could still cry.

"Why did she do that to me? Just tell me why." She leaned back in the seat. Her face was turning red.

"What is wrong with you? What are you talking about? Where did all of this come from?" This was the first melodramatic behavior that he had seen from her.

"I'm talking about my mother abandoning me. What the fuck do you think that I'm talking about?" Until she had seen her old building, she had been able to keep thoughts about her mother out of her forethoughts along with the situation.

"She wasn't in her right mind." He had answered a question that he would have preferred to have more time to answer.

"I'm not accepting that shit!"

"Damn, sis. What am I supposed to tell you?" He handed her a napkin. "Wipe the tears from your face."

She threw the napkin back at him and leaned forward. "Just tell me why," she said shaking her clenched fists in front of her face.

"Sis, I really don't know. She never talked to me about it, and I was too scared to ask her." He had forgotten about being anxious to get back to South Carolina.

She rested her arms on her knees. "I'm your damn sister. Why the fuck didn't you ask her?" She sat back and looked out the window.

She was reminded of all the nights in prison that she silently cried herself to sleep. Dealing with knowing that she had done the right thing by killing her mother's boyfriend—getting raped was out of the question—and being severely punished for it was the source of her greatest agony. Being abandoned was her second greatest source of anguish.

When she turned her head back toward her brother, she thought about why he was taking so long to answer her. She also thought about what it would feel like to kill her mother. In those few moments of silence, she felt that might be the answer to all her problems.

"Answer me, damn it!" she screamed at him.

Joey Lee took a deep breath. He wished that he weren't stuck in the middle. He wasn't prepared to answer.

"You had better answer me, Troy." She crossed her legs and shimmied in the seat.

"I wanted to ask her all the time. She always seemed to be talking about her dead boyfriend. So what could I do? I'm sorry, but I love you. Trina, we're a team now, and we have to look toward the future. We have some serious things that we have to take care of." He hadn't expected her to start out acting like this.

"That motherfucker who wanted to rape me is more important to my mother than her firstborn." They had just reached Fordham Road. She had a vision of herself shooting her mother, emptying an entire clip in her head. She put her head down and put her right hand up to cover her eyes.

The pain all came back at her.

"If you keep trippin', Trina, you are going to get us killed. I have plans to get you and Mother together." He was trying his best to keep her calm.

She wiped her face. "Well, I feel like killing somebody. Next stop is Virginia to get my weapons." She looked back up.

"I got you, Trina. I got you, Trina." He held up his hand to show his honor. "We're going to make this all happen."

"You promise that it's all going to be okay?" She reached for him, and they hugged on his side of the limo.

"I promise that it's all going to be okay."

"I love you, Troy. You are all that I have. Please don't let me down."

She felt better. "I'll kill for you and die for you. You have my loyalty, Troy."

She preferred giving her love and loyalty to Troy. Unlike having a relationship with a man, there was nothing that would come between them. After they handled their business, she planned to never set foot in South Carolina again to avoid her mother. She would make a life for herself in Atlanta and find herself a decent man. After that, she felt that she could go without killing or doing the drugs.

T.I.'s "What U Know About That" came from Troy's phone.

"Let me answer my phone."

"Okay." She wiped her eyes and sat back on her side of the limo.

"Yeah, yeah. This is Troy."

"Is this Troy the *Car Master*," asked Joey Lee.

"That's me. And who are you? And how did you get this number?" He was sure that the voice wasn't that of a black or white man.

"So you don't look at your caller ID?" He started laughing.

A streak of anger went through Troy as he looked at the caller ID. "Where is my mother?" he growled.

This made Trina look at him. His tone made her feel slightly jealous.

"Calm down, Car Master. She's okay for now. We're taking really great care of her."

"Who the hell is 'we'?" Troy screamed into the phone. He made eye contact with Trina.

"We're the Asian mafia, and we have a serious beef with you." He sat down and propped his feet up on a crate.

"Let me talk to my mother. I've never heard of an Asian mafia. Let me talk to my mother."

"Look at the picture." He took a deep breath. From here, he knew that the entire situation was under control.

Troy looked at it quickly. The condition that she was in scared him. He put the phone back to his ear. "If you kill my mother or do anything else to her, y'all will end up dead. Do you understand?"

"So you say."

"Turn my mother loose, motherfucker."

"You should be asking me what I want before I put a bullet in her head because of your disrespectful mouth." So far, because he had taken control, things had been going perfectly. Just a little while longer and he'd have more than he wanted from the beginning.

He looked at Trina again. The calm look on her face had much value. "So what do you want?" he asked in a calmer tone.

"That's much better. If you get me two-point-five million in cash, I'll let her go."

"If I do that, I'll have to borrow two and a half million. What makes me think that you will keep your word?" Trina had already instructed the driver to get back to the hotel in Manhattan.

"If you call the police, I'll kill her, just like I killed your main men. So what choice do you have? Maybe you don't love your mother."

"Man, fuck you. If she dies, you die."

"So mouthy. I'll call you in four hours." Click.

Troy dialed his mother's number several times. All he accomplished was leaving a few messages.

"So what do we have to do, Troy?" She was totally relaxed.

"He put out a ransom, but there has to be more to it than that." He was glad that she asked before he could work up the nerve to tell her.

"If he wants the money, he at least has to give you a location."

"Yeah, that's true. He told me that he killed Mike and Calvin. I know that he didn't mess up my stores and kill them just so he could get a ransom. Plus, I don't know anything about no Asian mafia." He made sure that he didn't use the word "mother."

"Remember I told you that it was the Asian mafia that put the hit out on y'all?" She rested her arm on the back of the seat.

"Yeah, I remember you telling me that. They must want all of my action."

She smiled. "That means that he plans to kill you and take your entire operation. We have the advantage."

"Please tell me what the advantage is." He frowned.

She smiled a little harder. "In the 'Art of War,' it says that a 'war is won in the head.' We know where they are coming from, but they don't know about me." It was just what she needed.

"We don't even know how many of them there are. They might be fifty deep." Troy was shaking his head.

"It only takes fifty bullets to kill fifty motherfuckers."

"I don't know." He leaned back in the seat and threw his head back.

"Just leave it all up to me, your little sister. The next stop is Virginia to get my weapons. Some fun with a few more Asians is what we are about to have."

They had fallen into an unlikely relationship. One hated the mother, the other loved her. They were on the same accord for different reasons. One was a little leery. One was extremely confident. It didn't matter to Trina that she didn't know the how many of them there were; she knew what they wanted, and she planned to take advantage of it. She also knew that they didn't know anything about her or how dangerous she could be. They were about to get clapped at by the clapper they hired. She loved the challenge.

Troy was sure that his sister was crazy, though in a good way. In a short period of time, he had experienced more drama than he had seen in all his life. His sister saving his mother's life didn't seem likely as his sister put it with her actions. Anyway, with the only assistance he could get, there was no room for complaining and arguing. She definitely had her heart in her work.

Let the game begin.

# CHAPTER 19

Martin had been studying everything about the case. He had all of Scott's notes and everything that he could find on Trina. There were moments that made him feel like giving up his search. Trina just seemed like a normal twenty-five-year-old who was living with a retired FBI agent.

He was almost home when the name Lattimore hit him. Her last name was Lattimore, and there was a Lattimore in the case files. Because it didn't register as being very important, he decided to wait until the next day to check it out. It really didn't seem like much at the time.

The first thing he did the next day was punch up Lattimore in Quantico's computer system. Seeing the picture was enough to make him stand up and pay attention. The resemblance was that serious.

He compared the picture on the computer to the recent pictures of her that he took from Patrick's house. He stared at the pictures for about five minutes.

The screen said that Troy was being investigated for running a car theft ring. His birth date was also listed. His South Carolina address was the only thing that threw him.

Her prison file listed Troy Lattimore as her twin brother. Her birth date was the same as his, but she was originally from the Bronx.

Next, he compared social security numbers. Their first three numbers matched: 011. So it seemed that their social security numbers came from the same batch.

At best, he felt that he was learning more about Trina. Whether they were twins or not didn't imply any kind of crime—and definitely not murder.

What he thought about next was obtaining both of their birth certificates, but that would take lots of time. He made a note to call the office of Vital Statistics in New York and South Carolina.

Next, he went into the file on Troy's rival. It was an Asian gang that was running a car theft ring in South Carolina. The gang had been under investigation by the FBI for two years. It all made sense. The hit had been put out on Troy as the rival.

He went back into Troy's file and put it aside with the Asian gang's. He concluded that the Asian gang wanted to get rid of Troy so they could take over his operation.

"Hey, this is Agent Jerry Martin with the FBI. I need to speak with somebody about an Asian car theft ring." He had called the South Carolina sheriff's office several times that day before he was able to speak with the correct person. Ten minutes later, he came on the line. "This is Arnold Smith. So you guys want to get back on a hot case?"

"I don't understand. I'm just calling for some information. I've never worked on this case." Martin was being diplomatic to get past the tension he heard in Smith's voice.

"A few months ago, the FBI dropped the case after y'all took over my investigation. So what do you want now?" He lightened up a little bit.

"I'm not doing that investigation, and I wasn't aware of it. This is totally different. I just need some information." He had just figured out most of the things in his head.

"Oh, yeah. That's what the last FBI agent told me before he took over the investigation." Because he had been handling it beforehand, he felt slighted about what had happened. He was right at the point of arresting the Asians.

"Accept my apologies, but there is a serial killer investigation that involves the assistant director of the FBI. I'm sure you've heard about it," Martin said.

"Yeah, I have. So what do you want to know?" He'd do anything to help convict one of their agents.

"I need some information on Troy Lattimore and his people and a few things on the Asians."

"We're looking for Troy ourselves. His top people got murdered along with a few Asians."

"Run that by me again," Martin said enthusiastically.

"Troy's people and the Asians are having a war. We don't know who started it, and we don't know where Troy is."

"Say again how his boys got murdered."

"From what I saw at the murder scene, Mike and Calvin went into the Asians' spot and started shooting with Uzis. Somebody cut them down with an AK-47. They were messed up."

"So have any arrests been made?"

"No." He hated to say that. "We pulled in a few Asians and a few of Troy's people."

"Did you get anything?" Things were matching up.

"Nobody seems to know what's happening, and we can't find Troy. He's definitely not in South Carolina or Georgia."

"Let me give you a little bit of insight. Some Asians put out a hit on Troy, but something went wrong." Martin liked the progress. More was needed.

"Maybe they killed him and buried his body. That doesn't help my case."

"I have a hunch that he isn't dead and that he'll be popping back up soon."

"What makes you say that?"

"I'll keep you posted. I may call you back in a few days."

"I'll be waiting." Click.

He remembered from Witherspoon and Patrick's conversation that something had gone wrong with a mission. From the way that they had been talking, what went wrong couldn't have been something as simple as a person not being there. He still didn't want to believe that Trina was a professional killer, but that was the only way that all the facts lined up. She had to have been there, and she messed up the operation because she found her twin brother. This still left him trying to figure out who the killer was. And not knowing whether Troy was dead added to the confusion. But he felt good knowing that some progress had been made. A little bit of information meant a lot.

"Damn, Trina, you always have us in strange places and doing strange things." Hiking was one of those things that he didn't care to do. They had been walking for almost an hour.

"Just work with me. The stuff that I have can't be just kept anywhere. Patrick and I did a lot of things together." She didn't want to tell him that they were also lovers.

"I didn't know that working with you meant being bitten by mosquitoes and maybe a snake or two." They were deep in the woods.

"What about wildcats and stray dogs?" She couldn't hold back her laughter.

"That ain't funny. I'm from New York; I just lived in South Carolina." He started looking around and behind him. "A dog ain't got nothing but some bullets coming. I don't know anything about wildcats. They'll die if they aren't moving fast enough."

"Stop trippin'. We are almost there."

"So Patrick really taught you a lot of stuff."

"Yeah, he did. It was two years of intense training, and I loved all of it." She used to push Patrick to push her harder.

"If you and he were so cool, why haven't you been telling me about him or y'all's relationship?"

"He taught me to be unemotional about things. Plus, the love that I had for him is the love that I'm now showing my brother. You can't stop being my brother. Do you understand? We're almost there." They walked into an open field of marijuana.

"Hey, I need some of this." He reached for one of the plants.

"Don't touch that. Marijuana farmers are the ones to be scared of." She grabbed his arm before he pulled off a large bud.

"They are nowhere around, and they are on your land." His eyes were wide open.

"It's a deal that Patrick worked out with a few people. We don't need another war. Let's go." She didn't want to be battlin' in the woods with people who knew the woods better than she did.

"Damn. All this weed and we can't get high? Ain't this a motherfucker." He hated to back away from the weed.

"We can't go into this with our senses dulled. Plus, they are going to call back in an hour." She pulled him by his shirt. "So let's go."

"Damn," he said as he turned around. "When are we going to get to this place?"

"It's a few more feet."

"It must be invisible or in one of those big-ass trees 'cause I don't see a damn thing." He didn't want to be there when it got dark.

"It's fifty feet from that tree that has the ax sticking out of it."

"Oh, y'all on some hidden treasure, pirate-type shit. What in the hell am I doing out here?" He preferred being in the jungle with a guide.

"Stay quiet while I count my steps." She mentally counted to seventeen, which amounted to approximately fifty feet. She stomped around and found what she was looking for. "There it is." She stomped a few more times.

"Oh, yeah. This only happens in the movies. You aren't from da 'hood anymore." He was trying to imagine what could be down there.

"I'm a killer for real. I'll be what I like. You'll like it down here." She pulled back a thick piece of dark, green plastic. Two doors were revealed. "Let's go," she stated as she opened the left door.

"Ain't no dude I know going to be able to hold you down." He followed her. He was beginning to feel like he was in some kind of black female spy movie.

When she got to the bottom of the steps, she pulled the latch on the portable generator. A few seconds later, the large room was lit.

"Nah. Tell me that this isn't happening." He had never seen so many weapons in his life at one time. "Where did y'all get all of this stuff?"

"Patrick was a trained killer, and he also purchased a lot of weapons. Just pick what you want. We have to leave quickly." For what lay ahead of them, it was all about using technology to her advantage. It didn't matter to her how many people were on the other side.

"Make sure you put on a bulletproof vest and a bulletproof T-shirt. I already have a plan." She strapped herself with a holster that could carry four 9mms and an assortment of other things.

"How can you make a plan that easily? You don't know how many of them there are." He was picking through the T-shirts.

"Oh, yeah." By the time that she had said "yeah," she had shot a playing card that was on a target wheel. It was of the ace of diamonds. Then she shot two more that were hanging up in different places in the room. One was the ace of spades. Then she shot the ace of hearts.

"Trina doesn't miss," she hollered.

Two hours had passed since Trina and Troy had left the safe house.

"I don't think that your son cares about your life. It's been almost two days, and he hasn't gotten back yet." Joey Lee was getting impatient.

"You are going to hell, motherfucker. My son loves me. He just got back from Africa, and it has only been a day." Vanessa was thinking that Trina had to be holding him up. An hour hadn't gone by that she hadn't cursed them out.

"When he gets here—if he gets here—we are going to end this thing. I'm tired of all the mouth that you have." He never thought that an old lady could talk so much trash. In a way, she was entertaining.

Lin walked into the old train station. "When is this guy going to show up with the money? I hope he can come up with the money." He understood that the guy had to get back in town, but this was taking a bit too long.

"You Chinese boys are supposed to be patient and shit!" Vanessa yelled. Lin had just given her a bucket of Kentucky Fried Chicken.

"We are not Chinese. Don't let me tell you that anymore." Lee wanted to smack her. He was thinking that Troy was waiting to see another picture before turning over the money. Hitting her might make the process take longer and get more complicated.

"Don't be so sensitive, Mr. Lee. It was just a joke. Just a joke." She knew that they were tired of her talking shit.

Lin turned toward Joey Lee. "I'm not liking this thing. It would be better if we were sneaking up on him. This isn't our home."

"I understand. We just need to put a few bullets in him. He said that he needed a few hours to get the money together. Like she said, we have to be patient."

Marvin Gaye's voice came from Vanessa's phone. "When I get the feeling, I need sexual healing." This was her favorite ring tone.

"That's him right there. He loves his mother." Joey Lee turned and smiled at her. "Yeah, what's up?"

"I'll have the money in six hours. Where do you want me to meet you?" He wanted to rest before they met, as Trina had suggested. Plus, it was still daytime.

"So what is going to take so long?"

"I still have to pick up half a million dollars. I've been on a trip around the world." He was tired and wired up on the verge of exhaustion. Trina keeping it together meant a lot.

"In six hours, I'm killing her and leaving town. You had better call back." Joey Lee hated being put off. The mother was beginning to bore him.

His eyebrows started coming together. "In five hours, I'll have that and be ready to meet with you." Trina had kept him calm.

Joey Lee hung up and smiled at Lin. "You see, it's going to happen. We'll give the location when he calls back."

"I just like being in more control of a situation. We could have just hung out until he comes, then kill him." Lin preferred to take it to his targets so that he kept the advantage.

"Just relax and be ready."

Lin walked back outside.

# CHAPTER 20

Witherspoon's suppression hearing lasted three days. Every angle of the situation had been attacked, examined, reexamined and cross-examined. His attorney brought in an expert witness. O'Malley did this to make him and his law firm look good on television, no matter the results. It was the fight that mattered. It was 5 o'clock in the evening when the court denied the suppression hearing motion.

Witherspoon clenched his fists as he eyed the judge. He was thinking about all the effort and time that had been put in and how easy it was for the court to just say no. Usually, it was him celebrating when a judge made a quick ruling against a defendant.

"So what the hell do we do," Witherspoon growled at O'Malley. He was looking up and wanting to bang on the table. If it weren't for the cameras, he would have.

O'Malley took his time sitting at the table. He saw that the marshals were being patient.

"I think that y'all would like to speak with me," Martin said. He sounded as confident as he felt and was acting more casual than usual. He promised himself that he would rattle Witherspoon to throw him off a bit.

Witherspoon turned his head in an attempt to hide the anguish on his face.

O'Malley looked up at Martin with a blank face. "Have you heard of attorney-client privilege? Would you mind?"

"Yes, I mind." He turned to Witherspoon. Witherspoon's head already being turned was taken as a weakness. "I believe we know who the girl is and will be arresting her in a few days."

Witherspoon still had his head turned. O'Malley decided that he wanted to hear this.

Martin continued. "Somehow y'all turned a girl from the ghetto into a killer. How y'all did this I haven't figured out." Witherspoon turned to face Martin.

"What the hell did you say?" Witherspoon sounded like his regular self.

"You and Patrick trained Trina Lattimore to be a killer, and Patrick was in love with her."

"That's the craziest thing that I've ever heard." O'Malley was thinking down the same line.

"She couldn't kill her twin brother, so that's why you and Patrick had that meeting," Martin bluffed.

Witherspoon stood up. "Understand this, and it isn't going to change: We're taking this case to trial. I hope you present that theory to the jury."

"I plan to do that, and I plan to win." Martin could tell that Witherspoon's confidence was built only on pride.

"Well, you also need to plan to find another job. The first thing that I'm doing when I beat this trial is firing you."

"You need to take this chance to tell me all that you can. We're not going to lose this case." He still had his cool. A chip at a time would do it.

"We're not going to lose this case neither." He raised his voice a bit.

Martin turned and walked down the middle aisle and out of the courthouse.

Witherspoon burned a hole in his back the entire time.

"We have to talk," O'Malley whispered in his ear. Several people had been intensely watching, many of whom were reporters.

"Not now." He was still looking at the courtroom doors. "I'm ready to go, marshals."

He'd had enough for one day. Losing the suppression hearing was enough. What Martin said ran his blood pressure up. He had to determine if Martin was telling the truth or bluffing. The truth could mean that she might decide to testify. He was scared of this, though he wasn't sure what she knew about him. Martin wasn't the kind he could ignore or just take for granted.

It was midnight, and he was still thinking about the situation. It was beginning to turn into a no-win situation. He wondered how he'd be able to beat the case if she was arrested.

The pressure from the entire situation caused him to age five years. At his age, that could be fatal. It also hurt that he couldn't see and be with his grandchildren. Being kept in a cell was beginning to take a toll on him.

"Okay, Trina, tell me what to do." Troy had just arrived at the meeting spot. He was communicating with her with a microphone and a clear listening device.

"I'm with you." She had been at the spot for about fifteen minutes when he arrived. They had given Troy thirty minutes to get there. "This is going to be easy."

"Oh, yeah." He opened the door of his truck. "Tell me something."

"There are three people in the area. One is upstairs. He looks like he has a rifle, so don't get in the light. Stay behind your truck if you can."

"What else?" He started dialing his mother's number.

"They're trying to kill you. I'll kill them first." She needed a longer relationship with her brother.

Joey Lee answered the phone. "What the hell took you so long?" He had a gun pointed to Vanessa's head.

"My watch says that I arrived a minute early. Where is my mother?"

"She's right here with me. Where's the money?"

"He's about three hundred feet away, and he has a gun to her head." Trina was using an infrared scope from about two hundred yards away.

"I have the money. I have all of it." Troy scanned the building.

Lin was trying his best to get a good shot in the dark.

Joey Lee felt good about the situation. "How do I know that you came alone?" Lin hollered to Joey to get him out in the open and into the light.

"What makes you think that I want to play with my mother's life? Do you see a SWAT team?" Troy was anxious to see more than darkness.

Lin wished that he had a rifle powerful enough to shoot through the truck.

"I need you to walk into the light with the money so I can see it and you," Lee said.

"No, Troy. The guy in the window upstairs is going to shoot you." Trina could hear Lee's voice from Troy's cell phone.

"I need to see my mother first. What's the problem with that?" He thought about how his sister was saving his life and his mother's life.

Joey Lee tried to think of something to maintain control. "Why can't I see the money first? I've been waiting for the longest."

A bag came sailing across Troy's truck. It landed in the light, where Joey could see it.

"Now let me see my mother and let me have her. That was the deal."

Trina was getting herself ready to shoot Joey Lee. "That's how you do it." She had one chance, and she had to make it count.

"A deal is a deal." Joey couldn't come up with anything to say to avoid going to get the money. His Plan B to take the money without giving up the mother was about to go in effect.

"So let me have her. Then we can go our separate ways, and there will be no hard feelings." His heart rate sped up. He sensed that Trina would shoot him when he came in the light.

"If you try anything funny, I'm going to blow your mother's head off, so don't make me angry." Lin told him that his plan was excellent.

"Okay." He waited for Lee to hang up the phone before he did.

"Troy, you can consider him a dead man." She was just waiting for him to move into the light so that she would hit only him.

"Please be careful." He wanted to say that was their mother.

Lee and Vanessa started walking. "I guess your son does care about you. He came with the money, and he came alone." They took about ten steps. They had about ten more before they entered the light.

"I told you that he'd be here. That boy loves me." She had been talking shit all day.

"I'm still going to kill you and him."

"Say what?" She had felt guilty because he wasn't playing fair.

"He's a dead man, and you're dead also."

"No, you ain't killing my son." She pushed back into him. When his arm went up in the air, she cut to the left. She preferred to die instead of letting her son get shot. "Run, Troy! They're trying to kill you!"

"Pow!" Before he could grab at her, a bullet was in his forehead.

It all took Lin by surprise. Troy pulled his gun. He could see that the figured had departed. Lin fired a few shots at Vanessa.

"Pow, pow." Trina hit him also. Lin fell out of the window.

"That's all of them, big brother. That was fun."

"I have to chase her." He took off running. Vanessa had tripped over a large rock. It took him about thirty seconds to catch up to her.

"It's okay, Ma." He was out of breath.

"You shot them, didn't you, baby?" She turned over and tears started forming in her eyes. "They wanted to kill you, so I started running. I couldn't let them kill my baby."

He lifted her up in his arms. "It's okay. Let's go home, Ma. The police might show up any minute." He turned around to make sure that the motorcycle that he heard belonged to Trina. He started walking his mother toward his truck.

Trina had scooped up the money and put it in the truck. To avoid Vanessa, she stood on the driver's side where their mother might miss seeing her. They were about ten yards away. Trina got back on her motorcycle.

It was a relief for Vanessa more so than it was for them. "Thank you for saving my life," she stated before she got in the truck. "Troy, I need something to drink and something to smoke."

"Okay," he said as he closed the door. He felt exactly the same way. "Ma, I have to tell you something."

"What, baby?"

"Trina is the one who saved your life. She's right behind you." Troy looked in Trina's direction.

Trina was still there because she wanted to tell her brother that he could find her in Atlanta—after she hugged him.

Vanessa looked at her, amazed. "Like hell she did." The way that she turned around and shook her head made it apparent what she was thinking and feeling. She didn't know that Trina was listening to every word. "You shot that fool in the head. You saved my life. Let's go."

Trina held her head down and gritted her teeth. She really didn't expect any better, but she felt that it would have been nice to have that small bit of recognition.

"Whatever you say, Ma. I'm ready to ride." It wasn't the time or the place. He walked to the other side of the truck.

"You did all that you could, big brother," Trina said to him as he cut the corner of the truck.

"Forget about that."

She got off her bike. "Only if I can get a hug from my brother."

It was that kind of moment. All of the tension that they had been feeling was released. They had pulled off a miracle. There was no need to say that they had saved their mother's life. They had done the thing like it should be done by twins.

"Look at me, Troy." He let her go and took a step back. "All I care about is you. I don't want to kill anymore." Vanessa looked at them for the third time and quickly looked the other way. "I need your help to live a normal life. I don't need her. I just need you and your brotherly love. Can I get that?"

"You got that. If I have to, I'll kill for you."

After she properly dismantled her weapon and destroyed it, she rode the highway like her motorcycle had a set of wings. At times, she hit 150 mph. It was time for a new life.

Tension causes headaches. Pride causes more tension. What seems inevitable makes the cycle seem to continue. Tension and stress take away the appetite. Pride brings out the murderer in a man. What seems inevitable brings on more negative emotions and pushes the cycle further.

Tension causes sleeplessness. Stress causes pains that can't be diagnosed . What's inevitable makes one puke, though there is nothing on the stomach. You want to win, but you know that you can't win. You want to fight, but you know there's no defense. You want to keep your pride, though pride is easy to swallow if it isn't the wrong kind. You don't want that pain that comes in so many directions you have to accept some of it as part of life, part of a sacrifice. In a way, you feel that it would be easier to just send yourself to hell to keep others from having that satisfaction. You want to keep your reputation and honor on your own terms, but freedom is telling you to let it go.

After looking at a quartet of light green walls, the walls seem to start closing in. Loneliness starts to cause a pain in the middle of the chest. Not the kind of loneliness that's caused by not having people who love you and empathize with your situation. It's the kind that's caused by not having a person to talk to who's in the same kind of situation or has been there.

It's all even worse when you are being knocked off a perch that seemed immune to incarceration. The further one falls, the greater the impact and the greater the pain.

After a while, the days seem to blur. You wake in the middle of the night and have no idea what time it is. When meals are served during the day, a sense of time is easy to keep, especially if you sleep all day. Confusion starts because all the days seem the same. Visits and telephone calls make one want the day to rush by. Confusion gets deeper because of rushing the days.

Then the anger sets in. Anger at the system for catching you, arresting you, putting you in front of the world as a criminal. Anger at your lawyer for not making the system do what you want to happen. Anger at all others who didn't do this or that. Nothing is your fault. You're too perfect. How could they catch the perfect criminal for the perfect crime? It couldn't be your fault because you weren't there when one of those people got murdered. What's more is you don't even know the murderer. Never even set eyes on her.

The doctor had just told Witherspoon that he had developed an ulcer. All they gave him for it was a shot of Maalox.

"We can't go to trial with this case. We have a two-out-of-ten chance of winning this thing." O'Malley looked at fighting it from every possible angle, and he was charging $500 per hour. His paralegal was making $100 an hour.

"What the fuck are you talking about? I don't even have a co-conspirator." Denial is a common stance for the defendant. It's a way of not giving up and looking for something that can amount to a good defense.

"What makes you think that Patrick isn't a co-conspirator? They have unchecked testimony. Plus, he's a trained assassin." Martin had sent over some very serious discovery that made it clear to O'Malley that they weren't playing.

"It's just a damn conversation. All it has are inferences. So what?" He was tired of thinking about the conversation. It had been the center of his attention for weeks. It was the one time that he had slipped and the one time that he should not have.

"Let's just say that he finds her and she decides to fill in a few blanks. What are we supposed to do?" He was also worried about the information from the computer. An expert had shown him that there was little that could be done to dispute the report.

"Damn, they haven't even arrested her yet. And who the hell says that she knows anything or has anything to do with this case?" It was one of those moments that he was becoming angry with his attorney and beginning to doubt his integrity.

"It's a matter of looking at the worst-case scenario. You don't want to be taken by surprise, do you? Martin feels like his life is also on the line." If she decided to totally testify, there isn't a jury in the country that would hesitate to convict him, O'Malley thought. The situation was already bad enough.

"So let's say that I plead guilty. I'm seventy years old. A ten-year sentence might kill me. A twenty-year sentence definitely will. So tell me what to do, counselor." It's moments like this when a defendant starts thinking about getting another attorney.

"We'll have to feel the waters out. If she gets caught, I'm sure they'd give you a ten-year plea. We'll push for the factor that you were only with one murder." At trial, he felt that he would have to argue that angle. That's how hard it would be to get around the tape.

"That's an attempted murder."

"When it comes to sentencing for either/or, it's going to be the same sentence. It isn't even a defense that can be used. We have to think about damage control."

Witherspoon was doing a great job of keeping a game face. In the face of turmoil, he knew that he still had to think about his image. His ship wasn't about to sink; it was about to be sucked to the bottom of the sea along with the entire crew. Even the life raft seemed like a sentence to death.

His kids had been telling him that he could start exercising to prolong his life. That didn't appeal to Witherspoon. Exercise hadn't been a part of his life since being at the FBI Academy.

They talked for about another hour. They decided on a strategy: pleading guilty to one count in exchange for a fifteen-year sentence. Maybe ten.

O'Malley didn't want the stakes to go up. Martin was for real, and the girl might make a quick decision to testify— even lie— and Witherspoon would have to deal with getting a life sentence. If she got arrested, it would be a matter of who decided to testify first. The circumstances said that she might be the most valuable witness if she was the real killer or knew the real killer. Plus, she'd be sinking a high-ranking FBI official. Not only would she get a reduced sentence— maybe significantly reduced—she'd also get paid for her services. Witherspoon would be bloody meat to starving sharks, and he wouldn't have a chance of survival or redemption.

O'Malley didn't hold any of this back from Witherspoon.

This left Witherspoon with a lot to think about. Witherspoon tried to argue and search for alternatives. There was nothing to be found or thought of. He had seen Lovett work a jury better than a minister could work his worshippers.

He was thinking that he had to take the plea. He was also thinking that he had nothing to lose by fighting it all the way. Hell, he was old and had lived his life.

Martin was still baffled, though he seemed to be getting closer and closer to the serial killer. "So what do you make of all this?" He had been at a morgue in South Carolina for three hours.

"I'm sorry that it took me so long. We had an emergency." Jefferson wasn't so pissed off with the FBI today. It was one of those times that he wanted access to their crime lab.

"So when can I see those two bodies?" Martin made the trip alone just because he was told that Troy had been seen in the area.

"Let's go. It's this way. First, like I told you yesterday, I know all the members of the Asian gangs. These guys aren't members. Both of them are from New York." This was surmised from their identifications.

"So what have the other Asians said about them? Or have you had a chance to question them?" He meant if he had any Asians on the inside who were giving up any information.

"One said that they might be with the Asian mafia."

"Never heard of such a thing," Martin stated.

"Neither have I, but I can't rule it out." They walked in the anteroom.

Jefferson walked directly over to box nineteen and pulled the latch as if he had a license to be there. "This is the one who was shot in the head." He pulled box twenty. "He was shot in the heart and also broke his neck when he fell out of the building."

"So what's so strange about this other than their being strangers?"

"They were shot with a high-powered rifle from a long distance at night. We don't have people like that in this area."

Martin put his left hand on his side and turned left to right a few times with his right hand in the air. "I think I see what you mean." Scott also was shot with a high-powered rifle from a long distance. The other FBI agents had been murdered with something sophisticated also.

Still, Martin was not sure of what to say or think. "Is there a girl who has been hanging with Troy?"

"No. I haven't heard about him hanging with a female. I did hear that he rescued his mother from some Asian kidnappers, but we haven't been able to substantiate this."

"Where is the crime scene?"

"It's about twenty miles from here."

"Is it still taped off?" Martin felt closer to cracking the case.

"Yes, it's still taped off. I thought that maybe y'all would want to investigate further." What he wasn't able to do was connect the entire situation together. His limited jurisdiction was one of the reasons.

"Where do you think that Troy might be?" Martin asked.

"He was seen at his stores that had been wrecked, but the easiest place to find him is at Club 112 in Atlanta. That's where he's most often seen. You can follow me in my car to the crime scene." He pushed the drawers closed.

"I'm definitely going to need to talk with Troy. It's strange that he shows up after these two get killed. I'm going to need pictures of them and your entire file on Troy."

"We don't have a file on Troy."

"Why not?"

"He's a resident of Georgia, and he seems to just visit his mother here in South Carolina." That was the most that he knew about Troy.

"Well, let me have her address."

"It's in my car." They were almost outside.

It seemed that Martin was getting a little closer yet a little farther away at the same time. What did the two dead Asians from New York have to do with the case and Troy? Their ending up dead and Troy popping up at the same time seemed to be more than a coincidence. Trina hadn't been back to Patrick's house. That had to mean something also. Making it all have something to do with Witherspoon was the objective. He was thinking that maybe the Asians were doing all the killing and somebody had gotten to them first. When he punched in the fingerprints and names, nothing came up in the FBI's database. It seemed that he had a few mystery cats. He made up his mind that Troy was going to tell him something.

"Troy, I love you to the ultimate, but I'm not smoking anymore hydro with you." They had been celebrating for almost fourteen hours. Trina had lost her desire to get high.

"What the hell are you talking about? We've just been building and having a good time." Once he found out the kidnappers were the ones who junked his stores, he felt redeemed. A lot of the Asian gang members wanted to call a truce because so many of them had been murdered.

"I just want to find myself a good man, get married, and have a few kids. This stuff–" She held the joint up in the air and took a drag. It took a few seconds to let out the smoke. "– is bad for my children."

"You see, you ain't from da 'hood. You have changed." He was thinking about how carefree she used to be years ago.

"Why the hell do you keep saying that? Damn, that's mean, bro." She was beginning to dislike getting high. She felt that she had changed but not to that degree.

"There ain't no housewives in da 'hood. It's just bitches, hoes, gold diggers and prostitutes. And some killas. Your ass wants to be a housewife?" He hadn't figured his sister out yet. How she could be so vicious and so soft had him confused. He didn't want to use the term "wifey" for her.

"I have to prove that I'm not a no-good bitch. I don't want to be remembered as a killer. Not that it wouldn't be fun. I just need all the love that I can get in my life."

"Who the hell called you a no-good bitch? I'll straighten that shit out. All these people know that you are my sister." He figured that she was just talking.

"She said it. Who the hell do you think?"

"Who the hell is 'she'?" Troy put his feet down and looked at her.

"Who is the only 'she' between you and me," she screamed.

The words and the scene had played over and over in her head hundreds of times. When she was in prison, every time she heard the word "bitch," she thought about what her mother said. It took getting high to block it out. As time passed, she learned to block out memories of her mother. Still, the anger of feeling neglected and lost persistently taunted her. That's what had caused her to take thrill seeking to the maximum. Every time that she killed, she felt loved, needed, wanted and worthy of being somebody.

Seeing her mother again made her think about being called a "no-good bitch." Ten years later, it didn't have the same impact. What impact it had made her want to prove her mother wrong, even if she never heard her mother say a word about it.

Saving her mother's life was just a start. She expected her mother to treat her like she didn't exist. Because she expected it, it didn't feel as painful. She hadn't given any thought to whether her mother could or would change toward her. She handled business for her brother. She just wanted to be a better person than her mother, though it didn't matter to her mother. Plus, kids would be a great source of love, and she wanted them to think the world of her.

"Damn, sis," he said like he was in the wrong. "I didn't know that." His mood had changed to a very serious one.

"I saved her life, and she didn't even want to recognize my presence, but I love you, so I can deal with it." She got up. "I'll see you tonight at the club. It's my last night for partying."

Troy just watched as she left his condo. He told his mother how wrong she was, but it didn't mean a damn thing. He hadn't realized how much hatred was really in his mother's heart for Trina. He had argued all that he could. Because of saying the same things over and over was the only thing that stopped an argument. His mother ranted, cursed and swore that she'd never have anything to do with Trina. Recognizing that Trina saved her life was the last thing on her agenda. She said that she'd prefer death than to ever think that was possible.

He was glad that Trina wasn't handling the situation badly. He didn't understand how she could just use the situation to move her forward. He didn't understand what it meant to have closure.

Trina did, and she knew how to use it to her advantage.

# CHAPTER 21

"**A**nd what the fuck do you want? I'm not buying anything." Vanessa had been drinking hard since her rescue.

"My name is Martin, and I need your assistance." Just looking at her told him that he was in the right place. He held up a picture of Trina. "Do you know this young lady?"

"If she's in some kind of trouble, I know that no-good bitch."

He pulled out a picture of Troy. "I presume you know him also."

"Yes, that's my lovely son. Is he in some kind of trouble? Who are you?" She stopped thinking about hurting her daughter to make sure her son was okay.

"I'm with the FBI." He showed his badge. "May I come in? I just need to speak with you for a few minutes."

She opened the door wider to let him in. "This way." She pointed toward the living room. She was sure that he was going to ask about the kidnapping.

He didn't accept anything to drink. "How did you get that scar on your face. It looks pretty nasty."

"Oh, that. I fell down a few weeks ago. I got a little tipsy at the time."

"It's important that I speak with your daughter. It has to do with an investigation. Do you know where she is?" A guard from the prison told him that there was no record of Vanessa visiting her daughter while she was in prison.

"Does Troy have anything to do with this?"

"No. It has to deal with something that happened in Virginia. He wasn't there with her, was he?" These were the easy-going questions to make her comfortable.

"No. My son is always in Atlanta or here with me. We actually don't see a lot of her." She had no shame in thinking about seeing Trina go back to jail. Nothing would please her more. Not even a good man.

"Can you tell me why your daughter was living with a man named Patrick in Virginia?"

"No. I don't know. She didn't want anything to do with us after she went to jail for murder." She just wanted him to know this.

"I see." He was caught off guard by the response.

"She killed the best man I ever had. She was fifteen at the time." It didn't occur to her that cops are able to find out at least that much.

"So do you know where I might find her?" Martin was thinking that his timing might be almost perfect.

"No, but my son might. He talks with her all the time. I can call him if you like." She was also going to call her son to tell him to stay away from her.

"You can give me the number later. Do you know anything about what happened to your son's stores?" He knew that she was lying and playing games. He suspected that she would.

"No. I only know that it happened. People were saying that some Asians had something to do with it." She was starting to wonder if he knew anything about the kidnapping.

"I was told by the local police that two Asians were found dead out in Charleston. Would you know of a reason that this isn't connected to your son?" Some female's hair had been found at the scene. He strongly sensed that she had been kidnapped for a ransom.

"I don't know anything about that. Plus, my son just got back in town a few days ago." She started acting irritated. Questions about her son always made her feel uneasy.

The more that he investigated, the more complex he knew the situation was becoming. Her protectiveness of her son was a barrier he felt that he couldn't get through. If only he could find a way to get her DNA so it could be tested against the hairs that had been found. His instincts said that she had been kidnapped. If he could prove that, an obstruction of justice charge would make her talk. There was a way to make it happen.

"I have at least one more question about your daughter. You haven't seen your daughter since she went to jail?"

"That is correct." She didn't mind the change in the subject and the change in her attitude being apparent.

"Do you think that she could kill again?"

"I don't see why not." She was praying that her daughter would get arrested.

Martin left with a brand-new perspective. Mothers don't abandon daughters, even in situations so serious.

Vanessa told him plenty. Why was the mother so against the daughter? What effect did it have on the daughter? It was time to find out. It should be going down, he thought as he left her house.

"Freeze! You are under arrest." He was pointing a gun directly at Trina, along with six other FBI agents. "Put your hands in the air and drop the bag." They had been waiting in the parking lot of the Hyatt hotel.

She did as she was told to do. She was happy that she didn't have a weapon on her. She wasn't happy that she was fully dressed in a beautiful red dress and matching stilettos.

She remained calm while they cuffed her hands behind her back. She listened attentively while they read her rights, noticing that nothing was being said about any charges.

Just as she decided to close those chapters of her life, again, something pulled at her. What it was, she didn't know. She had been trained to be a perfectionist, to not leave any evidence that was traceable. Still, she had to search for that one thing that might have been an error.

They left her in an interrogation room for several hours, just as she thought they would. Patrick had taught her about the tactic. He also taught her about the rooms being bugged and the two-way mirrors.

To keep her mind occupied, she paced the room as Patrick taught her. This was the most that she had thought about him since his murder. She wasn't missing him because her brother had filled the void. She would always pick her twin brother over Patrick. Patrick taught her a lot, and he had provided many things but that could never outweigh what she and Troy had from birth. She thought about all of these things and much more.

The length of time told her that they were speculating. What they were speculating about was what mattered to her.

"Good evening. My name is Martin." He walked in with a few folders under his arm. She had just turned right and was heading for her chair. "This may not take that long."

She was standing behind the chair. "I have a prior engagement. Do you think that I could just come back?"

"Please sit down." He was already sitting. "I'm sure you are innocent. So this won't take long."

"So you say," she stated in a sexy, sarcastic voice as she sat. "What is this all about?"

"This has to do with your twin brother. We believe that there was a hit put out on him."

"Do you think that I tried to kill my twin brother who I hadn't seen in more than ten years?" She was testing him as he was testing her. She knew there had to be much more to it.

"This also has something to do with Patrick. I'm talking about the Patrick that you were living with." He was trying his best to read her. So far, she was good.

"You sound as if I might be leaving my lover. Have you heard from him?" She crossed her legs to flirt with him a bit.

"I supposed you and your twin brother have been hanging out for the past few days." His objective was to get her comfortable and then confuse her. He needed evidence, at least.

"My brother and I have been trying to catch up. I was lucky to find him." She knew what he was doing. So far, she knew what he was investigating. She knew he didn't have enough to charge her as a serial killer.

"How did you finally run into your brother, if you don't mind telling me?" He was hoping for a lie.

"He's the *Car Master,* and I was in the market for a classic car. It's hard to not recognize your twin."

"When was the last time that you spoke with Patrick?"

"I'd say the day that I came out here. He seems to be missing." She paused for a second to check his demeanor. "Nor did I see him when I went back a few weeks later." She knew the times of the crimes and what he'd say if she was caught in a lie.

"Patrick trained you to be a killer, didn't he? You can tell me the truth." Her answer told him this. He could see the cold-bloodedness in her. Her eyes told him.

"Excuse me?" She rubbed her neck. "What did you say?"

He stood up. "I said that Patrick trained you to be a killer. It's the only theory that makes sense." He was at her side, just at the corner of the table.

"No. That doesn't make any sense to me. I'm just a black girl from the Bronx." She didn't think that he'd get so intense so quickly. It was telling her a lot.

"Four Asians were murdered in your house, and Patrick was already dead. So that leaves you." He had started walking back to his seat.

"So why haven't you charged me? You sound really confident. You aren't trying to frame me, are you?" She thought he had given this information up too freely.

"Oh, yeah, we have the sneakers that you wore in Las Vegas." He was still playing a game.

"Now what are you talking about? Maybe you should get checked out." This information was partially correct. She started wondering how they knew this.

"When you were abandoned by your mother, how did it make you feel?"

"What does that have to do with anything?" Damn, he had been digging really deep, she thought.

"It has to do with the making of a serial killer. That's what I think, and that's what you are." He spoke slowly and calmly in an attempt to scare her.

She remained silent. She knew that the more that she talked, the more he'd have to work with. He was the one searching, not her. She had seen his hand and the extent of his investigation.

She maintained eye contact to keep playing the game. Any other way would be a sign of weakness. She allowed him to continue to show his weakness.

"You and Witherspoon are going to be going to trial together. I have enough evidence to make a conspiracy work." He wasn't seeing or hearing the few things that he needed to hear or see. "You should just tell on him to save yourself."

She took a big breath and heaved her chest and shoulders like she was trying to flirt with him. "When you are finished speculating, I'll be ready to go to the club where I was headed." She looked at her watch.

"You'll be here for a while. You'll get a phone call in a few minutes." He left out to keep from hearing her response. Legally, he could hold her for three days. He had enough probable cause to do that. He had other things on his mind.

She just looked. The door slamming didn't faze her. She was confident that she won that round, though she wasn't going anywhere. For sure, she knew that she was about to have a long fight. She leaned back in her chair and waited for their next move. Instinct told her what might happen next.

Twelve hours seemed like two days to Trina. "Why the hell didn't you answer your phone last night?"

"Calm down, sis. This is a strange number, and I don't be answering them." Troy realized that morning that his sister had been arrested because of hotel personnel.

"You have to get me a lawyer. The FBI is dead serious." She looked around. Paranoia made her feel that the phone was tapped.

"I already did that. We have the best of the best in Atlanta. She'll be to see you before the end of the day." He had just made that call, not even an hour before she called.

"You got my back like that?" This was the first and most important test of their relationship.

"I'm going to take care of you like I should have taken care of you ten years ago. I'm the man in this family."

She smiled. "That's what I needed to hear. I have things to tell you, but not on this phone. I need you to visit me ASAP."

"I already called and asked about that. They said no. What's up with that?"

"All I can say is that they are playing a serious game. They are trying to make a sister out to be something that she isn't." This was her emotional side that seldom surfaced.

"Don't worry about that. I know what time it is."

An agent told Trina that her time was up. "I have to go, Troy. Make sure that lawyer gets here today."

"No doubt. I'm making sure of that. I'm going to." He was about to say that he would take care of her.

Trina expected the FBI to get at her if she had gone back to Virginia. When she got back to her cell, she figured that the investigation into Troy is what led them to her. She tensed up a little bit when she thought about them also arresting him. It was just something she chose to worry about.

It was frustrating to be in a weak position. Being let down before made it that much harder. She didn't want to doubt her brother. She wanted to know and believe that he'd be a man of his word. Most of all, she didn't want to be abandoned again. All that she wanted was peace of mind.

She was already thinking to herself what she'd do to him if he didn't do the right thing, especially after the loyalty that she had shown him. She tried to keep herself from thinking this way. It was no use.

There was also some wondering about how he'd be influenced by his mother. That's what she recognized her as: *his* mother.

An hour later, she ate her lunch and took a nap.

"It took you long enough to eat that small amount of food. I was beginning to think you don't like me." Martin would have waited another hour if needed.

Witherspoon sat next to O'Malley and looked him in the eye as a means of ignoring Martin and Lovett. "What the hell is this meeting about?"

Martin stepped forward. "We came for you. We have an offer that you need to take."

O'Malley slid closer to Witherspoon. "I think you really need to take this seriously." O'Malley looked him directly in the eye to let him know that things were getting worse.

Witherspoon looked at Lovett and Martin the same way that he had been used to looking at his subordinates. "What do y'all want?"

Martin laughed at the act. "We have the girl, and all you have to do is testify against her."

Witherspoon looked at O'Malley. O'Malley was still looking at Martin.

"Would you continue, Agent Martin," O'Malley asked politely.

"I'm talking about the girl who used to stay with Patrick." Martin was hoping to get some kind of reaction from Witherspoon.

Witherspoon leaned forward. "So why are you telling me this? I've never met her." This was the truth.

Martin stood up. "We can stop playing games. I'm going to indict her in a few days. She's the *Hydro Killer*." He made it sound very convincing.

"So that must mean that you are about to drop the charges against me." Witherspoon thought about pleading guilty to have the opportunity to testify against her. It was a fleeting thought.

After he pled guilty to the crime, he'd have to hope for a sentence reduction when he got sentenced. Of course, that would take place after the trial. This wasn't something that was guaranteed. He could get stuck with a much lengthier sentence than he bargained for. This meant he could get really stuck, especially if the girl didn't get convicted.

He wasn't ready to make that commitment and take that chance. As public enemy number one, he had to be extremely careful.

"You have to help us drop the charges against you. You know how this game is played." Martin was playing a high-stakes game. It was possible to take them both to trial and get them both convicted. Though that would be hard to do, that's the way that it might go down.

Chances were much better if one of them decided to testify. That was the usual objective. That's why cops hate those "stop snitching" T-shirts. In this scenario, Martin was dealing with two strong individuals, one he had known for a lifetime, the other he had just met and knew very little about.

He felt like he had the entire world on his shoulders. Many of his fellow agents had been shunning him. Many others in the bureau expressed their desire for him to resign. The threatening letters, memos and e-mails wouldn't stop coming.

He did have support from some. Most of them chose to stand in the shadows. Why should they commit political suicide? A few said that he might be guilty, but most thought that Witherspoon was innocent. If Witherspoon was convicted, then they'd say that they had Martin's back the entire time and they knew that Witherspoon was guilty.

At times, Martin felt that he should have allowed the CIA to handle it. This is what he got for trying to save the FBI some embarrassment.

What bothered him the most was the weak case that he had against her. So much had gone down that he couldn't figure out. His gut told him that she was at the center of the case. Logic told him that she wasn't capable of being a professional killer. If she was blamed, and he became a hero despite lacking sufficient evidence, it would just be another day at the office.

Witherspoon was thinking of all the things that Martin was thinking. "Next you are going to tell me that she's going to testify against me. I know the game better than you do."

"No, I wasn't. I want you to have the first opportunity at that. We haven't charged her yet."

This made Witherspoon raise his eyebrows. "Uhm. So you haven't charged her yet?" Martin felt that he was finally getting at Witherspoon's center. "That could mean something, and that could mean nothing." Not charging her yet meant, to him, that Martin didn't have enough evidence to do it. Witherspoon was also thinking that Martin wasn't about to have him or the girl testify against each other. Just get both of them to plead guilty. That's how weak Witherspoon saw the case. "What else do you have?"

Martin frowned. "You seem to think that we're playing. There isn't a problem with taking both of y'all to trial. If that's what you want, that's what we'll do. Let me say something. We'll be charging her and holding a press conference very soon." This is where Martin didn't want the situation to go. He still had not given up on her giving in.

Witherspoon had been shaking his head the entire time. "Martin, it's a good thing that you're a cop. You are acting terrible. If your case wasn't weak, you would have already charged her. There is no other way for me to see it."

The meeting ended a few minutes later. Witherspoon would have sat there all night. Martin didn't want to end the meeting in a manner that would make his case seem too weak.

Martin and Lovett talked for about fifteen minutes afterward. Lovett had been letting Martin call the shots because of faith. Because it was a tricky and high-profile case, Lovett felt that he could put the conspiracy on Witherspoon and make it stick. He didn't feel this way about the case against Trina. The biggest of the problems was her profile. It's hard to make even a convicted killer who's a good-looking female look like a serial killer. They still had to play their cards out.

# CHAPTER 22

It was 4 o'clock, and dusk was about to happen. One part of the city was about to rest while the other part came to life.

"Please excuse me for being late." She put her black bag on the small table and extended her hand to Trina. "My name is Ms. T. Funky. Your brother told me to make sure I spoke with you before the day was out." The "T" stood for Tallulah. She told people that it stood for tough. If she was flirting, she said that it stood for tasty.

"Please sit down. If my brother trusts you, then I have to trust you also. The first thing that I'd like for you to do is to get me the hell out of here." She didn't mean to send a nasty message, though it came out that way. It was typical for a person who's locked up.

"Sweetheart, this is a rather complicated matter." She crossed her legs and set about getting to know her client. "At the moment, they have a three-day hold on you, and this is only the second day."

"Well, does it matter that it's Saturday?" Trina was already thinking about calling her brother and getting another lawyer.

"No, it doesn't. And let me get straight to the point." Ms. Funky was known for speaking her mind and being funky about it. As a female African-American lawyer, she felt that she had to do things in a way that would make her stand out.

Ms. Funky continued. "They're looking to charge you as a serial killer." She almost couldn't believe what she was saying. "There's also something about you being a female killer for hire. I have to wonder why they haven't charged you yet because of the way that they were talking."

"Ms. Funky, is that all that they told you?" She sounded a little impatient.

"That is correct. I would love it if you told me more. I just need to know what the evidence says." Ms. Funky also had her mind on a date she had planned for 9 o'clock. At thirty-five, she was at her sexual peak and making sure that she enjoyed it.

"They want to make me the *Hydro Killer*. Have you heard about them charging the assistant FBI director with charges also?" Trina smiled at the thought of being famous and getting credit for her work. As illogical as it may seem, that's how the ego works.

"I know a little about it, but please make sure that I don't miss any details." She had noticed the bright smile. It really stood out in comparison to the frown she saw a few minutes ago.

"Agent Martin has tried to convince me to testify against Witherspoon. He thinks that I know him. That is something that I wouldn't do even if I knew him."

"Please continue." She preferred to work for clients who fought 'til the death. There were few things that thrilled her more than having a great defense.

Trina broke it all down to her in less than five minutes. She was beginning to trust Ms. Funky a bit more.

"So how do you know exactly what Martin is thinking?" She was thinking that this was the most unusual case she'd worked on.

"Martin asked me a bunch of questions yesterday. I know that this is unbelievable. So what do you think?"

"There must be some other things happening, but they definitely don't have a case against you." Trina started smiling. "You can believe that the FBI has something up its sleeve. So the first thing that you have to do is not talk to them anymore."

Trina slowly said, "So what do we do next?"

"Well, we have to see if they are going to charge you or let you go. They have to do it by Monday."

"So I have to spend another night in this place?" She didn't mean to scream.

"They're using an investigative tactic on you. It's a must that you keep cool."

"I understand." She had learned many things of this nature while she was in prison.

"Sweetheart, I can't see them making you out to be a serial killer. I haven't seen a pretty serial killer yet. If they don't charge you by Monday morning, I'll have you out of here." She stood up.

"So one way or the other, you are going to see me Monday."

"Ms. Funky will be here for you."

What stood out the most to Trina was Troy. He had kept his word and was handling business like he said he would. She was ashamed that she had some moments of doubt. She couldn't help it. She hadn't been shown a lot of love.

That night, she thought about all the people that she had murdered. She felt a little guilty because she had done it all for the wrong reasons. Over and over again, she saw herself firing off guns and rifles. She also saw how she had poisoned a few people. It was the first time that those thoughts had come back to her.

She didn't know if she was changing or just tripping. In the past, after she murdered somebody and got high or masturbated afterward, she put the entire thing out of her mind.

When she was searching to see if she had made any mistakes, she didn't think about the crime itself, just how she left the crime scene. Now she had to think about it because she was about to get credit for those crimes. She couldn't help being delighted at the thought.

She was tripping about how she was about to get away with it all. Getting credit for her work and getting away with it had an irresistible appeal. It was so good to her that she wanted to start laughing.

"So what took my son so long to get over here? I wanted you here this morning, and I called you all yesterday." Vanessa was watching her favorite program. Because "Soul Train" didn't come on anymore, she watched it on DVD.

He sat on the couch. "I had some real serious business to take care of. Something really serious has happened."

"What could be more important than your mother?" She cut the plasma television off and lit a cigarette.

"I had to get an attorney for Trina. She got arrested yesterday." He hadn't smiled since he had walked in the house.

She let out a puff of smoke. "So she is more important to you now than I am? That girl isn't any good. Troy, leave that girl alone."

"So what's up, Ma? Let me find out that you are jealous of your daughter. That would be a crime. Didn't you raise me better than that?" What Ms. Funky had told him about Trina facing the death penalty had him stressed. He had already made all the preparations to be there for her.

"You didn't answer my question," she screamed as she stood up. "You are sounding a bit disrespectful after all that I've done for you."

"Please sit down. It isn't a good time for us to argue. We need to get behind Trina." He was looking in another direction to let her know that he was upset.

She sat down slowly. "I knew that she was going to get arrested." She felt good saying this.

"Okay," he said as he sat back down. "What are you talking about?" He mentally prepared himself to remember what he had on his mind.

"An FBI agent came by here the other day. He asked a lot of questions about you and her. She's about to have you in jail with her. What did she get arrested for?"

"So what did you tell him?" He would not have believed her if she hadn't said FBI.

"I didn't tell him anything. I made sure that I made you look good. What was I supposed to do?"

"You were supposed to call me and tell me so—"

"What did you tell me about the phones?" She needed to present a defense that was solid.

"Ugh," he grunted. "What did he basically say about Trina? What did he ask you?"

"He wanted to know about a man that she was living with in Virginia. There was nothing that I could tell him."

"Is that all?"

"He asked about those Asians who kidnapped me. I told him that I didn't know anything. Can you relax now?" She tucked her legs underneath her.

He stood up. Troy felt even more compelled to do the right thing after hearing that. "Listen, Ma, Trina needs you and me. It's time to let what happened in the past just be something that happened in the past." She frowned at him. "That's right, Ma."

"She must have put something in one of your drinks. What the hell did she do to you?"

"She saved my life, and she saved your life. You know damn well that I didn't shoot those Asians from behind a truck. She had a rifle." This was the first time that he mentioned this.

"So what?" She was praying that Trina got the death penalty and would be all the way out of their lives.

"So this is what I'm about to do. Don't say a word. You are going to forgive and forget and visit your daughter. Or you are about to lose a son. They're probably going to try her in Virginia."

"What did you say?"

"You heard what I said." He walked out the door leaving her ranting and raving.

She let the statement run through her mind several times. Did my son really mean that? What did she do to him to make him do that? These were only a few of the questions that she asked herself.

She was surprised that her plan was backfiring on her. She didn't know that she had thrown a boomerang. Her son was supposed to abandon her and be grateful that he wasn't also getting arrested. He was supposed to thank his mother for keeping his name clean. She didn't get to tell him that part like she wanted. It wasn't supposed to be anywhere near what it was now.

She had to get herself a drink and snort a little coke to see if she would get the situation in perspective. It took about five minutes for the E&J and coke to start doing their thing. A euphoric feeling overtook the pain. Holding a lit Newport and still blowing smoke, she felt that she was ready to do some serious thinking.

She had to first determine if her son could really be serious about cutting her off. She knew that he had been extremely serious about most things since he was sixteen. That was when she had started seeing major changes in him. He had become the man of the house in every manner. He had started spoiling her and had kept her from having to work. She didn't ask any questions because he was bringing in plenty of money and whatever she wanted she got.

Though material things weighed in on her decisions, it mostly had to do with his determination. She had all the things that she wanted in the physical sense.

Her son withdrawing from her was an unbearable thought. He meant everything to her. He was the center of her world because she couldn't find a good man who would treat her like the tramp that she used to be. Some women love being abused. The men she dated were so scared of her son that they wouldn't dare mistreat her. To her, being abused was part of being loved. In another sense, she had no respect for the men she had been dating. Losing her son's love wasn't an option. Still, she had to wonder if she'd be able to forgive when it came to Trina.

Way before the murder happened, she had negative emotions when it came to her. From the start, Trina was the most beautiful of girls and attracted lots of attention. Trina's humps made Vanessa jealous. It was all coming to the surface. Nobody saw the signs, and Vanessa wasn't verbal about it. Vanessa knew that her ex-boyfriend wanted to get at Trina. If Trina hadn't been strong willed, Vanessa would have pushed Trina in that direction just to keep her man happy. It was a matter of feeling secure that the bills would be paid and that she wouldn't be lonely. It didn't matter to her what he did as long as he was there for her. Her attitude was you may do as you like, just as long as I get a little bit. With him dead, that changed everything for her.

All of the negative energy went straight to her daughter. There was no thinking that Trina was flesh and blood, that she came out of her, that she can find another man to replace him or that Trina had done her a favor.

There was no thinking. It was all emotional. If she had had a gun that day, she would have killed Trina right then and there. She had wished death on Trina on many occasions. She had also wished that she had seen it coming and done something to get rid of Trina. She thought many other similar things. She kept all of these feelings to herself, and she had no shame in despising her daughter. She had prayed to God that Trina would die while she was incarcerated.

During this time, Troy did not ask his mother a thing. He was too scared. All the letters from Trina that were meant for Vanessa and Troy ended up burned so that they were never found.

When people asked her about Trina, she told them Trina would be home soon. At times, it seemed that the entire neighborhood was asking about Trina. She told Troy the same thing on several occasions. Most of the time she could see that he didn't want to upset her.

It didn't take long after the murder for people to start saying that she wasn't supporting her daughter like she should have. There were other females in the neighborhood who knew about the things that Trina was doing. This prompted the move. Vanessa told Troy that she had found a better job.

It didn't take long after getting to South Carolina to forget about Trina. They found a brand-new life. Her son started hustling and messing with girls. She was glad that he had become preoccupied with girls, money and getting high. Hell, life had turned out to be far better than she could have imagined.

She blocked out Trina from her mind for years. All of the negative emotions came back when Troy said something about Trina being outside of her house. There was also some shock and surprise. She was also surprised that Trina was there when she got rescued.

For her son, she wanted to face Trina and make things up to her. It was just a fleeting feeling. She was only thinking about it because she had to.

She smoked. She drank. She snorted. And she put the thought out of her head. "My son will come around," she said to herself to get the matter off of her mind. She just wanted to enjoy her high.

# CHAPTER 23

When O'Malley arrived at FCI Petersburg at 9 o'clock on Sunday morning, he thought that he was about to lose his first federal death-penalty case. As much as it meant to him to win, he had to remain honest with himself and his client.

"To what do I owe this surprise visit?" So far, Witherspoon had spent more than $100,000.

"I have some really bad news." He shook hands with his client. Usually, he'd be in church.

"It's Sunday. So how could you have bad news?" He sat and wished he had something to smoke.

"On all the television stations, they're talking about how the FBI has arrested Trina Lattimore for being the *Hydro Killer.*"

Witherspoon wasn't sure how to react. He had played with the thought for several hours along with many other things. "I guess Martin had to do that. He really doesn't have anything on her that I can think of." It was more of a question than a statement.

"Y'all going to trial together isn't going to look that good. Patrick makes the perfect mediator between the both of y'all. I think that this could really work to your disadvantage." There was about to be more publicity. More speculation. More theories. More credibility for the taped conversation.

"Get to the point. Stop playing with words." Witherspoon wanted better service.

"You need to give serious thought to testifying against her. She just might do it to you."

"No matter what sentence I get, it's going to be like a death sentence. Then I'll disgrace my family by just pleading guilty. So what the hell can I lose by going to trial?" After a few weeks, a person gets used to being locked up. A person falls into a routine.

He was steadily searching for that way to win. So far, that meant winning at trial.

"So what does it mean to you to have the death penalty?" It was one of those things that an attorney has to say if that is the consequence.

"At times, it's best to go down fighting." He was also thinking about having to deal with the shame. "Hell, ten, fifteen years is like a death sentence to an older man."

"We have to use that as a bargaining chip. A ten-year sentence can be done in seven and a half years. And they can't put you in the pen with that kind of time. You have to think."

"You want me to think about testifying against a person I've never met? I'll look really great on the stand."

"That taped conversation that you had with Patrick implies that you know that she's the killer. All they have on her is that she was the woman staying with Patrick." He said the last statement with confidence to make the lie seem convincing.

"So you think that they can convict me because they cannot convict her? What sense does that make?" He was being emotional and filling in the blanks of O'Malley's last statement.

"Her presence may get you convicted while she walks. It has happened."

They were silent for ten minutes. Witherspoon was thinking. He was fighting giving in all that he could. He thought that he had pondered every angle. He figured that she'd go to trial because there was nothing on her. Her presence hurting him had slipped his mind.

What a paradigm, he thought to himself. As a cop, he didn't see her as dangerous to this situation. They could see him as innocent because they saw her as innocent. Rationalization. Rationalization after rationalization.

"There isn't a connection between us. What harm could there be?"

"The jury is going to know that there is a girl. They may think that it's her. They may think that it isn't her. And they may feel that just her sitting there gives credibility to the government's case. Whether it is or isn't her, he has to be guilty." He had been playing with scenarios in his mind since she had been arrested.

"If that isn't far-fetched, I can't think of much that is."

"We've both seen some verdicts that astounded logic. I think you had better think about not going to trial."

Witherspoon hated it when O'Malley said something of that nature.

"I understand and appreciate where you are coming from, but you are still going to be a lawyer after this. I really have to suffer the consequences by myself." O'Malley stood up. "So just relax and let me choose my own destiny. I feel that a hung jury may be easier to get than you might think."

"Just think about this. What happens if she decides to testify against you?"

Silence was the loudest thing in the room.

When certain clocks tick, they seem to tick agonizingly slow. Some are in a rush to get a trial done with. Some dread the days as they rush by. Making decisions have that effect, one way or the other, unless the person is insane. Or at least a little twisted. Life-and-death decisions are the kind with so much tension that many just break down under the pressure. For Witherspoon, things had reached the third quarter, and a new player had entered the game. All things had changed. The last thing O'Malley said made him recognize this. What do you do now, Mr. Witherspoon, was the question he asked himself.

He knew that putting his pride to the side would be a very hard thing. He had to ask himself that. He could only wonder if Trina would testify against him. He knew very little about her. It didn't take long to determine that her testimony would not help in the least. In fact, it could be very dangerous and lead the jury to think what they may.

This change in the circumstances weighed heavily on his mind until he went to sleep. He had to congratulate Martin for having the heart to take a person to trial with little evidence against her. This being done out of stealth was making him leery. Without any pretrial motions to be considered, the time for trial would be soon.

Witherspoon didn't sleep well that night.

Trina's preliminary hearing had been a major event. Her picture was all over the news, and she was the most talked about subject. Most were on the question of whether such a beautiful female was really a serial killer. Few were inclined to believe that she had killed more than fifty people and had done it in cahoots with the FBI.

Trina was extremely surprised that the case was causing so much hype. Ms. Funky had semi-prepared her for the publicity.

Instantly, Trina had become a celebrity. A few people had thrown up Web sites in her name. All she cared about was that Troy was right there in the courtroom with her. His presence alone made her feel safe.

"Hello, Ms. Funky, my name is Agent Martin. I'm the case agent in this case, and we need to talk." He extended his hand to her. He had been waiting for her to exit the courthouse.

"It's nice to meet you. What may I do for you?" She had read his name in a few articles. Her instinct told her what the meeting would be about.

"Your client has a grand opportunity to walk away from this thing and not do a day in prison." Half of this was a lie. She'd never walk away after pleading guilty to that many murders unless she pleaded to one count and relevant conduct was limited. Relevant conduct allows the court to sentence a defendant to crimes that he or she has not been convicted of.

She smiled to be professional and continued to walk toward her car. "It can't hurt to listen, and it won't hurt to tell my client what you tell me."

"We just need her to testify against the FBI director. It's a simple matter." Because of Trina's demeanor at the preliminary hearing, he knew that she'd make a great witness.

"I'm pretty sure that she's not interested in testifying. You don't even have a circumstantial evidence case against her. I plan to beat this trial the way that you beat your meat." She smiled a little harder.

"What did you say?" He had to look around because he had been caught off guard.

"You heard what I said. This case is weaker than an impotent who doesn't have any Viagra. In case you don't know what's impotent, it's a man who can't get a hard-on." She put her hands on her hips and stopped walking to face him.

"She had some participation in a murder that involved some Asians. One of her hairs was left at the scene. It's part of the evidence." He had done a DNA comparison with Trina's hair that had been found in her cell and her mother's hair that had been found at the warehouse.

"It takes a lot of murders to make a serial killer, and you seem to have nothing that would give you jurisdiction in federal court. Can you tell me more?" She had it all mapped out. At the preliminary hearing, she heard what she expected. They had nothing.

Martin wanted to say something about her mouth, but he couldn't because he had to stay on his mission. That meant getting to Trina. That meant going through her attorney.

"Ms. Funky," he said as he crossed his arms and took a deep breath. "We have a hair from that incident that matches hers. We have reason to believe that she was not only there but is the person who pulled the trigger."

"So how did you acquire some hair from my client? We have not authorized you to take any samples."

"We got it after she left her cell. We can search a cell all that we like when somebody is in our custody." This was one of the benefits of locking a person up for a few days.

"You can present that to a jury. I can't deny you that, and I wouldn't try. Will you be taking the stand?" She had in her mind presenting how the case was investigated.

"What I need to say is that we'll set her free if she testifies against Witherspoon. She's young and beautiful. Why get the death penalty or a few life sentences? What do you think?" He smiled so that he could make it seem like he was doing them a favor.

"While I'm telling my client that, I'll also be telling her that I hope that your sex life isn't as weak as this case. You should have never charged her. Get me that discovery and get ready to battle." She waited for him to say something else.

They stared eye to eye for quite a while. Martin couldn't think of anything else to say. She was being persistent to get some more information.

After accepting defeat, Martin walked away.

When he was about fifty feet away, Ms. Funky hollered, "I hope I didn't hurt your feelings!"

The first thing that all cops and prosecutors hate is an aggressive defense attorney, particularly a black one and especially a female. It worked opposite to how they wanted defendants to act: weak.

It was a surprise to Martin that Trina produced an attorney who was about fighting, especially so quickly. The off-handed comments that she made were enough to get his respect. She didn't even act like she recognized his bluff. While he had been staring at her, he couldn't think of any other moves to put down. He just started praying that Lovett was on top of his game.

On the minimum, he had found out that Ms. Funky had intentions of going all out. He searched for the positive side in this. Maybe, just maybe, he thought, Trina's presence would make Witherspoon look guilty.

It was time to find his favorite bar and ease his tensions. It was one of those moments that he wished he had not even arrested Witherspoon. His hand had been pushed, and an FBI agent had been murdered. He just couldn't let the CIA embarrass them. Some of his fellow agents felt that he made the right decision, but there were those who felt he had been premature. He expected all of this beforehand.

One drink, two drinks, three drinks. Not only did he get drunk, he accepted the solicitation of a prostitute. It was that bad. The tension level had gone up. Though he was drunk and sexing a stranger, he was still trying to think of a way to find more evidence or find another angle. He kept telling himself that there had to be something.

At times, he had to convince himself that Trina was really guilty. Guilty of something. It was a means to justify her arrest. At the moment, he couldn't even prove that she and Patrick were lovers. His instinct that she was the killer meant a lot in an investigation. It meant an acquittal at a trial.

In a sense, he felt that he had done the best that he could do. He smoked, drank, thought and sexed the night away.

# CHAPTER 24

Trina Lattimore had started feeling lonelier than she had in a very long time. Because of her status and instant celebrity, they placed her in isolation. Martin ordered it.

She brightened up when they called her for a visit. It was almost twenty minutes to ten.

"I didn't think that you were coming. And why so late?" she yelled into the telephone.

Troy smiled and ignored her. "They said that you couldn't have any visitors until visits for the other inmates were finished."

"Okay. I'm so glad to see you. I feel so much better that you didn't let me down. I love you, Troy. You're the best brother a sister could have." It meant the world to her that he had come when she most needed to feel his presence.

"I know that you like Ms. Funky. She says that she has this case beat."

"She's alright when she isn't talking about men. She had them mad today, so I like her." She started smiling.

"Tell me what you want me to send you to read. I already put some money on your books." He was thinking about how fast everything had been happening.

"You got your sister like that." She crossed her legs and tilted her head up a bit.

"On every day that I can visit, I'll be right here to keep your spirits up." He was thinking about how their situation should have been reversed.

"I want you to write me a letter every day. I don't care what you write me." She wanted him to make up for what he had not done for her in the past.

He gave her a strange look and tilted his head down. "I don't think that I've ever written a person a letter." The only time that he ever had any dealing with letters was when he had his secretary dictate a letter.

*"And?"* It sounded like she had breathed electricity through the phone.

"Ease up, sis. What is the letter thing all about?" He was really trying to figure out what he would write her.

"It's called having a relationship with your sister who's locked up. A stamp only costs thirty-nine cents, so what's the problem?" If he decided to say that she was overreacting, she would easily agree because he had been handling business for her so well that she dared not complain.

"I'll try. I have a laptop."

She started smiling. "That's what I love about my big brother. I'd do the same for you." One day she planned to ask about what happened to all of the letters that she had written him from jail and prison.

A guard hollered that the visit was over.

"I have to go, sis."

"You have to tell me that you love me before you leave." She had on one of those smiles that was hard to dismiss.

"I love you, sis." He rose.

"I love you, big brother." She threw a kiss at him and waved as he left.

For the rest of the night, she laid back and thought about the things that she'd do when she beat the case. With her gangsta-acting lawyer, she felt safe. With her brother on her side, she felt safer.

She knew that her brother would keep her supplied with plenty of reading material to keep her mind occupied. She didn't realize that she cared for her brother more than she cared for herself.

Ever since Trina went to prison, she wanted someone to love her for just being Trina. She never thought that she would find that love in her twin brother. She was happy with him just for getting her a great lawyer.

She wasn't thinking that he owed her for saving his life. Because he was a man, she would never bring that up and try to make him feel obligated to do anything. She wanted him to do things of his own free will. She also wouldn't bring up how she had saved his mother's life.

"So she allowed you to come back to South Carolina? Isn't that nice." Upon seeing him, Vanessa changed her mind about acting loving and caring. She had also changed the locks so that he'd have to knock.

"May I come in?" Troy had left Virginia that morning and wanted to be sure she was okay.

"Sure. You paid for the house and everything in it." She stood to the side and waited for him as he walked toward the living room.

He sat down on the couch.

She sat in her seat. "I didn't think that I was ever going to see you again. So to what do I owe the pleasure?" She picked her drink back up.

"Stop, Ma. Just stop. Your daughter is in major trouble, and you act like you don't care. I'm not about to give you lots of time." His voice was much cooler than the strength of his words.

"Damn, that's all you talk about these days is that girl. What da fuck has she done to you?" Her voice revealed that she had been drinking heavily.

"That's my twin sister and your daughter. She needs the both of us in her life. I need to know what you plan to do." He had been thinking about the situation since his first visit with Trina.

She looked at the ceiling. "Why do you have to make things complicated? I bet that she doesn't want to have a damn thing to do with me." She poured herself another drink and started drinking it.

"She saved your life."

She spit out some of the drink. "You did. She was just there. I wish that you'd stop saying that." The more that she had thought about it, the more she felt like it might be true. Admitting this would take a lot.

"You could have at least said thank you to her. You treated her like she was a disease." He was also mad with himself for not finding his sister sooner, like when they had first moved to South Carolina. Maybe he could have done something to save his sister from becoming a cold-blooded killer.

"Shit. Like hell I'll tell her that. She killed the only man I ever loved." She turned sideways in her seat. Her drink was done and so was the bottle. She was thinking about something a bit stronger, which she'd get to as soon as he left.

"Ma, suppose she dies. Aren't you going to feel something? *That's your daughter.*" He felt ashamed just thinking of telling people about this conversation. It wasn't supposed to be like this.

She let out a breath. Her expression said she wished he would just leave it alone. She lit up a cigarette and blew out some smoke. It was a long stream of smoke, as if her insides were made of it.

She shook her head from side to side. *"No,"* she stated like she didn't care what was said next.

He bit down on his lower lip and put it in his mouth. He banged his left thumb against his mouth. His eyes were cut to the right.

"I hope that you didn't mean that, Ma. Don't say a thing." He said the last part quickly while he took his left fist from his mouth. "She deserves to be treated better than we treated her. The way that we treated her caused her to be on trial, so we need to make that up to her." Moisture was forming around his eyes.

He held his head down. Those were only a few of the feelings that he had been suppressing. He felt worse and worse the more that he saw Trina. It was a matter of trying to do the right thing.

Would she ever say that he was correct? *Never*, she thought. And she had thought about it every time that she wanted to call him. It kept her from calling him. She figured that if she called him first, it would make her look weak. She couldn't imagine herself even speaking to her daughter, let alone talking with her or thinking that Trina had saved her life.

Though she was surprised and shocked, she just sat there and watched her son. She was seriously wondering what would happen with their relationship. They were close enough for her to do many things but not close enough for her to swallow her pride.

"Ma, I need for you to change your mind. That's just the way that it is." He still had his head down. He was afraid that if he looked up at her that his anger would intensify, and he didn't want that.

She remained quiet because she had never seen him act like this.

He waited for an answer for several minutes. He wondered if he should keep pushing the envelope. Was it the right thing to do? What his sister had done for him and how she had treated him gave him the answer.

He held his head up high as he stood up and walked over to her. "Ma," he said and let out a silent breath. To show some kind of love and affection, he knelt down to get below her eye level and continued eye contact. "By the end of her trial, we'll have to be a family. Or my sister and I aren't going to have a mother."

She looked deep into his eyes and into his expression to see if he really meant what he was saying. It was the first time that she had seen this expression. She had never seen tears on his face. It was as if there were a part of him that she had never known. She had more fear of his expression than she had for what he said.

They just stared at each other's faces and into each other's eyes for about forty seconds.

She wanted to hug him and tell him that she couldn't do it. She knew that she couldn't do it. She wanted to beg him to stop it, but something wouldn't allow her to say a thing. All she could do was look at him.

His face looked like it would close up at any minute. His lips were smashed together. His nose looked like it was closer to his lip. His eyes looked like they had dropped. And his forehead looked longer.

All he could think about was doing right by his sister. He was up and heading toward the door.

"I should have been the one who killed him and done the jail time," he said while walking. He didn't turn around. He had never been disgusted about anything in his life.

She wanted to call him back. Something just wouldn't let her.

Three weeks went by very quickly for Trina. Just as she and Ms. Funky expected, the government had very little on her. At the most, they could say that she was the female who stayed with Patrick. Ms. Funky told her and showed her that the case was a joke.

Ms. Funky felt that the second-most dangerous thing was the picture that was taken in Las Vegas. She was sure that the prosecutor would try to work it in there somehow to make it seem very relevant. She felt that it was a bit too complicated for her to explain to Trina. If necessary, she'd go there. Still, just like any good attorney, she kept her eyes open for surprises.

Trina was most happy about how her brother had been staying on point for her. She had been receiving a letter each day from him. Sometimes two. All the fan mail didn't mean a thing— and she was getting at least ten letters a day.

It seemed that every day a new article was being written about her. She laughed at how little they knew about her. It satisfied her that she was getting credit for what she had done and she was about to walk free. At the most, she had expected them to investigate her.

On the advice of Ms. Funky, she started planning her new life. She was young, beautiful, smart and filthy rich.

She had started to look at the situation as a temporary routine. She looked forward to the days that Troy visited. Other than that, she read, slept, ate and exercised.

She was ready for whatever.For whatever happened, she was ready. They definitely wouldn't see her sweat.

Martin had just told Lovett that he couldn't think of a way to make a better case.

"Stop it," Lovett hollered as he stood and rested his palms on his desk. "The more that I've thought about it, the easier this case looks."

Martin sat in the leather chair. "Please tell me what you mean."

Lovett sat down also. "She just might get away with it if my theory about Patrick training her doesn't work, but if she just gets away, we got Witherspoon." He leaned back in his chair.

Martin looked at the ceiling behind him and thought about Lovett's state of mind. What has him feeling this way, Martin asked himself. "You aren't talking this way because of the pressure. You weren't talking this way a few weeks ago. You haven't been drinking, have you?"

Lovett stood and started walking to the left to get to the front of the desk. "No, I haven't." He sat on the corner of his desk. "Two circumstantial evidence cases being tried together is a powerful thing."

"Okay. Would you please explain?"

"That conversation between Patrick and Witherspoon says a lot. Isn't it funny that a day later the FBI agent who's on Witherspoon's trail ended up dead?" He was indirectly practicing his closing argument.

"That makes a lot of sense."

"So who else is going to know where an FBI agent lives? The jury will have to think that it's Witherspoon. It also helps that Patrick and Gerald Scott ended up murdered also."

"Do you think that they'll buy that? She did the murder."

"No, not directly, but they might buy it indirectly. Why the hell was she always gone? Where the hell could she have been? That makes her part of the conspiracy even if she didn't pull the trigger." Lovett was getting excited.

"There is also the fact that a hit had been put out on her twin brother."

"So why wasn't he murdered like the rest, and why did the Asians end up dead at Patrick's house? They weren't happy that the hit hadn't gone down. That's good circumstantial evidence for both cases." It was mandatory that he have as positive an attitude as possible. What he was seeing was significant and meant something to the case. Whether he could convince a jury or not was another matter. He felt that he had to perform well no matter how weak the case was. A lot of eyes were going to be on him.

Martin walked behind the chair and leaned on it. He rubbed his lightly bearded face.

"Talk to me, Martin. It's almost crunch time. Say something. Say something." As the head attorney, he could devote all of his time to the case. That's what he had been doing.

"What you are saying sounds really powerful." He meant to use the word "strong." He turned around. "O'Malley and Ms. Funky aren't the weakest of defense attorneys. What they can do has me scared."

Lovett laughed. "It isn't like they have solid defenses. It's all about inferences on top of inferences. That's all that's needed for a conspiracy case." This didn't mean that he didn't want more evidence.

"Okay, Mr. Confident, we need one more crack at Witherspoon. What should we offer him?"

"I was thinking about just frying his old ass. He deserves it. He had an agent murdered. We just can't let him plead guilty and get away with murder. We would look like fools." Whatever they chose to do would be scrutinized to the max. Doing something that let it look like Witherspoon got away with murder was out of the question.

"I'm not as optimistic as you. Let him get ten years. That way, we get her as the serial killer." He was thinking about having all the insurance that he could get.

"We have to start with twenty, and let them work it down to ten." He knew how this thing works. He would simply make that promise and never keep it. Prosecutors were, at times, notorious for turning on snitches after they got what they wanted.

"Yeah." He smiled a genuine smile for the first time in days. "That'll work. That'll work."

"I'll see you later." Lovett appreciated the practice session.

"I'll be calling Ms. Funky before we go to see them. I'll love throwing this at her." On general principle, he wanted to have the last word when it came to her. Slapping her was out of the question.

"Maybe we'll be able to get the both of them to plead guilty. Then we could both move on to other things." They shook on that. They felt as if they had come up with a master plan.

Martin left Lovett's office almost feeling like a brand-new man. On the way to his car, he tried his best to think all the factors over. He couldn't help thinking about Ms. Funky's attitude. All the sources that he had checked with said that she was vicious in the courtroom. Nothing would let him take her for granted.

On the brighter side, he felt even more certain that Trina was the killer but still not certain enough for him to celebrate.

Usually, there was always that one person who could be questioned about a suspect. In Trina's situation, he hadn't found a person who was close enough to her to tell him anything significant. She didn't even keep a journal from what he could tell from the contents of her room and her computer.

All he knew for certain was that she lived with Patrick and that she was Troy's twin sister. Her being Troy's sister only told him so much. It made sense that Patrick and Witherspoon's problem emanated from her refusing to kill her twin brother. It all made sense to him and to Lovett.

But would a jury buy it? Here was a girl who they claimed was a serial killer, but they had not even caught her with a weapon. Her just having hydro in her system might not be good enough. He wanted just a little more to be certain.

All he could do was conclude that it would be a battle. With the next two moves that he planned to put down, he felt that he'd be able to reach that level of certainty.

Win, lose or draw, he had to roll the dice. Really, the dice had been rolled.

# CHAPTER 25

Trina walked in the visiting section with a smile on her face. "So to what do I owe the surprise? I didn't expect to be seeing you, Ms. Funky." She thought that her brother had somehow arranged a special visit.

"We have to do the attorney-client thing, and we have to do it face-to-face. So how are you holding up?" At times, she wondered if Trina took the situation seriously.

"I'm good. We're still supposed to beat the trial, right?"

"Now don't act surprised. I have to relay a few messages. It's some simple stuff."

"Okay, go ahead." Trina sat up a little straighter in the seat.

"Martin told me that they are offering you the chance to plead guilty." She put her finger up. "And testify against Witherspoon in exchange for a thirty-year sentence."

"Can I speak now?"

"Yes, you may."

"Tell them," she said as she rolled her eyes around in her head, "that I said I'm innocent and that they can go to hell. Straight to hell."

"That's what I already told them." They were both giggling like they were at a girls' slumber party.

"So what else is up? I know you sexed one of these cats in Virginia."

Ms. Funky pointed her finger at her. "Not yet, but I shall. I also have to tell you that Witherspoon just might testify against you."

"That old motherfucker has never met me. And I've never met him. What the hell is he going to do? *Lie.*" Trina knew that she had to at least think about it for a bit.

"I agree with you, but he'll say that Patrick told him that you were doing the hits. That's the part that I'll be waiting for at the trial."

Trina was shaking her head and thinking about what she had said.

"Witherspoon and Lovett are smart enough to not get caught in some simple lies." Ms. Funky was positive that she'd be able to find a few other holes that they wouldn't be able to fill.

"Since you still feel good about it, I'm ready to get it on with them. I'm innocent, and they can't prove that I'm not. Isn't the burden on them?" As the days went by, she grew more and more confident. She felt loved, wanted, appreciated and validated.

"We are going to show them that two black chicks can't be fucked with."

They high-fived each other.

Ms. Funky left the jail with a feeling of intrigue and inspiration.

Most clients acted emotional and irrational, especially when they were innocent or claimed to be innocent.

She had come up hating the way that the system and America treated her African-American brothers. Though, at times, she felt that African-American men treated their women terribly, she was willing to put her all in when it came to a criminal case.

Her tenacity was legendary in the federal court system on the East Coast. Her retainers were the highest, and she deserved it. What she loved to do was go to trial with a good case. That way, she could show her ass by playing close to the line.

She had won seventy-five percent of the cases that she took to trial. If the evidence was overwhelming, she worked out a great plea for her client, though she didn't always like this. She had to respect that certain people would turn on their comrades in certain cases.

Trina's case was her first high-profile case. She didn't count major dealers because there were so many of them and all of their cases were pretty much the same: Somebody on the inside was snitching and would make the prosecutor's case. Getting them the least amount of time possible was all she could do. Informants who can establish associations with pictures and phone calls were hard to slam in a conspiracy case.

With Trina's case, she felt that she was taking in fresh air. Before Troy called her, the case had caught her interest. She had already been thinking about how she would represent Witherspoon if she had the chance. But Trina's case was better than his.

She liked handling big things and making scenes while she was at it. That made a lot of people call her the female Johnnie Cochran. She deserved that title because she went that hard. All of the small matters were handled by the other lawyers and paralegals in her firm.

If necessary, she would have considered trying Trina's case for free or paying Troy to let her represent Trina. It was that tasty and delightful. She loved being the most watched defense attorney in the country. And she planned to put on a show that made them want to see her next performance. When reporters tried to interview her, she said, "My client is innocent, and I intend to prove it."

On a daily basis, she went over all the evidence. Even when she was taking a bath and handling other feminine things, she was thinking about the case. If a relevant thought came up, she jotted it down. She was on it like a client wants an attorney to be on a case.

When Ms. Funky had the chance, she planned to ask a serious question. She had to know if Trina really committed all of those murders. She just had to know. Her instinct told her yes. The evidence only pointed in her direction.

Her inquisitiveness was also driven by how Trina was handling the situation. It was the calm that was saying, "I know that y'all can't get at me. I didn't make any mistakes." There was just so much emotional control there that it astounded Ms. Funky.

It took O'Malley a week to convince Witherspoon to meet with Lovett and Martin.

Witherspoon had become more determined to beat the case. He had his heart totally set on it. O'Malley not knowing their offer was the only thing that made Witherspoon finally agree to meet with them. In his mind, they were truly the enemy.

"What is this meeting about," Witherspoon asked loudly and angrily as he entered the small room.

O'Malley was sitting and had an open seat reserved for him at the table. Martin and Lovett were standing against the wall. Before Witherspoon walked in, they were talking about strategy. They were all surprised by Witherspoon's tone. It was the same tone Witherspoon used as an FBI director.

Martin took a step forward. "It's a beautiful day, and we may have something really delightful for you." Lovett was already seated across from Witherspoon.

"If you are not offering me the chance to go free, you must be about to offer a plea bargain that I don't want." He had rationalized to the point that he knew that he would beat the case and resume life as it had been.

If the case wasn't that important, Martin would have said the hell with him and his attitude. "Listen, boss." O'Malley and Lovett looked up at him. "We just need to talk to make this matter simple."

Witherspoon had his hands behind his back. With the air of an Englishman, he held his head up and looked down at Martin. "I have the feeling that you are wasting my time." He was ready to battle unless they said something that he really liked.

"You used to tell us that it never hurts to listen. Why not hear us out?" What he was doing is what prosecutors usually did, and he was tired of doing it.

He tilted his head down and smiled a bit. "Okay, I'll grant you that, as I have so many times in the past." He had a timetable of being back at his job in less than ten months. He sat as Martin sat.

"I wanted to tell you this face-to-face. It wouldn't be right for me to let you get surprised."

"Would you please get to the point?" Witherspoon wanted to get back to his cell and think about his plans.

"Okay, Trina is seriously thinking about testifying against you."

Witherspoon immediately looked at O'Malley to see if he had knowledge of this. He may have thought that his reaction was safe and that it hid his emotions. He obviously had been snapped back to reality.

"She's seriously thinking about taking a twenty-year sentence and testifying against you." Lovett liked Martin's approach. Martin thought of it when he saw Witherspoon acting delusional.

About ten seconds later, Witherspoon turned his eyes back to Martin. "So what else do you have to say?" His tone had changed so dramatically it was obvious that he was majorly concerned.

"We can make it so that you only end up with a seven-year sentence. That means that you'll have to do less than five years. Actually, about four years. Really, three with the drug program." It was the first time that he had seen that window open, that window that reveals deep-seated fear.

"That's hard for me to believe. O'Malley and Funky have been talking extensively about strategy. She isn't a dirty lawyer." Witherspoon could still think fast. O'Malley sat up a little bit and started shaking his head.

Martin smiled and leaned back in his seat. "Listen to me good, Mr. Witherspoon, sir. This trial is about to go down in three weeks, and I don't have time to play games or babysit." His tone was on the verge of being nasty. "When she takes the stand, don't look back at me. Just get ready for that lethal injection." He stood and slammed the chair into the table. Lovett stood up also. "Let's go." They departed.

A classic example of saying what you have to say and just stepping off. It was the most confident that Martin had felt about the case. All of the doubt that he had about Witherspoon's guilt was now gone. He could already see Witherspoon taking the deal. The look he saw in Witherspoon's eyes told him all that he wanted to know.

Witherspoon, to say the least, was steamed. O'Malley could see it. Witherspoon stood and started walking the circumference of the room. O'Malley watched and waited for him to say something.

Witherspoon walked and bobbed his head. For minutes, he held his head down and walked. O'Malley could see that he was in deep thought.

"So what is it we should do about his?" Witherspoon asked to strike up a debate.

"What else can you ask for out of a plea bargain?" He would have asked for numbers that were higher.

"I know that I should. It isn't that simple of a decision. They made it all sounds so simple." His breathing had sped up a bit. That craving for something to smoke was kicked in because of the stress.

"We both know how these things work. It would be best that you let her be the star defendant in this trial." O'Malley seriously felt that this was the best thing for his client.

"Let's look at a serious hypothetical." He stepped into the middle of the floor and looked at the ceiling. "There's the possibility that she may not get convicted. Did you think about that?"

O'Malley hadn't. "You might be putting too much emphasis on that. They have a picture that looks like her from behind."

"If she doesn't get convicted, it means that I get stuck with fifteen years. I can't do that much time." He turned to face O'Malley. He was angry with him.

"There could never be a guarantee, and you know that. All the evidence and circumstances point toward her. What more could you ask for?" He didn't exactly see it that way. Still, he had a positive outlook.

"I could ask for some direct evidence. For all I know, Patrick could have been pulling off those hits and telling me differently. Did you think about that?"

"It was a female in Vegas."

"Suppose he had on a disguise?" Paranoid was the best way to describe Witherspoon's emotional state.

"There were dead people in his house after he was murdered." He wasn't expecting an argument. At this point, he was ready to do whatever. He wanted a sense of direction.

"I can see her walking, and I'll be stuck with fifteen years after pleading guilty. It might be better that I go to trial."

"Well, what about her testifying against you? Have you thought about that?" He took it seriously because he had seen the toughest of them turn around and testify.

"The only thing that they may have done is make an offer with a letter. If I were her, I'd take it to trial no matter what they offered unless it was a one-year sentence." As a police officer, he knew that he would have waited to arrest her. Would his testimony be the tipping factor? This was a tough question that he was trying to find an answer to. It weighed heavily in his decision.

O'Malley stood up and grabbed his briefcase. "No matter how long we talk, there are going to be pros and cons. Whatever decision you make, you have my support."

Witherspoon turned his back to him. "But you definitely would prefer that I took the plea and testified." These were just loud words to end the conversation.

"What's the use? They'll probably get convictions for the both of y'all. I can't see her getting an acquittal with your testimony. I'm leaving." He knew that it was wrong to walk out like that on a client, especially a rich one, but there was little else to say. He left wondering what Witherspoon would do.

Witherspoon was left to grapple with a decision that he had already grappled with and made—well, so he thought. It is never over until it's over, especially in a criminal case.

He couldn't escape the situation with a drink, a broad, a joint or even a good pinch of tobacco. Because of his position and the charge, no guards would let him get a play. His money didn't mean a thing.

For another hour, he paced the room. The guards had forgotten that he was in there. When a person is in deep thought, an hour can seem like a minute.

# CHAPTER 26

When the guards called Trina for her second visit, she was deep into *Keisha II - The Clit*.

Her brother had stopped in early that morning. She figured it had to be him or Ms. Funky. It didn't matter because it was a way to pass the day. She had instructed the guards that only family and her attorney be let in to see her. On her way to the booth, she figured two visits in one day would be a pleasant surprise. She and her brother had grown that close since they had started writing each other.

When she saw her mother sitting in the booth, her instinct told her to just turn around. Instead, she just stood there and looked eye to eye with her. Out of principle, she wouldn't walk or run away. These kinds of actions had never been in her blood.

Vanessa was very scared. Her right leg was shaking, and she felt like running out of the room. She didn't know how seeing her daughter face-to-face would affect her. There was a lot of guilt to go with the fear.

Vanessa had snuck in behind Troy that day. She didn't want him around, and she didn't want to listen to his comments and suggestions. When she told the front desk that she was Trina's mother, they didn't hesitate to let her in. She waited until the last minute for special visiting hours to end.

Trina didn't feel good about her. Trina didn't feel too bad about her. The thoughts that she had had about killing her came to mind. Still, she silently stared and looked over her mother's face. She squinted her eyes a little as she thought about her time spent in prison and what she had been through.

Vanessa wasn't paying full attention to details. She was using too much energy trying to keep her leg still. She wished that she had gotten high beforehand. She had made the first step of coming and facing her daughter. Just looking at her daughter made her feel like the worst mother in the world.

Without Trina's consent, her face began forming a frown. All the negative emotions came to the surface. She didn't want to act negatively, but what else could she do? What else could she feel? Thinking about her brother helped a lot.

Something inside Vanessa made her pick up the phone. She had a begging expression on her face. It was the weakest that she had felt in a while. With her head and free hand, she motioned for Trina to pick up the phone. She forced a smile on her face, the kind that begged for approval and acceptance, the kind that said don't make this any harder on me.

Be nice for Troy's sake. Don't be mean for the sake of Troy. Thinking about her brother made her feel a minute bit of pity for Vanessa. The word "mother" hadn't existed to her in years. The minuteness of her pity was so small that only she could discover it. She hated to see a person beg or act weak. She felt that pain should be sucked up. Going hard is all that she knew.

Trina slowly picked up the phone. She made the process take as long as she could. She thought about changing her mind. Being in the stronger position made her feel good—not that she wanted to see Vanessa in a compromising position.

She just had that feeling. She was still standing up. As she moved the phone toward the side of her head, she wondered what Vanessa would say and what she'd say back.

Vanessa balled her lips up in her mouth in anticipation of that time to speak. She couldn't read her daughter's expression. All she saw was a blank face. No warmth. No opening. No invitation. No love. Wanting it was different than experiencing it and desiring it and much, much different than deserving it.

When the phone was half an inch from Trina's ear, Vanessa said, "I'm sorry. I'm really sorry."

Vanessa wished that Trina would sit to make her feel a little welcome. "I'm sorry, Trina. I really am." It was all that she could think of to say, for so many things flashed through her mind, even thoughts about the day she had brought Trina home from the hospital. So many things that she hadn't thought about in years.

Trina ran the voice through her mind. She almost didn't believe this was real. She wondered why, but didn't think to ask. Nor did she desire to ask. She wasn't curious enough for that. She thought as she stared and thought some more. The sullen look on her face didn't change.

Vanessa felt trapped to the degree that she was totally paralyzed. Even her leg stopped shaking. Too little too late, she thought. She hadn't expected much from the situation. She only wanted to open the door. She wanted to do the right thing to keep from losing her son. Tears welled up in her eyes.

Trina was still just staring. She thought about putting the phone back in the cradle and walking away. They were about seven minutes into the visit. Though her facial expression hadn't changed, she was thinking some very deadly thoughts. She wanted to scream at Vanessa about how wrong she had been. That would have been proper if she desired to have a conversation and hear some more weak-acting things. She didn't.

Vanessa just made one expression after the other, hoping that Trina would say something that would start the process of them having some kind of relationship. She had already thought about doing whatever it took to make her son happy. She couldn't think of anything else to say. Being humble wasn't what she had much practice with, though she was doing it well.

"Listen," Trina said after she cleared her throat. Vanessa sat up. "What you did was an act of the heart. I can't forgive you. Don't come back." She put her eyes down as she let the phone drop to the desk. Seconds later, she was out the door.

Vanessa just stared as she wiped the tears from her face. There are boxes that should never be opened.

That night, for Trina, turned out to be one of the deepest thinking sessions, if not the deepest. She couldn't keep thoughts of her mother out of her head. She tried all the things she could. She couldn't read a book. She couldn't read her old mail. She couldn't read a magazine. Eating snacks didn't help

She was grateful to be alone so that nobody saw her state of being. She kept all of her desires, thoughts and actions to herself, just as Patrick had taught her and as she taught herself.

In a matter of hours, she relived all the pain. She remembered all the nights that she had quietly cried herself to sleep, all the praying she had done that she would just get one letter from her mother or brother, all the sexing and drugging to control the pain, all the murders to release her anger and suppressed emotions.

Until she saw her mother, her mind had been on how she would go about finally leading a normal life. It was easy to think normal when certain things hadn't been brought to mind. All the negative energy made her want to go out and kill again. She wished that she could change her feelings with a snap of her fingers. Her desire was to kill her mother so that all of the past would remain in the past.

She paced her cell with these thoughts until she got tired. Then she lay down. Her anger was so intense that it put her out for several hours.

When she woke up, just before dawn, she asked herself if she had said the right thing to her mother. She decided that she couldn't have a relationship with her and she couldn't be around her. Her brother was the one whom she couldn't hurt.

She couldn't see things being any other way.

It was a week later. Troy and Ms. Funky walked into the courtroom just in time. Because it was so crowded, they had to play the back. Ms. Funky decided to use her cell to get a good view of the front.

Troy and Ms. Funky chartered a private plane to make it to Richmond to be with Trina. All the morning news channels had been talking about Witherspoon pleading guilty that afternoon.

It had come to the point that Witherspoon had to plead guilty or go to trial. Martin and Lovett had sent messages that they were not accepting it after a certain date. Witherspoon had waited until the day before the deadline to make the decision. It was the fighter in him that made him fight and hold out until the last minute.

"Mr. Witherspoon, would you tell us how you plead to the charge of conspiracy to murder FBI Agent Jason Scott?" The court spoke loudly and clearly.

Martin and Lovett were filled with anticipation, just as the audience and media were. It had been an overwhelming consensus that Witherspoon would take it to trial and maybe win. The world was in suspense.

Would he plead guilty? Would he change his mind? Would he stand there and hold the world's attention for as long as he could? Would something unexpected happen? They were also wondering what had made him change his mind. What was on Trina's mind? Would she also plead guilty? Would he also testify against her? Was he really guilty? Was he pleading guilty just to skip the death penalty?

From the moment Witherspoon walked in the courtroom's side door, his body temperature dropped. It didn't matter that he looked elegant in a custom-made suit with all the accessories and shoes to match.

So far, he had done an excellent job of ignoring the overcrowded courtroom. Still, he had to think that most of the personnel were once close friends of his. He hadn't said a thing for thirty seconds.

He actually hadn't heard what the court had been saying the entire time. If he hadn't been the defendant, he would have soaked up every word and nuance.

Most of what had happened in the past few days had been a blur to him. The deciding factor was his grandchildren. He wanted to be around for them as long as he possibly could.

Ten seconds later, the court spoke with a raised voice. "How do you plead, Mr. Witherspoon?" If it weren't for the media, he would have revealed the disgust in his voice.

Witherspoon was barely fazed. He turned to his right to look at the audience, intentionally not looking to the left to avoid the eyes of his lawyer.

Lovett and Martin were glad that they had put out a press release. At minimum, they wanted him to walk into the courtroom. This would be a relevant factor to jurors unless they didn't follow major events.

After Witherspoon scanned the audience, he turned back to the judge. The nasty look that he saw didn't mean much to him. Making them wait didn't mean much to him, though he knew better than to make the judge mad. He was dealing with a situation of don't look back. The trial was scheduled to go down in a little more than a week. "I'm doing this for my grandkids," he kept telling himself. Pleading guilty was not for him. He'd turned from the idea that he could beat the trial.

"Mr. Witherspoon, you have five seconds to plead guilty or be ready to go to trial in a week." He spoke fast and let his impatience be heard.

Witherspoon felt that he had made them wait long enough. Out of principle, he wanted it to look like he had been forced.

"I plead gui—" He paused and waited for close to five seconds. "Guilty."

Martin and Lovett clinched their fists to celebrate. It was as if they were more than halfway there. The other half would be getting the person who pulled the trigger.

A tidal wave of murmuring rushed across the courtroom. The judge decided to save his energy instead of trying to quiet them down by hitting his gavel. He felt that all were ignoring him, and he was happy.

Though it had happened live for the world, it still had to be put in print.

There would be more opinions about this trial than the O.J. Simpson trial.

Naturally, people were voicing their opinions and doing it arrogantly to win arguments.

A few reporters caught Ms. Funky and Troy before they left the courthouse. "Ms. Funky, would you please tell us what you think of the situation?"

Saying "no comment" was not her when confronted after a significant event. "What you saw and heard is what you saw and heard. My client isn't going to plead guilty."

"So are you expecting Mr. Witherspoon to testify against your client?" The loud female reporter was expecting to get a raise for this exclusive interview.

"I can't wait to do him. Why else would he plead guilty? And make sure you print that." She put her palm up to the camera, then to the microphone, then to the reporter's face. Everything else being said was ignored.

Ms. Funky grabbed Troy by the arm and headed for the jail.

# CHAPTER 27

"**Y**ou made the right decision." O'Malley had come to talk to Witherspoon before the marshals took him back to FCI Petersburg.

Witherspoon was looking at the floor when the comment was made. He let it sink in for a few seconds. He hadn't told O'Malley that he did it for the love of his grandchildren.

"What is there that you can tell me, Mr. O'Malley?" He held his head up to make eye contact. On so many occasions, he had taunted defendants who were in the same cell.

"We're still in this together. I think you made the right decision."

Witherspoon slowly stood and walked over to the gate. "When this is all said and done, you'll still be a lawyer. A lawyer who's making over two million a year. By the morning, I'll be disgraced to the fullest."

"You have to understand that is better than getting the death penalty or a few life sentences." For the sake of adventure, he wanted to go to trial with the case, and with the tape, but not with Trina's presence.

"If this doesn't work, I'll be blaming you and suing you." He still wasn't accepting any more blame than necessary.

"You'll feel better after you testify against her and she gets convicted." He left on that note. O'Malley hadn't expected much other than that kind of conversation.

Witherspoon had accepted defeat with all the graciousness that he could. Not an easy thing.

Politically, it was over for him. He was now an outcast and embarrassment. At times, he reasoned with himself that he'd lived his life. It was the best attitude for him to adopt. He also wanted to see how many of those outside his family who depended on him for free financial support were true friends. Inside, he prayed that the five years would go fast. So what he had gotten caught with his hands in the cookie jar. He had already put the money in a trust for his grandchildren.

"And what took you so long to get here? We've been waiting on you." Ms. Funky was excited to get the trial started. She'd already planned what she'd wear every day of the trial.

"Hey, Troy." Trina went over and kissed him. Ms. Funky had told the jail that Troy was her paralegal. "A sister was taking a nap. What's this surprise for?" She sat next to her brother.

"We came to tell you that Witherspoon just decided to plead guilty. Well, he did plead guilty," Troy stated as she sat.

Trina shrugged her shoulders and looked at Ms. Funky. "What is that supposed to mean?"

"We can bet that he's going to testify against you." Ms. Funky still had a smile on her face.

In a surprised tone Trina responded, "But he doesn't even know me. We already talked about him."

"Yes, we did."

"So to hell with his scared ass."

They high-fived each other like they had been having grown girl talk.

"We have to hang after I beat this thing. I know where all the hot spots in Atlanta are." Ms. Funky was dead serious.

Trina laughed. She loved the way Ms. Funky carried it. "May I speak with my brother for a minute? Those visits are far too short for this topic."

"Okay. I'll keep the guard busy." Might as well get herself a date for the night. Just because a lady has to work doesn't mean she can't get her party on. She politely closed the door and made sure that her skirt was in place.

"Can your sister get a hug?" she said as she stood up with a smile on her face. It had been weeks since she had been able to put her hands on the man who was the center of her life. She hugged him tightly. "Okay, we have to talk."

"Tell me what's up."

"You know that I'm ready to deal with whatever happens in this situation." Her demeanor had changed to semi-serious. If she were speaking with anyone else, she would have been aggressive.

"We already talked about that, so tell me what is really on your mind." He could not think of anything other than the trial that could be important to her, but her tone made him think that it had to do with something else.

"You know that I plan to beat this trial and be with you in Atlanta."

"Yeah. I know this. I hate to rush you, but get to the point."

"Okay. I'll do that. This is hard for me to say because it might hurt you, so I've been keeping it all to myself." With any other kind of situation, she would have been direct.

"You must have AIDS or something. Damn, sis."

"Hell naw. Boy, you crazy."

"What the hell is it that you are talking about? Just say it."

Not knowing how he'd feel also kept her from being direct. "No matter what happens, I can't stand to be around her. Do you understand?"

He almost asked whom. Instead, he thought about it. There were only two females that they had in common. "So what brought all of this on?" He had planned to bring the subject up long after the trial was over.

"She came to see me."

Troy waited a minute to get his thoughts together. "So when was this, and what happened?"

"Tell me what you are feeling first. Then I'll feel comfortable about this."

"I did have plans on making us a family. You deserve to have a real family."

Hearing him say something of that nature meant so much to her. The surprise of it threw her off. "It's nice that you feel that way, but I can't do that for you. Not even for you. I wish that I could." Trina had more concern for his feelings than for hers.

Though he figured she'd go in that direction, he knew where she was coming from. "Whatever you say. It's all about you."

"Are you sure that you understand? I need to know this." She felt badly about not being able to give her brother something that he wanted.

"I understand, and I want you to know something."

"Are you sure that you understand?" She reached over and touched his knee.

"Yes, I'm sure. I never thought that she'd come to see you. I'm surprised she came. Can I tell you something?"

Trina nodded her head.

"It shouldn't have been you that killed him. It should have been me. This shouldn't be happening. I want to be able to make this up to you, so tell me how. Whatever you want, sis. I'll make it happen."

The emotions made her catch a lump in her throat. Now that she felt totally loved and appreciated, she felt ready to pass to the next world if need be. She knew exactly what she wanted and how she wanted it to happen. At the moment, she wasn't able to say it.

Troy was patient. He had finally told her how he felt. He needed her to relieve his mental.

"I want something very simple. Are you ready for this?" She started smiling. It was an idea that had come to her in a dream.

"Girl, you saved my life. If I have to—and if I can—I'll give my life so that you can live." He had never felt this way about any female other than his mother.

"Okay. Good." She clapped her hands. "I want a nightclub in Atlanta that's named after me—*Trina*!" She hollered her name as if the club would be the best present that she could ever receive. "Will you do that for me?"

"Yeah, girl. I've been thinking about starting a nightclub anyway. I'll put three million into it. It'll be the baddest night spot in the ATL." Putting his sister's name in lights was the perfect thing to do. He would argue to his death that she deserved it.

"Oh, I love you Troy." She jumped on him and started hugging and kissing him.

"Ease up, Trina," he hollered and joked. It meant the world to him to have her happy.

"It's going down once this trial is over. They ain't got shit, and he ain't never met me. I love you."

"I love you too."

Brother and sister had become as one, as twins definitely should be. It would have been easy for people to mistake them for lovers by the way they were acting. They laughed, joked and talked about the future until a guard made Troy leave. It turned out to be the best visit they'd had.

The significance of having somebody to love who loved you back had affected Trina in a strange way. If she would have given deep thought to the situation, she would have realized that her relationship with her brother was more important to her than death. Things that she had said similar to that were deeper than she meant. She was the happiest that she had ever been and had ever expected to be. She had been good to her brother, and her brother was being good to her.

So what she was facing the death penalty? She had thought about killing herself on many occasions while she was getting high and doing hits. That emptiness inside and feelings of abandonment had gotten to her on many occasions. She had felt as if she had nothing to live for and that nobody cared about her. She struggled through it by killing, getting high and pushing Patrick to love her more and more. She had only found temporary fulfillment and hoped that things would get better.

In the middle of the night, it was easy to feel lonely and forget about what hope is. On many occasions, she held her gun to her head and prepared herself to die. It was something that she never told anyone, and she never would. Only one thing would keep her from pulling the trigger: She couldn't allow her mother the chance to say that she was nothing but a worthless bitch who should have killed herself earlier. Trina kept trooping on.

All had changed for her. People were showing respect for the homicidal acts, though they didn't know for sure that she had done any of them. She had already been made into a living legend. Her name would be placed amongst the most vicious of killers. She was getting more mail as the time came closer for her to go to trial.

It had become important to her to get credit for the things that she had done, just as it is for most criminals.

If she died, she wanted to make sure that her name was kept alive. She had faith that Troy would do that for her.

She was fully ready for those twelve people to get in that box and rumble, and nothing would change that.

The next day, Troy made it over to his mother's house. Instead of knocking, he used the key that she had given him the other day.

"So you finally made it here to see your mother. You don't even call me back anymore." She had a drink in her hand. If she wasn't drinking, she was snorting cocaine.

"I've been really busy, Ma." He sat. He had never seen her look this bad. If she had slept in the past few days, he couldn't tell. He almost hadn't come over because he was feeling so good about his relationship with Trina.

In a spinning motion, her drinking glass was sailing through the room toward Troy. Just above it and slightly behind the glass was the rest of the E&J that was left. She threw the glass just high enough for it to reach him, along with some of the contents. "Crinch," the glass sounded when it hit the wood floor on the other side of the couch.

Troy ducked the glass, but that didn't keep him from getting wet.

"I bet you had time to go see that bitch!" she screamed at the top of her lungs. Disgust soaked ever word and every syllable.

Troy just stared at her. He was surprised that she had disrespected him like that. It couldn't be his mother who was acting like this. It was the first time that he had seen her act violently. Hateful he had seen. He had to ask himself was this his mother or someone else?

"Why the hell did you have me do that?" To fulfill the look, all she needed was a butcher knife—or even better, a chainsaw.

He wanted to check her and tell her to calm down. "What are you talking about, and what has gotten into you?"

"I'm talking about that bitch." She had never recognized what she called her daughter. "I went to see her, and she talked terribly to me. It's all your fault."

He stood up. "How could it be my fault? What did she do to you?" Though he was talking loudly, he wasn't talking as loudly as she was.

"She told me that she never wanted to see me again." Those weren't the exact words, but she had interpreted them correctly.

"So why are you acting like this? You haven't cleaned the house in days." He spun around. "This place looks absolutely terrible. You are acting like ... damn."

"She made me feel bad. What do you think? You could have left things alone. You want us all to be a family." She sat in her chair. She held her head down and put her left hand over her eyes to hide her tears.

"We abandoned her. We owe her. How would you feel if that had happened to you? She's my twin sister, and you are her mother. We're supposed to be a family." He sat back down in his seat.

Her mix of emotions had her stuck. How she treated her daughter had kept her up many nights and made her feel like life wasn't worth living. It didn't help that she could also lose her son's love. She had been feeling that way because he hadn't returned any of her calls.

After about five minutes, she held her head up, making sure that she wiped her eyes. "So y'all want to make y'all selves a family and exclude me? Is that the plan? To hell with your mother, huh?"

He leaned back on the couch. His right hand hit a wet spot on the couch. He looked at the ceiling while he moved his hand.

"Mr. Runs Everything can't talk. I saw you on television with the attorney lady. You can run to that—"

"Don't call her that again." He had his finger pointed at her.

The look on his face stunned her. Her pain pushed her forward. "See what I'm saying? I've been your mother all of your life, and this is how you want to treat me. You've chosen your sister over your mother."

"No, I have not."

"Oh, yes, you have." She had leaned forward to make that statement.

"If we hadn't abandoned her, we wouldn't be going through this. So you need to get it together. She's up for the death penalty." None of this was part of the plan. Life is such when emotions are involved.

"So you are on her side. That's what it seems like to me."

"It isn't like that. I was trying to do the right thing for all of us, and you know that."

"Not calling your mother back isn't the right thing to do, but you flew on a plane to see her. What are you talking about? What are you telling me, Troy?" She screamed the last sentence so loudly that it was almost inaudible.

"I'm still with you, Ma. All I wanted for you to do was try, and you did that. Thank you, Ma." He was thinking that he wouldn't be able to stay calm much longer.

"What has she ever done for you? I'm your mother. You can't turn on me."

"Oh, boy. She's going to be in Atlanta, and you are going to be at your house right here in South Carolina. So what's the problem?" He wished that he had left the situation alone.

"And you are going to be in Atlanta also. Tell the truth." She took a drink from the E&J bottle.

"That's where I've always been. That has nothing to do with her. That's where I'm getting my hustle on."

"So I'm not the most important female in your life anymore? All because of that ..." She put a unit on her face. "Homicidal maniac. She might get the death penalty. Then what?"

"Ma. You are making far too much out of this." He couldn't tell her the truth and hated what she said.

She stood up. "It's all your fault. I have to use the bathroom." She walked off at a medium pace.

What a situation, he thought. In the past sixty days, he had made some of the toughest decisions of his life. Everything that he had experienced was totally unprecedented to him. Most of the decisions concerned life and death.

He had enough excitement to want to retire and relax, but he wouldn't be able to relax until his sister was free and his mother had calmed down. He figured his mother would accept the situation after a while and just do her.

More important was that his sister didn't get laid down by the feds, though he knew that she was guilty. His stress level was limited because Ms. Funky was not only on the case, she was excited about handling it.

He had also grown tired of the hot-car business. Without his best men in the game, things just didn't seem the same.

That made his sister that much more important to him. Nothing could be more of a priority.

It had been five minutes since his mother left out of the room. He expected her to come back two minutes ago when he heard the toilet flush.

He had to decide what to do with his mother. He couldn't have her going around acting like a crackhead. He also didn't want her to feel like he was neglecting her, especially not for Trina. But over the next two weeks, he'd have to be there for Trina, no matter how his mother felt.

Troy wanted his mother to understand the situation. He was furiously thinking of a way to make her understand, no matter how impossible that seemed. He thought about going in the bathroom to see why she was taking so long.

He planned to spend the next few days with her to make her feel loved. He definitely decided that's where he'd start. He'd just fly to visit Trina in a few days.

"Hey, Ma? What are you doing?"

No sooner than he started walking in the direction of her bedroom did he hear a loud boom and the clank of a gun hitting the floor.

"No!" he hollered as he rushed to her bedroom.

All he could do was stare. The .45-caliber bullet had blown her brains and head across her bed and onto the light purple–colored wall. Red and light purple didn't make for a great sight for the eyes.

He wanted to reach out and touch her. "You didn't have to do that, Ma," he said several times. There was no need to wonder if she was dead.

What started out as a lovely day had turned into a terrible night. Because of who he was, he couldn't just leave the house and call the police from down the street. He had to wait. Because of who he was, he was given an extra hard time. The police questioned him until Ms. Funky arrived.

She got there as fast as she could. There is nothing like the presence of an attorney to make police officers scatter.

Still, after they allowed him to leave, the house was taped off as a crime scene. They wanted to search the place for clues to Troy's car business. They knew that he hadn't murdered his mother.

Powder burns on her hand told them enough to know that it was a suicide. Police will always be police.

Troy took his mother's suicide very hard. He felt that if it hadn't been for his pushing that she wouldn't have done that. He didn't understand what she had gone through when they left New York. He didn't know what kind of box he had opened.

He was glad that Trina understood why he couldn't visit her for a few days. She wrote back and told him to do what he had to do.

She felt badly about Vanessa's death because it hurt Troy, but she still felt that karma had come home to rest.

A lot of people came out for the funeral. Mostly to support him. Troy cried at the funeral. One of the only females he loved was gone. Gone forever.

He blamed himself for the entire ordeal. He felt that he should have been man enough to pull the trigger when he was supposed to. That way his ladies would be together. He felt that it would have been better for him to serve a life sentence.

Wisdom doesn't come without experience, so the young seldom have its advantages. He'd just have to suffer with those regrets and stand by Trina. The trial was going to start in less than twenty-four hours.

# CHAPTER 28

C ould a girl so beautiful be the one who killed so many people? That was the question that gave the case so much attention. Theories on top of theories had been presented. Of course, there were a few that felt she was capable. They pointed to so many other beautiful women who had been homicidal maniacs. Some went so far as to say that she had been specially trained by the FBI and that they were going to murder her soon to cover it all up.

Most felt that she didn't do it and wasn't capable. By far, the biggest argument was that the murders were just too sophisticated for her to commit. There was also the argument that she used too many drugs to be able to get away with all those murders in different cities. Reporters dig deep when a criminal defendant becomes a major celebrity. That's exactly what Trina had become.

What little that was known about her caused a large amount of intrigue. Her mother's death added to the intrigue. The most that they knew was that she'd done time for murdering her mother's boyfriend. The public had fallen into the vacuum and wanted more information.

If they found out that she did it, they would still love her. If she hadn't, they'd still love her. If she was acquitted, they'd feel like she got away with murder, but the whole world would adore her—something cops hate about dealing with criminals.

Trina and Ms. Funky had gone over every facet of the case with ultimate care. Ms. Funky had played the devil's advocate most of the time. She knew the case like it was a book that she had read ten times. Trina and Troy knew that Ms. Funky was ready to kill.

The inevitable is inevitable when it comes to a trial date. It takes an act of God—like the courthouse catching on fire or an area evacuation to take place—to stop the wheels of justice. And if it's a major case, like the one at hand, other cases will be set to the side.

Lovett was on top of the case like no other in his career. He had spent the last five days preparing Witherspoon and Martin to testify. The rest was circumstantial evidence that would be presented through them. This would allow him to make his presentation that much more memorable. He planned to hit hard and fast with an impact that couldn't be erased.

He meticulously picked out the things that he would emphasize and the things that he'd leave alone. It was his only project, and he'd been studying it day and night as if his very life and career depended on it. Never had he wanted a conviction so badly. It didn't matter if she had or hadn't done it. A courtroom is still a jungle, except only the prey can die.

The first day of the trial started right on time, like major events are supposed to. The courtroom had been cleaned from top to bottom. The court's image was important.

Ms. Funky was dressed in an expensive three-piece black skirt suit. She was wearing a tie to look feminine yet masculine.

Trina wore a white dress with a big button in the front. With a pair of designer glasses, she looked like a secretary or a college student, the intended effect. Her a murderer? Imagine that.

The court didn't waste any time. Jury selection started immediately. Many are of the opinion that trials are won and lost during this process. Ms. Funky didn't leave anything to chance. She brought in the best African-American sisters that she could find to help her. Della and Deloris. Together they weighed more than five hundred pounds. Both had a Ph.D.s. It cost a whopping $100,000 to bring them in. Della and Deloris had memorized the jury poll two days before the trial.

They came in just after the first set of jurors had been seated. They sat to the right of Trina so they could take notes and pass notes to Ms. Funky and whisper if necessary.

Most figured that they were bodyguards. Because of their size, a lot of people paid more attention to them than the jury.

Ms. Funky and her team wanted to make sure that as few cop lovers as possible made it on the jury. They also had to watch out for outright racist people. Della and Deloris had something to say about each and every juror. All things mattered, from the way that they were dressed to how much jewelry they had on to what they carried in their hands to their facial expressions.

Lovett only had the one assistant helping him. He wanted to make sure that no fans of Trina's or sympathizers made it onto the jury.

The court asked the potential jurors an array of questions. Hands went up. More questions were asked. Many stated that they couldn't vote for the death penalty. Lovett made sure that he had them excused for "cause." Many stated that they couldn't give an unbiased judgment. Depending on how the juror looked and the reason, either Ms. Funky or Lovett had him or her dismissed.

Each one threw jabs and quickly weaved and bobbed in an attempt to leave favored jurors on the panel. Out of the first ten, two made it.

Lovett felt weary after only the first round.

More potential jurors were seated. The process continued. Della and Deloris made sure that they liked the jurors who had been picked to stay.

So far, none of the prospective jurors was African American or a minority. There were some coming up, and Ms. Funky and her team made sure to have room for them. Della and Deloris stuck to their reasons for every juror. It was their job to be as critical as possible. It was as simple as talking about people.

An hour and a half later, two more jurors had been added. Ms. Funky challenged a few she liked just because Lovett liked them. She wanted to see how easy it would be to get under his skin. Some that she couldn't get then, she'd get later. It was ten-forty-five.

Della and Deloris naturally became excited when they saw four African Americans seated. They planned to be critical in a manner that would allow the right ones to stay. Just because a person is black doesn't mean that he or she is for African Americans.

Lovett didn't act like he was fazed. Trina was doing her best to keep up with what was happening.

Neither party used any of their preemptory challenges, which were limited. If Lovett decided to strike all the blacks, he knew that Ms. Funky would jump all over him. Neither party needed to state a reason for the use of a preemptory challenge, but an apparent racist motive can be challenged by the opposing party.

Lovett got rid of two blacks for "cause" because they already had opinions about the case. Two of the seven prospective jurors were black. At that time, they called for a recess.

By the end of the day, another minority had been chosen. A Puerto-Rican female. She just happened to be from the Bronx.

The first day of trial was complete. Each side seemed to be satisfied.

Lovett didn't sense that any of the jurors had succumbed to Trina's celebrity. He was most concerned about the jury because he had to convince the jury beyond a reasonable doubt. If one juror had doubt, it could be means for a mistrial. With a burden like that and going up against a defense attorney like Ms. Funky, he didn't want to chance one juror causing a mistrial. Even worse, he could have a deadlocked jury, one half going one way, the other half going the other.

Though Ms. Funky's burden wasn't as high, she acted like it was. Her job was to create doubt in the case. To her, that meant making the prosecutor's case look as silly as possible. It was a matter of poking holes in cheese. Before she arrived, she had picked her holes.

She was happy with the jury. She had already started establishing a rapport with a few of them. It was also important to watch for potential leaders on the jury. Jury foremen have proven to sway a jury just by being placed in a leadership position.

Opening arguments would start in the morning. The prosecutor would get to go first and last because the burden was on him. All audiences would perk up to hear what strategy the prosecutor would be using.

The next day, like clockwork, the jury was seated at nine-forty-five a.m. It took two hours for the judge to read the jurors their duties and what they could and couldn't do.

Trina was wearing a black dress that looked very casual. With the same eyeglasses, she looked like a girl who should have been in church.

Ms. Funky was dressed in a dark gray two-piece skirt suit. Her silver silk blouse made her look like she was ready for combat. She wanted the change in her dressing style to intrigue the jury. Having the jurors' attention could make the difference.

Troy was sitting right behind them in a dark brown suit by Sean John. Every once in a while, Trina turned around to wave at him. Most thought that they were husband and wife or something.

At 1 o'clock, right after lunch, it was time for Lovett to deliver his opening statement.

"Ladies and gentlemen of the jury, what you are about to hear is like nothing you have ever heard." It was important to use the first sentence to capture the jury's attention. "This is a murder-for-hire conspiracy that involved three parties. I don't have to tell you that former FBI members are involved in this case. There are two members who were active members of the FBI. One of them is dead. One of them is going to testify." He stopped for a second. So far, he had them opening up.

"Well, there's a third party. It's the defendant. She's a part of the conspiracy. She lived with a former FBI agent, and she was pulling the trigger."

"Objection. Objection." Ms. Funky waved her arm like an orchestra conductor. She was standing like she had been offended.

"Why are you objecting, Ms. Funky," the court inquired.

"He's testifying to something that isn't in the evidence. This is a trial, a circumstantial evidence case. Thank you, " she said, sounding insulted. She sat down.

Lovett was staring at her with disgust.

"Sustained." The court was impressed. "Please rephrase that statement."

Lovett smiled to make it seem like he wasn't fazed and that he had committed an innocent mistake. Trina and Troy were pleased.

Lovett continued. "This is a circumstantial evidence case." She made him change direction. He said what he had to say to get where he was going. It was his first mistake. "That's right, ladies and gentlemen. This isn't a direct evidence case where we have eyewitnesses who saw a crime being committed, but we have indisputable evidence that points in her direction. It infers that she was the one pulling the trigger in all of the murders we present. There are more than fifty murders in this trial.

"Don't let that innocent look lull you into disbelief. You are going to hear how the FBI director went into Quantico's computer and found customers who wanted their rivals murdered or their potential snitches murdered. He would give this information to Patrick. Patrick is the absent defendant because of his death." He was certain to say little about his death. "Afterward, the target would end up dead, but we know that Patrick wasn't the one doing the murders."

Ms. Funky thought about objecting. It was too close of a call.

"Mr. Witherspoon is going to testify that Patrick made the deals and had the defendant do the murders. This is what we call a simple murder conspiracy. Mr. Witherspoon is going to testify that he wanted the defendant murdered because her drug use had started an investigation.

"But the connection doesn't stop there. We have a tape. On the tape, you'll hear a conversation about how a hit didn't go down. That hit was on Trina Lattimore's twin brother, Troy Lattimore." Now he had to be careful. "This is where the conspiracy started to have problems."

"We have another tape— a videotape that reveals that the killer is a female. A female who wears a size eight shoe. The female had just committed the murder of a Colombian drug smuggler. Along with the evidence, we'll have expert witnesses who'll allow you to make an informed decision."

It was time for him to clean up the Ms. Funky situation. "Just as Ms. Funky informed you only minutes ago, this is a circumstantial evidence case. Yes, that means nobody saw her pull any triggers. Yes, nobody has heard her confess to the crime. But does that mean that we don't know that she didn't do it? No, it doesn't.

"A circumstantial evidence case is a simple matter of reasoning. When we see a pregnant woman, is it necessary to ask how she got that way? She could have been artificially inseminated, but more than likely that arrow points in the other direction. If you see a dead man and a man standing over him with a gun, do we need to see a video to know who killed him? We simply have to look at what the facts add up to.

"I now turn this over to Ms. Funky."

He felt that he had done well, and he had. Some of the jurors were considering whether Trina could have really done it. They felt suspense driving up and down their spines.

They were also interested in what Ms. Funky had to say. Many sensed that there were going to be very few dull moments.

Ms. Funky stood up as soon as Lovett sat down. She stared him down. He started conversing with Martin.

"Good morning ladies and gentlemen of the jury. I'm having a beautiful day, and I'm proud to be able to represent my client. Please look at her and ask yourself if she looks like a serial killer."

"Objection." This is what Ms. Funky wanted.

"What is your objection based on?" The court could see in his face that he was trying to get her back.

"She's trying to influence the passions of the jury. She should stick to the law and facts. This is a criminal trial."

"Overruled." It was not even close to the line. "Please continue, Ms. Funky."

"Thank you, your honor." She turned to face the jury. "This is what's called a case of convenience. According to the evidence, there's a serial killer who smokes hydro marijuana and is supposedly a female." She smiled and moved from behind the defense table.

"Well, let me tell you a few things about this case that you can be thinking about." She turned her head toward Lovett as she talked. "It's their theory that FBI Agent Patrick trained her to be a professional killer. Then he sent her around the country to kill people." People started to chatter.

The noise prompted Lovett to holler "objection."

"Overruled." There was nothing negative in the statement, though it caught everyone's attention.

Ms. Funky had officially drawn first blood. She knew that this had to be his main theory. He had allowed her to mock his strategy and get away with it.

She wasn't finished. "Now I must propose to you that Patrick may have been the killer the entire time. It could have been Patrick who murdered FBI Agent Jason Scott, not Trina Lattimore." She paused to allow them to think about that. So far, the audience was feeling her style.

"I promise that I'm not going to force you. It's my job to punch holes in this case. This is simple for you to think about. Trina did live with a former FBI agent who was a trained assassin. Yes, he was involved with murdering people for hire. Yes, there is a female involved in this case somehow. Yes, there's a witness who pleaded guilty to this charge already. Yes, these are major facts that Lovett plans to present to you. With all of that— or shall I say, none of that points to my client being a murderer. That's what I plan to prove to each of you. At the end of this trial, it shall be revealed that they know very little about my client. You may even wonder why they charged her." She went over the line by mistake.

"Please keep in mind that I'm not here to prove that she's innocent. It's my job to show that she isn't guilty. That may sound like the same thing. There is, however, a large difference. It's my job to show doubt that she isn't guilty. I only need to show a crack in the house, not blow it off the map. This I shall do. That I promise to you. Just remember that every crack that I show you is doubt. And there are lots of cracks. Thank you." She sat with the feeling that she had accomplished her mission of getting their full attention.

She was tempted to say that Witherspoon would take the stand and tell a few lies. It wasn't the time. What she had done was set the perfect stage for the defense. Everything had been put in the context that would make them doubt the government's case, and that was all that was needed.

Lovett was still pissed with the statements that she started with. She revealed a major part of his strategy and stated all the facts that he planned to present. It was all that he had to present.

Per the rules, he finished his opening. He did his best to recover from her vicious attack. He talked about Patrick a bit to convince the jury that Patrick was an ally to his case. He went deeper into how certain pieces of evidence would point to her guilt. He ended up talking longer than planned because the jury members were giving him blank looks. Trying to reverse what she had said proved to be too hard.

He accepted that he had lost the second round. In law school, he had been taught that his opening statement could be the most important part of the case. It was that tricky of a case that if he had gone in another direction, it could have also been the wrong way. Going forward was all that he could do.

When he was finished, the court felt that it was too late to call the first witness. Court was adjourned at three-twenty.

# CHAPTER 29

"So tell me how you feel about the situation." It was the first time Troy had been alone with Trina since the trial had started. He had been with Ms. Funky every time that she had visited.

"When the prosecutor started talking, I got a little scared. I felt better when Ms. Funky started talking. The jury was listening to her like she was a celebrity." She wanted to say something about the depression that he was in. Because she knew why, she kept it to herself.

"I have all the faith in the world in her. All she talks about is beating the case. She wants to shine in front of the cameras also." Ms. Funky had been using him as a sounding board.

"Let her shine. She's good, and she deserves that. All she has to do is what she's been doing. So what is the first thing that we do after she beats the case?" Whatever she and her brother talked about wouldn't change the outcome of the case. She wanted him to have a better disposition.

"Maybe we should make plans. Ms. Funky said the trial would take three more days at the most. So we should make plans." His tone hadn't changed. "You tell me what you want to do."

"We need to travel, then get my club as tight as possible for a super-big grand opening." The building had already been purchased, and the work on the inside would start soon.

"It doesn't matter to me. I just want to see you out of here. I can't lose you also." He secretly blamed himself for his mother's death. He also blamed himself for what was happening with his sister. It was hard for him to smile about anything. His self-imposed depression had a lock on him.

"In a few days, I'll be walking out of here with my favorite man. If I'm not stressing and they are trying to kill me, then you shouldn't be stressing. So can your sister get a smile?" It was okay with her that she was the one with the nerves of steel.

He made the best smile that he could make. When a person is full of negative energy, it's really hard to fake looking happy.

"Now that wasn't that hard. Ms. Funky has a playlist for this trial that you wouldn't believe. She's told me a few things that she hasn't told you. We're all about to be famous. So throw me a kiss and get some sleep."

Trina felt the pressure far more than she was saying. She had paid attention to every word and sentence that was said. She understood that all it took was one thing to impress the jury to find her guilty.

No matter how innocent a person is, in the same position, she has to recognize the possibilities of what could happen. Even the toughest of characters have to feel something when somebody's trying to kill them. Trina did feel something, but it wasn't fear of death. Whenever she had gone out on a mission, she did it knowing there was a possibility that she could be murdered.

She was handling the situation with caution. With her glasses on, she was able to hide much of her concern. If she had to die, she just wanted to see Ms. Funky put up the best fight possible. If she went down, she wanted to go down like a champion would.

So far, she was able to keep her emotions under control. Ms. Funky had told her the significance of making things look good in front of the jury. It would be much harder for her because she was worried about her brother's mental. But she was strong enough to hold the both of them down.

That night she thought about her brother's mental more than she thought about her own.

Early the next day was work call for Lovett. It was 5 a.m. when he started going over his strategy. A presentation of witnesses had to be in a precise order. Above all, a jury couldn't be left confused about the relevant facts—unless the confusion created inferences that benefited his case. In a circumstantial evidence case, all the inferences had to be correct. One misstep meant the case would blow up.

While a presentation is being made, the most important consideration is cross-examination. At no point can a prosecutor take an aggressive defense attorney for granted. In Ms. Funky's case, he knew that he had to be extra careful. He had to take the position that if he coughed the wrong way, she would be all over him. There was more fear than there was caution.

Trial started right on time. Lovett felt he was fully prepared. He walked into the courtroom with a big smile on his face. He purchased a brand-new suit the day before. It was light gray with black pinstripes.

Ms. Funky was dressed in a dark purple two-piece skirt set. She also had on some schoolboy-type glasses to make herself look preppy. Trina was wearing a plain white dress that looked like it was glowing. Troy was sitting behind them.

Just like a writer, when introducing an audience to a foreign subject, it's best to lay a simple foundation.

Lovett started with an FBI agent who was at the most important crime scene: the site of Jason Scott's murder. Martin usually would have been called because he was in charge of the crime scene. Lovett used another officer because Martin was one of his main witnesses. Presenting him twice would limit the impact of Martin's presence.

Lovett also had another strategy in the mix. He was using two-three witnesses to make Jason Scott one of the focal points of the trial. The murder of an FBI agent is a hard thing to ignore.

He managed to catch the jury's attention. The jurors were all on the edges of their seats as they listened to how the murder happened. Lovett went to the extent of using a bit of forensic science to create a visual that was easy to visualize. Lovett used an hour and a half on this part of his direct examination.

Ms. Funky clapped lightly when the court asked her if she had anything.

Lovett almost allowed himself to get mad. He felt that she was patronizing him. He felt slightly belittled when he saw that the jury was amused by her antic. Still, he managed to keep his game face on.

Ms. Funky continued to clap her hands as she stood up and looked around at the spectators. A few in the audience started clapping.

The court wanted to say something, but she started speaking before he was able.

"I only have questions for you, sir, but first I'd like to congratulate Mr. Lovett for a great direct examination." She was looking directly at Lovett.

"That won't be necessary, Ms. Funky. Please do your cross-examination." The court suspected that she was acting for the cameras.

"Okay. I'm sorry, your honor." Ms. Funky acted as if she had been busted, and she would act correctly for the rest of the trial. "Sir, my questions are few and simple. You did state that the killer used a high-powered rifle, correct?" This was the wade in.

"That is correct." He had a smile on his face because of the clapping antic. Plus, he felt that she couldn't catch him in any lies. It was all crime scene stuff.

"You also stated that you've had many years of experience with murders and murder investigations, correct?" Another wade-in question.

"Yes, I've been involved with at least a hundred of them in my fifteen years." He stated this on direct examination.

"Out of all of these murder investigations, in how many did the murderer make sure that the victim was definitely dead?" She had statistics with her about murderers that would be used if he said the wrong thing. Some of the information had come from the FBI.

"Not very many that I can recall."

"Thank you," she said in a sexy manner. She had put her lips and all into it. "Would you agree that Jason Scott was shot at point-blank range to make sure that he was dead?"

He didn't want to agree with the question because of her aggressive tone. "I'd have to agree." Sounding stupid wasn't an option.

"You also stated that he didn't die from the first head shot because he had on a bulletproof helmet, no?" This question would fully get her there.

"That is correct."

"Would you agree that all the facts of this murder say that the murderer had to be a professional?" She was at the top of the steps.

"I'd have to agree."

"Thank you." She sat with the inference that she had won that round.

Lovett started out with a bang, and so did she. What she was attempting to do wasn't above him. He wasn't surprised that she had attacked the weakest part of the case in a chipping manner. All he could do was press forward with the stage that he had set.

Ms. Funky felt that she was handling the case with finesse and nearly perfectly. She wanted him to come on with it.

Lovett called the Las Vegas detective next. This detective was next because of the picture and the evidence in the carpet.

Lovett made sure that he only used necessary questions to lay on the inference and a reference point.

The last thing that he did was introduce the picture. It was undisputable that the picture was one of the killer and that it was a female.

Ms. Funky had spent days examining the picture. She had also consulted with a few experts. The picture scared her more than anything. She had a gut feeling that it was Trina. It was the hips and the walk.

In a pretrial hearing, she had deflected the government's request to dress Trina up in the same gear and take a picture.

She bypassed her cross-examination. There was nothing that she could accomplish other than hurting the defense. Rehashing the same evidence wasn't the thing to do. Silence can also be a defense.

Lovett liked the way that she had bypassed. He felt that he had accomplished keeping her quiet for once. It didn't matter that he would have done the same thing.

Before lunch was called, Lovett called a detective from New York. This detective testified as to how the killer made sure the victims were dead by cutting their throats. It was also established that hydro marijuana was found in the carpets.

After Ms. Funky declined cross-examination again, the court called for lunch recess.

To the average citizen, it would be appalling that a defense attorney was lying back after two police officers testified. People want to see blood, sweat and tears. They want to see anything and probably wanted to holler "do something!" They want to hear some fancy questions being presented.

Ms. Funky had explained to Troy and Trina why these witnesses were dangerous to try to rattle. There was the chance of establishing something that the prosecutor forgot. Also, asking simple questions would be a waste of the jury's attention. There would be no changing facts.

Ms. Funky wanted the jury to pay her the utmost attention when she had something to say. She knew that she had them in suspense. Making the most of that was mandatory.

The next two people to testify were also homicide detectives. One was from Florida; the other was from New Jersey. They both testified about the homicide scenes.

Of course, they mentioned the hydro ashes in the carpet and the slit throats. Ms. Funky didn't cross-examine either of these witnesses. But she kept a sexy smile on her face.

She and her behavior were getting more attention than the witnesses. A few speculated that she had lost her funk because she allowed all of that testimony to go unchecked. Even the jury gave her a few suspicious looks.

It had a lot to do with what had already been established. With four witnesses, a killer's pattern had been established before the world. The jury knew that there was a killer who always made sure the victims were dead: one shot to the face, three shots to the back of the head and a throat cut with a jagged-edged knife. And hydro ashes were in the same spot at each murder scene.

There were other crime scenes that could have been presented also, but all parties agreed that would be repetitive and serve no purpose. Ms. Funky didn't mind at all because she knew that the extra testimony would bore the jury to death. Lovett wanted to keep the action going in his case. He was the one who came up with the idea. Sentencing-wise, it didn't matter how many counts Trina was convicted of. The first count carried a death sentence. That was Jason Scott's murder. The rest of the counts carried life.

Lovett was satisfied with the results of the day. The jurors would have most of the pertinent murders in their minds. It was like the end of the first quarter of a very important basketball game. He felt strongly that he was ahead by about ten points.

Many felt the same way that he did, though they knew that the trial was far from over. It was hard to not be thrown off by Ms. Funky's behavior. People were waiting and expecting for her to act funky. Instead, they interpreted what they saw as docile.

Some saw her as cunning. Most of them understood the process of a trial. They understood that the evidence couldn't be disputed. They didn't want to see miracles like the average citizen did. Actually, this was a common strategy of some defense attorneys.

# CHAPTER 30

Lovett was anxious the next day. He made a hard decision that he felt he might regret. In most trials, prosecutors love to call expert witnesses to bolster their cases. Lovett wanted to do this just to strengthen the foundation of his case.

He wanted to have an expert speak about the background of the typical serial killer. The major problem with this was his lack of psychological information on Trina. Plus, she wasn't exactly on trial for being a serial killer. She didn't exactly fit any kind of profile of a serial killer either. He couldn't take the chance of Ms. Funky reversing things on him. Usually, prosecutors know so much about their prey that character assassination is easy and compelling.

Ms. Funky whispered "let the games begin" in Trina's ear when she saw Martin heading for the witness stand. She was dressed in a black pants suit that had a tight collar. Her hair was pinned up to make herself look harmless. Trina was wearing a black dress.

The beginning of Martin's testimony made him seem like just another police officer. Lovett solicited the simple stuff first.

"Were you familiar with FBI Agent Scott?" It was the time to get to the relevant evidence. Lovett sounded confident and liked the vibe that he was getting from the jury.

"Yes. I was very familiar with the young agent."

Meticulously, Lovett and Martin went through how Jason Scott had determined that Witherspoon had something to do with the murders. Computer analysis always intrigues audiences. Lovett felt like he had the jury in the palm of his hand. Everything being laid on the table was perfect for the platform that had been laid.

Of course, everyone wanted to know if it all connected to Trina.

"Do you recall a carpet that Jason Scott retained from Las Vegas?" Lovett felt comfortable.

"Yes. Agent Scott had the carpet brought over from a Las Vegas hotel crime scene. He had it thoroughly examined."

"Did he come to a conclusion?"

"Yes, he did, and he wrote it in his report."

"Would you please tell us the conclusion?"

"The murderer had been in the room for several hours and wore a size eight in female sneakers." This was the part of the case about which he felt the strongest.

"Was he also able to determine what kind of sneakers were worn?" He felt that this made the situation seem much more reliable.

"It was determined by forensics that the murderer wore a size eight sneaker made by Avirex."

Lovett sent documentation to the jury to show how he arrived at this conclusion. Ms. Funky agreed to stipulate to the finding. There was no way to get around that piece of evidence. Still, she wanted Lovett to present it. Lovett felt that her stipulating helped him to save a lot of time; now he didn't have to call an expert witness.

Lovett's next move was to bring out how Witherspoon had been investigated. This led to the recording being made and the introduction of Patrick.

The jury was a little confused about Patrick. Hearing about how he had been an assassin didn't seem to fit in the case for them.

Ms. Funky noticed the jury's anxiety. She was shaking her head.

Lovett had introduced Patrick the best way that he saw fit. He had to just put him out there and make sense of it later.

He went back to the surveillance of Witherspoon. A few questions were asked about how they managed to record the conversation. This perked the jury back up. A perfect time to play the tape, Lovett thought. He did just that.

There was only one more place to go. "Agent Martin, are you familiar with Trina Lattimore?"

"Yes, I am, sir." He sat up in his seat a bit.

"I presume that you are the officer who arrested her."

"That is correct. She's the female who was living with Patrick." He volunteered this information. Because it was going to come out one way or another, Ms. Funky didn't object.

"Do you know how long she lived with Patrick?"
"For at least four years."

"Where did you get information to support this?"
"In Patrick's house."

Lovett submitted some documents to establish that she lived there for four years. It was mostly receipts from credit cards and car registrations.

He continued his questions. "Did you determine what size she wears in sneakers?"

"Yes, I did. All the sneakers under her bed were size eight."

"In your investigation, did you find anything else that connects Trina Lattimore to this case?"

"Objection! That's leading," Ms. Funky hollered as she stood up and stomped her right foot.

"Sustained." The court ordered Lovett to ask the question in a different manner.

Many were glad to see Ms. Funky come to life. They didn't just want to see a trial, they wanted to see blood.

"Did you find out the target that Witherspoon and Patrick were talking about?"

"Yes, I did."

"Would you please tell us who?"

"A group of Asians had put out a hit on Troy Lattimore, AKA the *Car Master*."

The last name caught everybody's attention.

Lovett submitted documents that showed Troy was in the computer database. "Is Troy Lattimore related to Trina Lattimore?"

"Yes. They are twins." Martin felt that Lovett was handling it nicely.

Ms. Funky expected that to happen. The reaction didn't surprise her. Her plan remained the same.

"Do you know if the hit was successful?"

"I do know. He's sitting behind the defense table in the front row." He went so far as to point at Troy. This was noted in the record. Ms. Funky smiled as she looked at the jury.

Lovett wanted to stop there, but he had to get in another fact that would paint a better picture.

"The first time you went to Patrick's house—would you tell us what you found?" This was another leading question.

"There were four dead Asians in the house."

"Is it possible that Patrick murdered them?"

"No, it isn't."

"Would you tell us why?"

"He had been dead for at least two hours before their times of death."

"I have no more questions."

Nobody would debate that a serious and vivid picture had been painted. Lovett handled direct examination in a manner that would allow a tenth-grader to keep up.

It took close to two hours. The court let out for lunch because it was close to 12 o'clock.

"Good afternoon, Agent Martin. My name is Ms. Funky. I hope that you are having a good day." She was putting on an act to make it look good and to bait him properly. She needed the jury to see how he acted under stress and without it.

"I'm well. Thank you." Like most cops, Martin tensed up a bit before aggressive defense attorneys.

"Isn't it true that you had Patrick under twenty-four-hour sur-veillance?"

"That is correct. That is after we taped the conversation with Mr. Witherspoon." He offered the extra information that she was going to ask for next. He went against the rule because he was sure of where she was taking him, and he wanted to make him-self look more credible.

"So on the night of his murder, wasn't the FBI watching him?"

"Yes, we were."

"Weren't y'all also watching his house?"

"That is correct."

"Isn't it correct that his house is gated and only has one driveway?" She loved it when she found shabby police work.

"That is correct."

"So can you tell me how those Asians got in that house?" She almost growled the question.

"No, I can't." This was what the audience had been hoping for.

"So you can't tell me who killed them, can you?"

"No, I can't." Trina felt that Ms. Funky was being very slick.

"All of that is interesting." She looked down at the floor and shifted on her hips as she shuffled her feet. "Maybe I should change gears."

Lovett almost fell into the objection trap. Ms. Funky wanted Martin to linger in his ignorance for as long as possible.

"I'm sure you are familiar with CIA Agent Gerald Scott." She felt that she was about to enjoy this a lot. She knew that she should have worn a tampon. She thought about wearing two to keep the juices from leaking down her legs. She was that wet already.

"I'm familiar with Agent Gerald Scott."

She smiled. "Isn't he related to FBI Agent Jason Scott?" The name caught everyone's attention.

"Yes, they're related." He hated to say that. Though he didn't know where she was going, he knew that she had a plan up her sleeve.

"Would you please tell us how?" She could have asked in a different way, but it wouldn't have had the same impact.

"Gerald Scott was Jason Scott's older brother." He had to at least make it sound professional.

"Thank you for that information. We're still working with things that you know." She paused and shifted on her hips a bit so that she could tease him and model a bit. "Isn't it true that Agent Gerald Scott is also dead?"

"That is true." He had to wonder how she knew that. That part had been redacted from the report. Still, he couldn't take a chance on getting caught lying.

"Isn't it true that Agent Gerald Scott actually shot Patrick at the beach?"

"Objection." Lovett could barely hold it. He was out of his seat.

"What is your objection based on?" The court was very interested in the answer.

"It's all part of the investigation." Ms. Funky was in her element.

"Overruled." The court turned to Martin. "Please answer the question."

"That is correct." He almost took the chance of lying.

"Was Agent Gerald Scott overly concerned about his brother's murderer getting arrested and whatnot?"

"Yes, he was concerned." He had the worst feeling a cop can have. Making sure to not get caught in a lie can be stressful. It was also seen on his face. This is what Ms. Funky wanted. She had a devilish grin on her face.

"Do you know why he didn't try to kill Trina?" She didn't care what he said or did, and she had only just begun to chop him up.

"Objection, your honor." Lovett was out of his seat again. "That would be hearsay." This is usually when a defense attorney would holler.

"Sustained." The court still knew that it was too late. It didn't matter. He understood that the jury couldn't ignore the comment. It's impossible to ignore something the prosecutor fears so very much.

Ms. Funky's devilish grin hadn't left her face. "I'm sorry, your honor," she said in a humble voice. "So we can assume that Agent Gerald Scott knew a lot about this investigation, right?"

Martin let out a breath. "That sounds reasonable."

"Did you and he talk about the investigation?" She was slowly tearing the case apart.

"Yes, we talked about it."

"Did Patrick come up in y'all's conversations?"

"No. We didn't talk about Patrick." It would sound too unprofessional to tell the truth.

"So he suspected Patrick's involvement because of his own investigation?" It was time to hit another angle.

"I really don't know." He understood that the jury had been left to think what it liked. He also understood that this wasn't good for the case. Chip. Chip. Chip. Chip. And he hated it.

"We're going to switch up again, Agent Martin." Lovett was beginning to hate how she was throwing comments out there. She was pushing for a change in his expression. "Did you do a thorough search of Patrick's house?"

"Yes, I did."

"Did you find any Avirex sneakers that would fit Trina?"

"No, I didn't." He said this to make sure he kept his demeanor and tone the same.

"Did you find any weapons in her room?" She skipped establishing that Trina had a room. It was implied in the question.

"No, I did not."

"Before you entered the house, did you know when was the last time she had been in the house?" She was glad that Trina hadn't given them any information.

"I don't know."

"So she came to your attention because she may have been staying with Patrick?" She was slowing taking Trina out of the picture.

"Objection, your honor. That isn't relevant." This question would make the case look really weak. He had to do something.

"Overruled. Answer the question."

"That's basically true."

She loved it. "Is it possible that Patrick didn't want to kill Trina's twin—"

"Objection. Patrick isn't on trial."

"Sustained."

Ms. Funky smiled at the attention. "I have no more questions." The way that she crossed her legs when she sat said a lot about what she was feeling.

The absolute silence represented the applause the jury and spectators wanted to give. Martin represented cheddar cheese in the worse way. Lovett felt the pain also.

Lovett did all that he could to repair the leaks. Too many factors had been presented that made it look like they didn't know what they were doing. There was nothing that could be done to reverse the effect of Gerald Scott's murder and the murder of the Asians. These murders created lots of curiosity and lots of doubt about Trina being a hit girl.

Lovett was surprised. He hadn't expected these factors to come up. He didn't think that they knew. It told him that he was correct about Trina being the hit girl. It had to be somebody on the inside that knew these things. If she knew anything, that meant she was guilty. But there was no way for him to prove a thing. Ms. Funky would protect her at all costs, and there was the attorney-client privilege.

Ms. Funky knew about all of these things because Trina filled her in. They had that kind of relationship and trust.

"That bitch is about to walk up out of here because of the way that you prosecuted this case." Martin had just sat at the prosecutor's table. They were all waiting for Witherspoon to be brought in the courtroom.

"Witherspoon's going to put her in the case in a manner that she can't get out of it." Lovett didn't exactly believe this himself. He was praying for a deadlocked jury so he could try the case again.

"It's a damn good thing that we tricked him into pleading guilty. That Ms. Funky is vicious." He hated feeling that Trina was about to walk, but a hunch just isn't good enough for a conviction.

"Have a positive attitude." The court had just finished swearing Witherspoon in. Short, sweet and to the point was his plan.

Lovett started out with Witherspoon's credentials. It was nice to have the jury's full attention. They were sucking up every detail. Witherspoon's face had been in the news a lot. Here was a man who didn't look like a criminal or act like a criminal and didn't have the credentials of a criminal. But he informed the court and the world of how he orchestrated several murders with Patrick's assistance. He went into how Patrick had convinced him to get into it. It all sounded absolutely fascinating.

Lovett didn't think that the jury might be more concerned with being entertained than with the case. He was just moving ahead with his plans.

The pivotal point came when he played the tapes. Things were going exactly the way that Ms. Funky had expected.

"Did you and Agent Patrick have a lot of these meetings?"

"Yes, we did, sir." He acted as if he was testifying as an innocent police officer.

"This female who y'all referred to—did y'all speak about her often?"

"Yes, we did, and I met her a few times." The last point was a lie.

"Do you see her in the courtroom?"

"Yes, I do, sir. She's at the defense table." He pointed to her. Martin started feeling better.

"So is she the one who committed all of the murders?" He had arrived at that place.

"Yes, she's the girl we counted on to do the murders." He looked directly at her. "Trina Lattimore is the *Hydro Killer*." Ms. Funky had a reason for not objecting.

"That'll be all."

A strong comeback had been made. The finger had finally been pointed at Trina. The pointing had been done by an authority figure. He was still seen as such, though he had pleaded guilty to murder for hire.

At the least, people saw them keeping the government in the game. Some waited patiently before coming to a conclusion.

Ms. Funky felt that the testimony was pretty tight. She had just received his statement before he took the stand. It was one of those times that she had used her ability to think fast.

"Good evening, Mr. Witherspoon. I'm Ms. Funky." She had her left leg extended so she could rock back and forth while she calculated her next move.

"Good evening to you. I'm fine." He sounded like the epitome of a gentleman.

"You didn't think that y'all would get caught, did you?" This was a slight ego stroke.

"I didn't see it coming."

"I understand. You weren't even at one of the murder scenes, were you?"

"No, I wasn't."

"You just put together the research for rivals and talked to Patrick?"

"That's pretty much correct." He felt that he was doing a terrific job of answering her questions.

"I imagine you were always at work or with your family. Is that correct?"

"At times, I did go fishing."

"You didn't go fishing anywhere near any of the murder scenes, did you?"

"Of course not."

"So that means that you weren't with Patrick either during these murders, correct?"

He sat up a bit because he saw the hole. "No, I wasn't with him either." He had made a commitment two questions ago.

"So you were extremely safe until Jason Scott started the case?"

"I'd say that."

She was presenting a diversion before the knockout. She was a professional at reading body language. "With Jason Scott out of the way, there'd only be Patrick to testify against you."

It bothered him that he wasn't sure of where she was going. "I suppose that's true."

"So the time that you met Trina, y'all didn't have a discussion about murders?"

He had made another commitment. "No, I never discussed murders with her." He was wishing that she'd hurry up. He hadn't expected her to be that good.

"Did you have any discussions with her at all?" This was a safe question to which she didn't know the answer. No matter the answer, she'd use it in her closing.

"No, I just saw her the few times that I visited Patrick." He couldn't think of a lie that would fit better.

She loved the answer. "So it's safe to say that you only knew about Trina what Patrick told you?"

"That's pretty much so." He was internally cursing her out.

"Have you ever seen her fire a weapon?"

"No, I haven't."

It was time to blister him. "So you never saw her at a murder scene?"

"No."

"So you don't know if she killed anyone, do you?"

"Yes."

"Yes?" She laughed and smiled. "So how do you know?"

"Patrick told me." He had been sunk.

"Couldn't Patrick have lied to you and have done all the murders himself?" She felt herself getting moist again. She hadn't had this much fun in a while.

"Yes." He quickly decided to retreat. "No."

"Didn't you say that Patrick was with the FBI and that he trained her?"

"Yes, I did."

It seemed that she had rescued him. "How could one train to kill and not be a killer?"

"I don't know."

"So you don't know for sure that she killed anyone, correct?"

"No. That—"

"Thank you. No more questions."

Ms. Funky was nuttin' on herself and about to scream. Her smile said it all. She felt that she gave one of her best performances to date. She felt so good that she didn't care if she ever tried another case. While Lovett was trying to clean up the situation, she was barely listening and wanted to start laughing.

Suspense had built. There was a bit of tension on Witherspoon's face. There was no denying that he had been tarred, feathered and dragged through the mud. A small bit of his humiliation had been saved by Lovett asking him a few more questions. There was only so much that he could do.

Trina was compelled to tell Ms. Funky that she was satisfied with her performance. She learned a lot from the experience. She learned a lot about herself, her brother and the legal system. She was glad that she had taken all the precautions Patrick taught her.

When the case went to the jury for deliberation, she felt only a small bit of tension. As usual, she was ready to accept the consequences, whatever they might be. What mattered the most to her was that her brother had shown her the kind of love that she had wanted and needed. What he did mattered even more after his mother committed suicide. Troy having her back meant the world to her.

The jury deliberated for a little less than three hours.

A month later was the grand opening for Trina's. A celebration with free food and free entry kicked things off. Trina was one of Atlanta's biggest nightspots.

Ms. Funky and Trina stepped out of a limo in the most expensive dresses that they could find. There was little left for the imagination. The crowd went crazy when it saw Trina. She was that home girl that had committed many murders and had gotten away with it.

Ms. Funky was having the time of her life. Her status had been bumped up as far as it could go. Organizations were paying her $50,000 just for speeches.

Witherspoon ended up with a life sentence because Lovett refused to move for a sentence reduction. There was nothing that could be done about his discretion. Lovett hated that Trina got acquitted.

"Trina, you have to tell me something." Ms. Funky loved posing for the press. "Since I got you acquitted, you can tell me something."

Trina waved at her brother. So far, she hadn't met that man who fit her qualifications. "What is it, counselor?" They started walking in. Troy was walking toward them.

"Did you do all those people?"

Trina smiled. "And I'll do it again!"

# ABOUT THE AUTHOR

Darrell J. DeBrew is a North Carolina native. DeBrew's experiences with the criminal world and the criminal justice system drove him to show people the game and educate them; he wants people to be entertained by street life without getting locked up or being adversely affected by the streets. He is the author of Stacy, and Keisha.

# COMING SOON!

DC

4X

A KILLERZ
AMBITION

A NATHAN WELCH EPIDEMIC

# PRELUDE

"They done let the wrong motherfucker out of HELL!" I snickered, as I exited D.C. Jail with a second chance at life.

Six months ago, I was sitting in a United States Penitentiary in Marion, Illinois trying to beat the sweltering heat, and just reaching a decade on a 46 year-to-LIFE prison term for catching a homicide, and an armed robbery beef.

Fortunately, this time my appeals got my convictions over-turned on a legal technicality, and I damn sure wasn't about to go to trial for a second time, once I learned that the same hot mo-therfuckers were willing to come to court, and sing like a canary again! Instead, I took a 10-to-25 year Manslaughter plea agreement, and walked with time served, because the judge suspended all but ten years that I had served.

With my newfound freedom, I had a purpose to serve. There would be no more hustling for peanuts, and expensive designer clothes; It's a damn shame that I have to quit hustling, but some things more important had to be handled for the forgotten men on lockdown. I've been through several correctional facilities across America, and there hadn't been one guy that wasn't rotting in prison because of a SNITCH!

I even went to the extent of getting those guys contact information just in case they made it back to the streets before I did.

But as you know, I, Carmelo Glover made it first, and I must keep a vow that I'd made the second after I'd got convicted-BY ANY MEANS... And that was, eliminate every hot motherfucker in the streets that I could.

Like every top-notch killer, I had a plan, and as soon as I get them guns, I would begin executing it. Although this time, things were much riskier, but I loved challenges, and this was the biggest one of my life!

Hell, if motherfuckers could lie, snitch, and send good men to prison for EONS, then why I couldn't kill their weak asses, and get street justice and revenge for the forgotten ones?

If you're feeling me, then come, and take a ride with me in THE CITY WHERE IT GOES DOWN AT!!!

# COMING SOON

By
# RJ CHAMP

"Beware of DC's charming
man...you never know
whose path you may cross"

# A BEAUTIFUL SATAN

A NOVEL

DC BOOKDIVA PUBLICATIONS

# PREFACE

## The Breaking Point...

The bluish glass window shimmered in the afternoon sun, casting rays of dancing sunlight upon Angel as she slept – warm sunbeams flickering across her eyelids began to awaken her. Slowly, Angel emerged from her sleep. She rolled over in bed, a tired frown etched in her face as long black tresses fell over her eye. Angel felt fuzzy, like she hadn't gotten a wink of sleep.

'What's this?' Her hazel eyes focused now on a crumpled note paper laying on the pillow beside her; the name – NATASHA – scribbled at the top.

The note was a letter from her husband, Rafael.

'Will I ever see you again?' Angel's inner voice wondered as she reflected over the recent loss of Rafael.

"Why, Lord? Why would you allow me to fall in love with a man so deep, then allow Satan to intervene in our lives? Father, you let Satan take my love away. Why??!!" Angel cried out, tears of pain swelling in her eyes.

As if all her energy had just been sucked right out of her, Angel's head collapsed on the pillow. Dazed, Angel stared – spellbound – up at the ceiling, staring off at some distance in the middle of nowhere.

---

Suddenly the sound of a smooth jazz melody came drifting into the room. Startled, Angel turned and gazed tiredly at the door.

'Where's the music coming from?' she silently mused. Shivering, Angel pulled herself to her feet. As she stood, Angel felt a cold chill rise up and through her entire body.

Kenny G's 'Songbird' came floating from the open doorway leading into the master bedroom, as if trying to drown out the pleasurable moans of a woman in some kind of synthetic coup.

Angel lingered in the hallway; a concoction in Whipped-Cream fragranced candles saturated the air outside the master bedroom. Angel's trembling fingers moved along the wall as she reached for the door.

The blonde with crystal-blue eyes, Natasha, was inside the master suite on her hands and knees, doggy-style. She was getting her world rocked by Angel's cheating-ass-husband, Rafael.

Gripping Natasha firmly around her waist, Rafael pounded her insides – pushing all 12-inches of his throbbing organ in to the hilt.

"Yea, that's it, bitch," Rafael hissed through clenched teeth. "Who's your daddy now, huh, bitch?" A smug grin spread on his lips – Rafael got off watching Natasha's rump jiggle every time he gave that ass a slap.

Angel stood in the doorway with pure rage simmering in her eyes, grinding her teeth as an icy chill ran down the back of her neck. She let out a scream at the top of her lungs, and then lunged across the room like a woman who had totally lost her mind.

"You dirty-dick-sonofabitch!"

Angel leaped on Rafael's back like a panther with the intent to kill. She hissed, exposing a perfect set of pearly-whites, and sank her sharp teeth deep into the thick-meaty muscle bulging atop Rafael's shoulder.

Sudden shock and fear exploded on Rafael's face. He howled like a wounded wolf and stumbled backward twisting and turning with Angel strapped to his back. It took Rafael all the strength he could summon to pry his crazy wife's arms from around his throat. Rafael spun around and slung Angel toward the bed. His heart dropped instantly and Rafael cringed inside when he realized his mistake.

Angel hit the king-size sleigh bed poised on all fours when she landed; she resembled a ferocious feline preparing to attack. Operating on sheer impulse, Angel licked her lips and pounced on the frightened woman. Natasha tried to leap across the bed to escape the clutches of Angel. But Natasha moved to slowly and her attempts at escape were futile.

"Oh no, bitch!" Angel snarled aggressively. "You ain't going nowhere... fucking ho!" Angel grunted, as she tore into Natasha, death gleaming in her eyes. She mounted a vicious assault using fist, teeth, and nails, exerting pain and punishment on Natasha's nude body. The attack was so severe; Natasha swore she was being attacked by more than one woman.

Rafael rushed to Natasha's rescue. "Let her go!" Rafael screamed while locked in a heated struggle – wrestling and tussling to save his battered and bruised lover from the death grip of his enraged wife.

Angel's uncontrollable rage had her adrenaline pumping in overdrive, her strength was uncanny. Rafael had to use all 220-pounds of his muscular frame to lift Angel in the air. He was stretched to the limit, all six feet of Rafael stood erect. Rafael gave one last forceful push breaking the death-hold Angel had on Natasha.

When Angel released her grip, Rafael felt the wind knock out of him from the full impact of Angel's weight crashing on top of him.

Angel bounced to her feet immediately when she realized Rafael was injured. She hovered over him, glaring.

"You like laying with sluts!" she yelled rancorously.

"You dirty-dick-bitch!" Angel cocked her right foot back, aimed for Rafael's dick, and kicked him as hard as she could. With a snide smirk twitching at the corners of her mouth, Angel leaned over Rafael's face, coughed-up a snotty blob of phlegm, and hawk-spit right in his face. "You and your whore can burn in hell!!!"

Moments later, Angel could see herself standing in the doorway just outside the master bathroom staring across the dark interior as if she was having some weird out-of-body experience. Angel could feel an eerie presence radiating from the still darkness inside the bathroom like there was some kind of unforeseen and ungodly force lingering in its space. Angel focused straight ahead on the large walled mirror and saw the silhouette framed in the doorway was her own reflection.

Angel took a step inside the bathroom and was surprised at how chilly the air was inside. With caution in her every step, Angel walked to the mirror and gazed at herself. Angel looked discombobulated when she noticed a bright white t-shirt covering her torso. She couldn't remember putting on the shirt. Angel looked down at the white tee, her fingers trembling as they brushed against the wet cotton. NATASHA was finger-painted in fresh blood on the front in large crimson letters. Angel froze, utter horror and disbelief radiating in her expression. Slowly her head rose towards the mirror and Angel's eyes twinkled strangely with an insanity that made her inwardly cringe. An ice cold sensation pierced Angel to the core when she saw the inverted reflection of Natasha's name in the mirror! Spelled in fresh blood, the word 'AH-SATAN" seemed to leap off the shirt. The crude painted letters were all Angel could see. She stared at herself in the looking glass and realized with terror the woman looking back was a total stranger.

Suddenly the fog lifted from Angel's eyes and she was brought back to reality. She realized she was still on the bed, gazing up at the ceiling. Shaken, Angel bolted upright and reached out to yank open the top drawer of the nightstand. She pulled out a prescription pill bottle with the narcotic Oxyline printed on the label.

Angel popped two pills in her mouth, tossed the pill bottle back in the drawer, and then closed her eyes tightly, exhaling deeply...

"Father-God, I pray for you to vanquish the bad dreams, the bad feelings and the bad demons that I feel surrounding me and taunting me. Please, oh Lord, I know that I am nothing without you. So please have mercy on me... I put no other above you. I'm begging you, Lord, please bless me with a real man so I can move forward with my life and forget Raphael. Help me purge my husband's unclean spirit from my soul...Help me Father-God, I need you...please!"

# COMING SOON

THE HUSTLE

NOVEL BY
FRAZIER BOY

# Order Form

DC Bookdiva Publications
#245 4401-A Connecticut Avenue, NW
Washington, DC 20008
dcbookdiva.com

**Name:** _____

**Inmate ID** _____

**Address:** _____

**City/State:** _____ **Zip:** _____

| QUANTITY | TITLES | PRICE | TOTAL |
|---|---|---|---|
| | Up The Way, Ben | 15.00 | |
| | Dynasty By Dutch | 15.00 | |
| | Dynasty 2 By Dutch | 15.00 | |
| | Trina | 15.00 | |
| | **Coming Soon!** | | |
| | A Killer'z Ambition | 15.00 | |
| | A Beautiful Satan | 15.00 | |
| | The Hustle | 15.00 | |
| | Q, Dutch | 15.00 | |

**Sub Total** $_____

Shipping/Handling (Via US Media Mail) $3.95 1-2 books, $7.95 1-3 books, 4 or more books-Free Shipping

**Shipping** $_____
**Total Enclosed** $_____

**FORMS OF ACCEPTED PAYMENTS:**
Certified or government issued checks and money orders, all mail in orders take 5-7 Business days to be delivered. Books can also be purchased on our website at dcbookdiva.com and by credit card at 1866-928-9990. Incarcerated readers receive 25% discount. Please pay $11.25 per book and apply the same shipping terms as stated above.